my brother's best friend

Bad Boys of Redwood Academy

emilia rose

Cover by: The Book Brander

Editing by: Jovana Shirley, Unforeseen Editing

Emilia Rose

emiliarosewriting@gmail.com

content warning

This book is considered a dark romance and includes murder, decapitation, sex trafficking, sexual assault, nonconsensual sex, and more. If any of these things makes you uncomfortable, I suggest not reading.

To all the good girls who love gushy, warm feelings in the chest ... and in other places too.

1

maddie

"HERE'S to the start of an undefeated Redwood hockey season!" my brother, Oliver, shouted over the rap music blasting in my parents' living room.

I ran a hand over my face and groaned through the phone at the noise ... and at the scene unfolding in front of me.

Oliver's entitled man-whore best friend, Alec Wolfe, stood next to him on the coffee table, throwing back a shot of tequila while a group of half-naked hockey groupies and teammates roared wildly around them.

I held my phone to my ear and glared at Alec fondling Sandra, his ex-girlfriend and one of the popular girls at Redwood who made my life a living hell.

"God," I growled, hand tightening around the stupid piece of metal in my hand. "I hate him so freaking much."

"Why don't you come over to my house?" Vera, my bestie, asked through the phone. "It's quiet, and it doesn't have smelly-ass boys in it. They probably didn't even shower after that game. I can smell their BO from here."

Alec licked the last drop of tequila off his lips and hazily gazed

1

in my direction with his dark, hooded eyes that I fucking loathed seeing every day. And then this dickhead had the *audacity* to smirk.

To smirk at me!

I wanted to kill him.

So many Redwood groupies had been graced with the infamous Wolfe smirk, but Alec had barely even *looked* in my direction since he and Oliver had started hanging out five years ago. I didn't know what this little smirk was all about tonight.

We hated each other. Well, mostly, I hated him because he was a disgusting man-whore who couldn't keep it in his pants, he was fine as hell, and he couldn't spare me a single moment out of the damn day.

Ugh, whatever.

"Too distracted?" Vera hummed, a small giggle escaping through the phone.

"Yeah, sure," I said sarcastically. "Distracted by Alec grinding up against three girls." My hand tightened around the phone, and I glared harder at him so he'd look away, but he didn't. I gritted my teeth. "I'll be over soon."

This was exactly why I left the house anytime Oliver threw a stupid party.

Alec hopped off the table, grabbed a red Solo cup from one of his teammates, and stumbled in my direction, his gaze on me the entire time. Not even glancing back at a cheerleader who pulled off her top.

Wanting to distance myself from him, I swallowed hard and made a beeline for the kitchen. "See you in a half hour, V."

I slammed my finger on the End Call button and slipped into the other room, hoping that Alec somehow lost his way in my parents' fucking mansion.

After grabbing a cup, I filled it with water from the fridge and chugged it. All I had to do was grab some overnight clothes from my bedroom and force my way through the crowd of smelly boys in the living room, and then it'd just be me and Vera for the rest of the—

Someone seized my waist from behind and tugged me closer until I collided with a hard, taut chest. The scent of Alec's cologne that I knew all too well drifted through my nose. Alec grazed his nose against my ear, the stench of alcohol coming off him in waves.

"Looking for me, Cupcake?" he murmured into my ear.

A wave of heat ran through my entire body. *Fuck.*

I twirled around and slammed my hands into his chest, my fingers brushing against the thick muscle that lay underneath his V-neck. I clenched my jaw and ignored the warmth building between my legs. "What the hell are you doing?" I whisper-yelled, not wanting anyone to see.

Alec Wolfe had never touched me like this, had never even looked twice in my direction … when he was sober. Now that he was hyped up on hard liquor, I bet he thought I was another one of his little groupies.

Probably couldn't even see straight.

Stumbling back, he drunkenly grinned at me. "What does it look like? I want to dance with the sexiest girl at Redwood tonight." He stepped closer to me, his large hands resting on my waist again. "Come here."

I pushed Alec away and ignored those sultry eyes that he was giving me. He was drunk and mistaking me for someone else because popular guys like him *never* liked nerdy, awkward girls like me. Except in Vera's case with her skateboard-loving bad-boy fling.

"Why don't you go back out to the living room with your girl-friend?" I huffed.

"Girlfriend?"

"Sandra?"

Alec stepped closer to me and laughed coldly. "Sandra isn't my girlfriend."

"Well, she's telling everyone that you're still together."

Which might've—definitely—been the real reason that I had been pissed off since the end of the game tonight. I couldn't care less about Oliver throwing another party; I had gotten used to sleeping on Vera's couch when he did.

Alec tucked a strand of hair behind my ear. "You think I would go back to her when I can have you?"

I scrunched my nose. "I don't know how you get any girls with pickup lines like that."

Though the thought of Alec actually meaning those things …

I shook my head. No. He was just drunk. He didn't mean it.

"You don't like my pickup lines?" he slurred, his cheeks reddening from the alcohol.

Because Alec Wolfe *wasn't* blushing. Not because of me.

"No," I scoffed and crossed my arms. "Do you even know who you're talking to?"

"The only girl who I can't get up the fucking courage to talk to while I'm sober."

Warmth exploded through my chest. "What?"

He paused for a moment, then leaned against the counter, sipped his beer, and smirked at me again, like he hadn't just said anything, like he was talking to Sandra or Nicole from the cheer squad.

I waited for him to explain what had just come out of his mouth.

But he continued to smirk.

"Go stumble back to the half-naked cheer team in the living room," I said, clenching my jaw and turning away. Why'd he have to go and say that?! Now, I wouldn't be able to stop thinking about it. I hated the way I felt about him. "I'm sure you'll have fun with them."

"If I wanted to," Alec started, "I would've slept with them already."

"And here I thought you were actually a decent guy," I snapped, anger boiling inside me.

Lie.

I thought he was the biggest player Redwood had ever known.

"And here I thought, you were smarter than to believe all those rumors Redwood Academy spoon-feeds everyone," Alec fired back, stepping back into my vision and tilting his head down at me. He drew his tongue across his lower lip.

And all I could imagine was him drawing his tongue up my inner thighs, slipping it between my legs, and—

Stop it, Maddie.

Straightening myself out again, I sucked in a deep breath. "You being the school slut is not a rumor. I've seen it with my own eyes."

Before I could stop him, Alec placed his hands on either side of my body and trapped me between him and the counter, his muscular frame towering over me. And those eyes—those freaking brown eyes—trapped me.

"Don't look at me like that," I said.

"How am I looking at you?"

"Like you want to ..." My mouth dried. "Want to ..."

Alec grasped my chin and forced me to look up at him. "Like I want to do what?"

Heat engulfed my entire body just from the mere touch. I inhaled sharply and pressed my thighs together. I hated how my body reacted to him. He was my brother's best friend and had annoyed me since middle school.

"Hmm?" Alec asked, his breath fanning across my mouth. "Speechless, Cupcake?"

"Can you stop calling me that?" I managed to get out.

"Alec!" someone shouted from our right. "There you are!"

Sandra, Alec's ex-girlfriend or new fling or whatever the hell she was to him, walked into the room with her arms crossed and her gaze shifting from Alec to me. She narrowed her beady brown eyes.

"What are you doing here?" she asked him.

Alec stepped away and smirked. "Just teaching Oliver's little sister a lesson."

"Well, come on." She tugged on his bicep. "The party's out here. Not here with her."

Sandra wrapped her arm around his, but he pulled himself away from her. After throwing me a heated glance, Alec grabbed another beer from the counter behind me and walked out of the kitchen and into the living room with her.

I balled my hands into fists and glared at her retreating figure. I hated her too.

Instead of pouring another glass of water, I took a red Solo cup from the kitchen and filled it with whatever kind of spiked punch my brother had made today. Nobody here should've even been drinking. We were all underage, but …

"Come on, baby," Sandra shouted in the other room. "Dance with me."

Fuck it.

I downed the drink and stomped up to my bedroom.

I was not going to watch Alec's ex-girlfriend rub herself all over him.

After slamming my bedroom door, I changed into a pair of shorts and a T-shirt to wear over to Vera's house, collapsed on my bed, and sighed.

Alec hadn't even looked like he had mistaken me for someone else tonight.

But he must have, right? And I mean—

My bedroom door suddenly swung open, and Alec Wolfe walked in.

2

maddie

"MADDIE WEBER ..." Alec walked farther into my room with a smirk on his chiseled face and sin in his dark, hooded brown eyes.

He wanted something, and I feared that he wanted *me*. But ... nothing could happen.

It couldn't.

"What the hell are you doing here?" I sucked in a sharp breath, shot up from my bed, and covered my pajama-clad body with a thin blanket. I used it for another layer of protection from the Redwood hockey star because ... I knew that my guard was already down. "Get out!"

Instead of listening, Alec grabbed my hand, made me drop the blanket, and tugged me closer until our chests met. He dipped his head and drew his nose up mine. "Make me, Cupcake."

I tried hard to yank my hand out of his, but he was too strong.

Or maybe I just didn't try as hard as I could.

"I said, make me. What are you waiting for?" Alec taunted.

"What is your problem? Why can't you leave me alone tonight?"

I finally gathered enough strength to pull myself out of his grip and shoved him against my bedroom door, but he easily switched places with me, his taut body pressing against me like I had always hoped it would.

"I'm the one who can't leave *you* alone?" Alec asked, humming in amusement with that smug grin on his face. "Do I gawk at you during every class, at lunch, while you're playing hockey?"

My cheeks burned in embarrassment, my breath hitching. "I don't gawk at you."

Lie.

But honestly, the only way he knew that I stared at him was if he stared back.

"If you catch me staring, I'm just wondering how an idiot like you got into AP Calc," I said.

Instead of getting angry with me, like he usually did, he wrapped his large, callous hand around my throat and roughly stroked my jaw with his thumb, a low chuckle rumbling from his chest. "You know what I think?" He moved closer. "I think you're a liar." He gently maneuvered his knee between my legs and pressed it against my core. "I think you want me to trap you like this and take you like *you think* I take all those slutty girls downstairs."

"As if," I managed to say. "I hate you."

Another lie.

Alec Wolfe was the sexiest senior at Redwood Academy.

And I had had so many dirty dreams of him doing exactly this.

"Is that why your nipples are so hard that they're poking against your shirt like this?" he asked. Loosening his grip on my throat, he trailed his fingers down the center of my chest and over my nipples, the feeling sending a rush of heat between my legs.

I tried to press my thighs together, but his knee stopped me.

"You're not saying anything, Cupcake …"

With my lips pressed into a tight line, I refused to let any moans escape my mouth. No matter how good his fingers brushing across my nipples felt, no matter how hard I was clenching, no matter if Alec got on his knees and begged for me, I still hated him.

Alec captured both of my nipples between his fingers and tugged.

Alec had pulled on my hair in grade school, tripped me plenty of times in middle school, and even shoved me against the lockers a few times this past year, but he had never touched me like this. He had never once dared to come on to his best friend's little sister.

"Do you like this so much that you have to hold back your moans for me?" he asked.

"Alec ..." I whispered.

I balled my hands into fists and squeezed my eyes closed.

I hate Alec.

I hate Alec.

I hate Alec.

That was what I told myself. That was what I wanted to believe.

"What about this?" Alec asked, trailing his fingers even lower and grazing them over the hem of my silky shorts. "Do you like this enough to moan for me?"

I sucked in a sharp breath and whimpered softly. *Fuck.*

"Spread your legs like a good girl for me," he ordered.

And for some ungodly reason, I spread my legs. He pressed the bulge in his jeans against my thigh and gently cupped my pussy, his fingers strumming against my wetness and making me clench even harder.

"You're wet for me."

"Alec, please ..."

After grasping my hand, he placed it on the front of his pants. "Tell me you want this."

Fuck.

He was so big. So fucking big.

"You're my brother's best friend, and I ..." I started, my knees almost buckling underneath me. "I ..."

I moved my hand up and down his length, imagining him inside of me. He would feel so much better than my fingers.

"You what?" Alec taunted.

"I hate … y-you."

Alec groaned, "Tell me you hate me again as you're jerking me off like that, baby."

I moved my hand up and down his bulge again. "I hate you."

It was a lie that we both saw through.

Alec picked me up, tossed me onto the bed, and crawled up after me, pulling his shirt over his head. Moonlight flooded in through the window, glistening against his muscular, tanned chest. He slipped his hand between our bodies and pushed down his jeans, and I could do nothing but gasp.

"Spread your legs."

I pressed my knees together. "It's not going to fit."

"Cupcake, you're soaked right now," Alec said. "It might be a tight fit, but I'll slide right into you."

Fuck …

I spread my legs for him again, desperate to feel him inside of me.

This was wrong.

I was supposed to hate Alec, but I couldn't stop.

I had wanted this for longer than I should admit.

"Fuck…" Alec grunted, pulling my oversize shorts to the side, rubbing himself against my entrance, and thrusting himself into me slowly. "I didn't think you'd be this tight." He continued to push himself into me until all of his cock was buried in my pussy. "You feel so good."

Once the pain subsided, I wrapped my legs around his waist to draw him closer and moaned into his mouth. Pleasure rushed through my body, making my legs tingle, and I clenched harder on him.

"More," I moaned. "Please, more."

Alec pumped into me and gently rubbed my clit through my wet panties.

He hadn't even been inside me for a couple of moments yet, but I was close. So close.

I dug my fingers into his muscular shoulders and arched my back, about to explode all over his cock. But then the doorknob jiggled, and I froze.

3

maddie

"MADDIE, WHY IS YOUR DOOR LOCKED?" Oliver shouted over the music from the hallway. He shook the doorknob again, as if his drunk ass really thought it would magically unlock because he shook it harder this time.

Oh my God! Why is he up here?!

I stared up at Alec through wide eyes and tightened around his huge cock, but Alec didn't stop thrusting into me. Instead, Alec kissed me just below my ear, his slight stubble tickling me.

"Answer him," he murmured to me. "Before he comes in here and finds me fucking his little sister's tight cunt."

"What d-do you want, Oliver?" I managed.

"Have you seen Alec?" he asked.

Alec sucked on my soft spot, sending chills down my spine. I slapped a hand over my mouth and moaned into it, clenching around Alec as he continued to pump into me. I furrowed my brow, trying to find my voice.

"Maddie?"

"No. I—I haven't seen—" I started.

Suddenly, Alec thrust into me so fast and so hard that I couldn't think straight. I gripped on to his shoulders, fingernails digging into the taut muscle.

"Alec ... we need to st-stop," I whispered.

"If you see him, let me know." Oliver paused. "Nobody is bothering you tonight, right?"

A couple of moments passed, and I pressed a hand harder against my mouth to hold back my whimpers. All I wanted to do was to cry out for Alec. As much as I hated this dickhead, I had wanted to be with him for so long.

But nobody could know about this, especially Oliver.

Hell, I didn't even want Alec to know how much I enjoyed this. With all that he had drunk tonight, I doubted that he'd even remember this tomorrow. But still, if he even remembered a glimpse of me moaning for him, I would never hear the end of it.

"N-no!" I shouted to Oliver.

"And, uh, are you okay in there?" Oliver asked. "You sound like you're in pain."

"I'm fine!"

"All right."

Once I heard Oliver's boisterous footsteps disappear down the hall, I let my hand fall from my mouth and whimpered into Alec's ear as quietly as I could. I wanted to stay quiet, but I couldn't hold back anymore.

"Fuuuuck," he grunted loudly into my ear, making me tighten even more.

After thrusting himself all the way into me, he stilled, and I couldn't help the leg-trembling orgasm that ripped through my body. He looped his arms underneath my shoulders and slammed even deeper into me.

"You're mine now."

"Yours?" I asked, wave after wave of pleasure rushing through me.

My mind was high. I wasn't thinking straight. I couldn't.

"All"—he thrust deeper—"fucking"—even deeper to push his cum inside me—"mine."

After a couple of moments, Alec pulled out of me and collapsed onto the bed beside me. His chest heaved up and down, his hazy gaze focused on the ceiling. I let out a low breath and pulled the blankets up to my chest.

Fuck.

I had just slept with Alec Wolfe, the man who I claimed to loathe the most in Redwood, the player, the douchebag, the man-whore who slept around with anything that moved, the asshole who had barely spared two glances at me before.

Why? Why is Alec really here? And why am I now his?

Hands balling into fists, I gritted my teeth. Because of the alcohol.

"Get out," I snapped, shooting up in bed.

I must've been some kind of game to him. *How many beers do I have to drink in order to sleep with my best friend's little sister? How blackout drunk do I have to get? How easy is she to bag?*

Alec Wolfe was friends and teammates with my ex-boyfriend, Spencer. And I would never forget how that had turned out, the damn horror he had put me through after he slept with me for the first time.

"What?"

After leaping up, I grabbed his hand and his clothes, then dragged him to my bedroom door. He stumbled after me, nearly planting face-first into the wall.

"Get out of my bedroom. This never happened."

"The hell you mean?" he asked, refusing to let me push him out the door.

"This. Never. Happened," I said between gritted teeth. "Now, get out."

Alec stared at me for a few moments, his hazy expression twisting into a mix of anger and … the same expression he always had when he lost a hockey game. Then, he slid his tongue across his lower lip and tugged on his shorts. "Fine. It never happened, Sandra."

Anger rushed through me, and I smacked him hard across his

face. My chest tightened, hot tears welling in my eyes. I didn't want him to remember that he had slept with me, but had he really thought he was with Sandra this entire time?

It hurt like a motherfucker.

"Get out," I growled, shoving him out of my bedroom and slamming the door.

When Alec finally left, I pressed my back against the door and cursed out loud for allowing myself to be another one of his fuck-toys. It was stupid. *I* was stupid. I shouldn't have fallen for that arrogant smirk of his, should've made him leave as soon as he came into my room.

My phone buzzed from my bedside table, and I ran a hand through my messy hair.

Fuck, I am supposed to be at Vera's.

I snatched it and peered down, expecting to see Vera's contact, but instead, I was met with an unknown number.

Unknown: Stay away from Alec Wolfe. He's mine.

4

alec

I SHOULD'VE NEVER FUCKING TOUCHED her.

Growling to myself, I stumbled down the stairs and pushed through the grinding bodies. After picking up a random red Solo cup from a side table near the alcohol-stained white couch, I threw it back and let it burn the back of my throat.

Even while I was drunk, her rejection still hurt like a fucking bitch.

Why couldn't I keep my hands off her? Stay away from her? She was my best friend's little sister, who I had barely talked to in the five years I had known her. But, God, she was beautiful—fucking beautiful—and it pissed me off most days.

Because I could never fucking find the words to say to her.

And the one night I had … she had kicked me out of her bedroom and told me that this never happened. I'd said Sandra's name just to piss her off, like she had me, but when her face dropped, I'd felt even more like an asshole.

"Alec," Sandra screeched, dragging her claws all over my chest. "Come dance!"

When she wrapped her arms around my waist and drew me

16

closer to her, I pushed her back. "Get the fuck off me, Sandra. And stop telling people that we're dating," I growled, annoyed that she was such an insecure bitch that she had to lie. "We're not."

She dropped her hand and grazed it over the front of my jeans. "You don't want—"

"I said to get off me," I snapped, ripping myself away from her and storming toward the back door. I grabbed another drink from someone else—my vision was too blurry to see straight anymore.

"Alec," she cried, following after me, "we need to talk about what happened!"

The fuck is she talking about? Us?

Nothing had happened between us since Maddie and Spencer had broken the fuck up because I thought I finally had a chance at winning her heart. But I'd been pussying out on talking to her for the past year.

And now, I'd screwed it up.

I threw the beer back and grabbed another one from a shelf. "Leave me alone, Sandra."

"But—"

When she reached for me a third time, I twirled around. "Don't make me say it one more time," I growled and grabbed on to the wall to balance myself. My vision was suddenly spinning, a piercing pain shooting through my head.

"Fine," she said, crossing her arms and stomping through the crowd. "I hate you."

"Good," I said and turned back in the direction of the back door.

"Hi, Alec," another girl purred, wiggling her fingers at me.

I threw the alcohol back, wanting to get as fucked up as possible right now, but not wanting to deal with another groupie, another fan, another fucking annoying bitch from Redwood Academy who wanted her hands on my dick.

Jesus fucking Christ. I have to stop going to parties.

"Dude, where were you?" Oliver asked, grabbing my shoulder.

I highly doubted that he'd be okay with me saying something

along the lines of *fucking your sister,* so I shoved him off me, too, and headed into the backyard to get some fresh air. After sucking in a gust of chilly air, I collapsed on some padded lounge chair away from the hot tub, where girls were fooling around with each other and I could be by myself near the pool.

At least, I thought I was by myself until I saw a couple fucking in the pool without a damn care in this world. Forty-five degrees outside, and kids were banging in the water of a pool that wasn't theirs.

What a time to be alive.

Closing my eyes, I sipped the plastic cup and sighed. *Fuck.*

I shouldn't have come on to her so strong, especially not after what Spencer had done to her last year. Of course she had thought I didn't know who the hell she was.

God, what the fuck is wrong with me? I had gotten up the courage to say—*do*—something with her, and I had fucked it up.

"Lonely out here?" a girl said from the door, walking over.

I placed my hand on my forehead, my vision like fuzzy static. I blinked a couple of times in an attempt to see straight, but the world spun around me, the pool and long, skinny legs walking suddenly above me, heading in my direction.

The woman climbed right onto my lap and straddled my waist.

"I already told you to get off me," I murmured, vision too blurry to make out her face.

"You haven't said a word to me tonight, Wolfe," she whispered.

A low grunt escaped my lips as I tried to lift my gaze to her. She drew her small hands over my shoulders, then down my chest and to my abdomen. Over and over. Driving me insane—and not in the same way that I felt about Maddie.

"Get off me," I growled.

God, it was so hard to stay awake. My eyelids were heavy.

She giggled again.

"What did you do to me?" I asked.

I had gotten blackout drunk many times before while thinking about Maddie, but I had never hallucinated, and it sure as hell hadn't felt like this. I opened my mouth and inhaled deeply, my chest restricting.

She ground her pussy against me.

"What are you doing?" I asked.

"You won't remember by morning," she whispered into my ear, trailing her hand down my abdomen and slipping it underneath my waistband. "Don't worry about it, Alec. I hope you enjoyed Maddie's pussy because you're mine for the rest of the night."

"S-stop," I mumbled, my mind fading and my limbs so heavy. "G-get off."

She unzipped my pants and pulled out my cock, covered in Maddie's juices. I grasped her hand, my fingers too weak to hold it at all.

She giggled and stroked it up and down in an attempt to get it hard. "Stupid jock."

"Please, stop," I mumbled. "Get off m—"

The last thing I remembered before I blacked out was her lips pressed against mine.

5

maddie

AFTER SHOWERING to get Alec off me, I dried my hair and grabbed an overnight bag for Vera's house. I couldn't believe that I had stupidly fallen for Alec Wolfe's charm. Out of all the jocks who were here tonight, it'd *had* to be him.

I balled my hand into a tight fist and stood at my door, taking a deep breath.

Come on, Maddie. You don't even need to look around the party, just slip out the side door.

My phone buzzed in my pocket, and for a moment, I thought it was that weird, threatening number again, but Vera's name popped up on the screen in our group chat with Piper, the third friend in our little nerdy group, who I'd met last year during the Math Olympics that our school hosted. They had been texting all while I had been with Alec.

Vera: If you're both staying over, one of you will prob have to sleep on the couch.

Piper: Ugh, I don't know if I will be able to make it. My dad is being annoying.

Vera: What happened?

Piper: Something about Poison and the mob? Maybe someone died or something. I don't know. He ran out of the house in a rush, almost forgot his gun and badge here too. Anyway, he told me that if I left, he'd have my ass later so ...

Vera: 😶

Vera: Are you still coming over, Maddie?

Peering up at the door once more, I typed back.

Me: Yeah, I'm leaving now.

Vera: Mmhmm ...

Me: What?

Vera: You said that an hour ago. Get distracted? 😏

For a mere moment, my lips curled into a smile. But then I wiped the grin off my face—because I couldn't get distracted by some chiseled abs and a heartbreaker's smile. Alec Wolfe was a dickhead, and I was standing by that.

Me: No, I was showering.

Vera: Showering in cum?

I bit my lip to stifle a giggle.

Me: Get your mind off those smutty stories of yours. I'll be over in fifteen. Want anything from Cumby's while I'm out?

Vera: Gatorade, pls. <3

Me: Blaise wear you out? Need to replenish with some electrolytes?

Vera: 😒😒😒

Vera: Hate you. Bye.

My phone buzzed again, but this time, Vera texted me in our private chat.

Vera: And a Hostess CupCake from Cumby's, pls, pls, pls. <3 I will love you forever!

Me: Only if you tell me how it was with Blaise tonight. 😏

Vera: ...

Vera: Deal! Get me two.

Once I finally deposited the phone into my pocket—for good this time—I grasped the doorknob and flung the door open. I was on a mission to ignore anyone and everyone tonight because I did not want to see Alec getting handsy with Sandra again.

I would hurl ... something at them probably.

Keeping my head down, I hurried down the stairs and pushed through the sweaty jocks. Because I was a damn masochist, I scanned the crowd for Alec and Sandra and growled when I couldn't find them. That was what I got for fucking someone who wasn't mine.

Stupid jealousy.

When I arrived at the door, I scanned the crowd once more. No sign of either of them.

Teeth gritting together, I stomped out of the house and through the grass to my car that I had parked on the street after the game because I had known that I wouldn't be able to get down the driveway with everyone and their sisters at this party tonight.

Alec and Sandra were probably sleeping together in one of the spare rooms upstairs or fucking in the pool.

"Hey!" someone shouted from the front porch.

I twirled around, heart racing at the *thought* of it being Alec, but I found my brother instead. "What?"

"Where are you going?"

"To Vera's."

Holding a red Solo cup in his hand, he arched a brow. "To Vera's?"

"Yes, to Vera's house," I repeated.

Ever since Spencer, Oliver had been acting like nothing but an overprotective parent to me. He always had to know where I was going, who was going to be there, and if I would be safe. And Oliver didn't technically love that Vera lived in the slums.

"Oliver!" a girl shouted, stumbling onto the porch and grabbing his free hand. "Come on."

"Text me when you get there," he said to me, letting the girl tug him back inside.

After blowing out a breath, I continued to my car and slipped into the driver's seat. I sat in silence for a few moments, then glanced out at the house, wishing that Alec would stumble out front to get some air, alone.

Hell, I knew that I'd needed air after what happened.

But the longer I waited, the more my hopes fell.

His car still sat in the driveway, and he was still inside, getting drunker by the second and probably letting Sandra suck him off in the bathroom or something. Maybe I should've done that? Not that I had ever really given a blow job before.

Spencer and I had ... gone far, but we had never done that.

I would've probably fucked it up so much that Alec would've *known* that it was me.

Maddie Weber and not stupid Sandra.

Tears welled up in my eyes, but I blinked them away and started the car. I didn't care about what Alec was doing right now. I drove down the street toward the slums. I didn't care at all. I stopped at the Stop sign at the end of my road and glanced into my rearview mirror. Not at all.

6

alec

SOMEONE SLAPPED me hard on the cheek. "Dude!"

I lifted my head off my shoulder, my head pounding, and opened my eyes. Oliver and some of my teammates stood around me, all laughing and some holding their phones in my direction, their flashlights shining brightly in my face.

"What's going on?" I asked sleepily, glancing around at them. "What happened?"

And why the fuck were they recording? I got that we joked around and shit on the team, but I had been sleeping. What the hell was so funny that they had to record me while I was half-drunk, half-hungover, and sleepy as fuck?

"Who'd you fuck out here?" Frazer asked.

"I didn't sleep with anyone," I mumbled, not daring to even look at Oliver.

I had been good at keeping my little crush on his sister a secret. It would never go anywhere—especially after tonight—but I still didn't want him knowing about it. He had become way too protective of her after her piece-of-shit ex-boyfriend, and I didn't blame him.

"Must've been good if you couldn't even stuff it back in your pants," Caleb said.

Eyes widening, I peered down at my jeans and saw my soft cock covered in dried pussy juices and blood hanging between my open zipper. While we had all seen each other naked in the showers, I quickly scrambled to stuff myself back into my underwear and jeans.

The fuck happened?

The last thing I remembered was—my chest tightened—a girl climbing into my lap.

I stood up and shook my head. "I-I didn't—"

"Dude, come on." Caleb laughed. "You're probably too drunk off your ass to remember."

"Y-yeah," I whispered, dropping my gaze to the ground and shaking my head. "You're probably right."

But he wasn't. He fucking wasn't.

"I-I'm going to head back inside and get something to drink."

I grabbed on to the house so I wouldn't stumble and headed to the back door.

"Hey," a drunk Oliver called from behind me, pointing his finger. "No more beers, or you'll end up sleeping with the entire town."

The guys erupted into a fit of laughter behind him.

"Leave some girls for us."

"As long as you assholes don't share pictures of my soft dick online," I called, forcing myself to smirk and play along.

They wouldn't share shit. They would probably use it to attempt to blackmail me, but I didn't care about that right now.

My head was spinning, my throat closing. I stumbled into the house.

Instead of heading toward the kitchen, I sprinted up the stairs and slipped into the bathroom. As soon as the door closed, I clasped the porcelain bowl and leaned over the sink, breathing heavily. My heart pounded fast. I turned on the cold water and splashed my face.

"I wanted it," I affirmed. "I wanted it. I wanted it. I wanted it."

The cold water did nothing for me. I ran to the toilet and puked inside the bowl, my throat burning from the bile.

I wanted it. I wanted it. I wanted it.

I ripped off my clothes and stepped into the shower, turning on the cold water to ground myself.

When I was younger, I used to do it for my anxiety attacks, but it wasn't working now.

I slammed my fist into the tiled wall and split my knuckles. "Fuck!"

I needed to get out of here. I couldn't breathe. My head was spinning again. My hands shaky.

Nobody could see me like this.

So, I wrapped a towel around my waist—because I wasn't putting those filthy clothes back on—and hung another towel over my head, then hurried down the long hallways until I found Maddie's room. I didn't want her to see me like this, but everyone knew that this room was off-limits during parties.

It was the only damn place that I could go.

My breaths were short, ragged. I could barely breathe. I grabbed the doorknob with a shaky hand and yanked it open, hurrying into the room and locking the door behind me. I placed my back against it and sank down to the floor, shoving my hands through my hair.

"I wanted it," I said to convince myself, rocking back and forth. "I was too drunk to remember that I … that I …" I wanted to finish the sentence with *asked her to do that*, but all I remembered was telling her to crawl off me.

I couldn't even remember who the fuck it was.

Did she get me hard? Did I come inside her without a condom?

I crawled over to Maddie's bed and used the rest of my strength to hoist myself up onto the mattress.

She wasn't here. *Why isn't she here?*

I pulled one of her pillows to my chest and sank my nose into it, inhaling her vanilla shampoo deeply. My shoulders relaxed slightly, and the facade that I had desperately attempted to hold up slowly faded.

Fuck.

Fuck, fuck, fuck, fuck, fuck, fuck, fuck.

Fuck!

Heavy tears threatened to spill down my cheeks.

"I didn't want it," I murmured. "I didn't fucking want it."

7

maddie

"SO, do you think that lover boy will be down to see you today?" I asked, leaning against the front counter in the library on Saturday morning as Vera checked in books that had been dropped off last night.

Vera arched a dark brown brow at me. "No."

I hummed and smirked at her. "Suuure."

With a small smile on her face, she continued to scan in the books and ignored me, which meant that Blaise Harleen—Redwood Academy's bad boy—would probably show up at the library at some point today to flirt with Vera.

"I have to work," she said, lifting her gaze to me. "You can't loom over me all day."

"Pleeeease," I begged. "I don't want to go back home."

She stared at me blankly. "Maddie, you literally live in a mansion. All you have to do is enter through one of your thousand side doors and make it into your room before Alec even sees you. Plus, I doubt that he's still there." She looked down at her computer. "It's ten."

"You don't understand," I said, summoning my inner drama

queen. "Those boys sleep in until two in the afternoon on the weekends. They're probably littered around my house with a bunch of girls and beer all over them."

"Vera!" an older woman called from the bookshelves in the back. "Can you help me with these books?"

Vera smirked and walked out from behind the counter. "Have fun!"

After she disappeared behind the shelves, I slumped my shoulders forward and dragged my feet out of the library and to the street, where I'd parked. I slipped into the driver's seat, started the car, and sat there.

I didn't want to go back home and face Alec. I'd do anything.

So, instead, I whipped out my phone and texted Piper.

Me: Please tell me you're free.

Piper: Sorta?

Piper: My dad's teaching me how to hack into someone's computer. Haha.

Piper: Perks of having a corrupt policeman as a father. 😬

Piper: I can probably hang out later tonight.

"Noooooo," I drew out and rested my forehead against the wheel.

After Kai Koh from Poison—the most dangerous gang in Redwood—had hacked into everyone's phone at the school last year to spread Poison propaganda, Piper had been obsessed with learning how to be a better coder and hacker than Kai.

And I didn't doubt that she would do it one of these days.

She had utterly destroyed me at the Math Olympics last year, had aced every one of her coding classes at Redwood, and had taken up way too many robotics projects in her free time. She barely had time to hang out.

But I didn't blame her. I blamed stupid Alec for making *me* want to not even spend time in my own house because he was always there. It was totally that dickhead's fault that I found every excuse not to be home on the weekends.

Me: What time?

Piper: Five? Maybe.
Me: Sounds good.

Once I deposited my phone into my purse, I pulled off the side of the road and headed home. I wasn't going to be caught dead hanging out at a restaurant or a local coffee shop alone. Definitely *not* in Redwood.

When I pulled into the driveway, there were still about ten cars parked near the house. I blew out a low breath, spotting Alec's, and parked my car the farthest away from his so he didn't get any ideas.

I could only imagine how trashed the house was after that banger last night, which was not something I wanted to deal with. So, I grabbed my backpack, stuffed with dirty clothes from Vera's house, and my purse.

As soon as I stepped out of the car, the stench of alcohol drifted through my nostrils. I pinched the skin between my eyebrows and walked to the front door because it would be the quickest route to my room. I didn't want to waste any time sneaking in through the side door and scurrying around dirty underwear and empty bottles.

Using my sleeve to turn the knob so I wouldn't accidentally catch an STD—yes, I really was that much of a drama queen—I stepped into the house and scrunched my nose. Three guys were sprawled across the living room floor, another sleeping half-naked with a girl on the couch.

"Ew," I whispered so I wouldn't wake them and continued weaving through the room.

Beer cans were littered across the floor, the white rug stained with alcohol and what looked to be … dirt, mixed with piss. I gagged and averted my gaze, heading straight for the stairs. Oliver must be in his room with that girl from last night. I didn't see him anywhere.

I also didn't see Alec.

My hands balled into fists as I ascended the stairs, glancing over the railing at the living room for him one last time. But still, no sign of him or of Sandra. Usually, I always saw Sandra in the mornings after a party here.

Jealousy bubbled inside me as hot tears built in my eyes.

Alec Wolfe had fucked me senseless last night, and this morning, I was nothing to him.

I should've freaking known the moment he walked into my room, drunk off his ass. I should've pushed him away, made him tell me that he was lying about all those dirty little things he had whispered into my ear before I let him inside me.

At least, that way, maybe I would've been able to shout at him that I didn't want it.

But I had. Badly.

I gritted my teeth. No, I hadn't. My head was just messing with me.

After making it out of the sea of hockey guys and their groupies, I sighed in relief, closed my bedroom door behind me, and leaned against it.

Thank God I didn't—

My eyes widened when I caught sight of messy brown hair on my pillow. I ran over to my bed and ripped off the blankets to see Alec Wolfe lying in my bed, curled up in a ball and completely naked.

8

alec

"WHAT ARE YOU DOING IN HERE?" Maddie asked, shoving my shoulder to wake me. "And why the hell are you naked? Please don't fucking tell me that you slept with someone else in my bed!" She slammed her hand into my shoulder again, turning me over. "I swear to God, you'd better not have done that shit, Wolfe."

I blinked my eyes open and stared up at a mess of frizzy red hair. "A good morning would have sufficed."

Maddie yanked the pillow out from underneath my head and smacked me across the face with it. "If you slept with someone else in my room, I will kill you! You're a disgusting piece—" The rest of her voice faded as she smacked me again. And again.

"Maddie," I said between slaps.

Another mouthful of pillow.

"Maddie!"

Smack.

"Maddie!" I shouted, yanking the pillow from her hand and quickly turning us over in the bed so she lay underneath me. I pinned her wrists to the mattress and blew a strand of hair off

32

my forehead. "Settle down. I didn't sleep with anyone in your room."

She sucked in a sharp breath and stared up at me through wide eyes, tears forming in them.

"What?" I asked.

"B-but you slept with someone else?"

My body stiffened as I thought about what had happened last night. I hadn't slept with anyone, except her—at least not willingly. But, hell, I wasn't about to tell her that. Because I ... because how could I have let that happen? I should've been able to push that girl off, to protect myself.

A part of me ... must have wanted it if I couldn't even do that, right?

Right?

I squeezed my eyes closed and shook my head. "I didn't sleep with anyone but you."

Her eyes widened. "Y-you remember?"

Again, I froze.

Last night, I had led her to believe that I thought she was Sandra. It was the easiest thing for both of us to believe, apparently. But I had wanted to be with her for so fucking long.

And now, I would never be able to.

Not after ... not after what had happened once I left her room.

What if I had come inside the other girl? What if she had gotten pregnant? Maddie would never want to be with someone like me, who had gotten an anonymous chick from Redwood Academy pregnant. And, fuck, I couldn't be a dad now. All my chances at playing hockey in college would be flushed down the fucking drain. It was bad enough that the guys hadn't believed me last night.

I stared down at Maddie, not knowing how to respond.

Guilt, shame, and fucking pain simmered inside my body. I wanted to hurl again, wanted to collapse into her arms and cry as I told her everything. But would she even believe me? She hated me —and for good reasons.

I had always been a dick to her because I couldn't tell her how I felt.

"Oh, yeah," I said, playing along with the stupid lie I'd told her last night.

Because I couldn't deal with rejection right now.

"Yeah, you and Sandra both look alike," I said. "Sorry."

"We don't look alike, Wolfe," she snapped. "I'm literally like the whitest-white girl at Redwood with frizzy, bright red hair!"

A smile tugged at my lips. God, I fucking loved her frizzy hair.

"And?" I asked.

"And Sandra is Asian!" Maddie exclaimed, staring up at me like I was crazy. And when I didn't respond, she continued, "She literally has, like, the prettiest, thickest black hair ever. Clear, glowing skin. And she wears black eyeliner that scares me half to death with how sharp it is. Do you not see a difference?!"

Play along, Wolfe.

"Not when I'm drunk," I said.

She slammed her hands into my chest. "Get off me."

"Are you going to hit me with a pillow again?"

"Maybe." She glared at the wall to her right. "Besides, why are you in my bed, naked?" she asked, crossing her arms and shaking her head. "You know that my room is off-limits during parties. If Oliver catches you in here, he will literally beat the shit out of you. Have you been here all night?"

What the fuck do I say to her?

Someone took advantage of me while I slept, and I lost it, so I ran upstairs like a fucking coward to cry into your pillow? That would make me sound like a weak piece of shit who couldn't protect himself, who couldn't control his emotions.

Besides, I wasn't planning on telling anyone about what had happened. Not after my teammates recorded me with my cock hanging out of my pants last night.

"Huh?" she asked, then pressed her lips together.

I tore my gaze away from her and scrambled off her. "None of your fucking business."

Because I had dumped my dirty clothes in the bathroom, I stormed to her walk-in closet to find something to wear. I needed to get out of here and go home, never return to a fucking party again after what had happened.

I felt so dirty, so disgusting, so fucking ashamed that I had let this happen.

"Hey!" Maddie shouted, leaping up from the bed and following me. "What are you doing?" She grabbed my shoulder as I completely ransacked her closet, tossing clothes everywhere in an attempt to find something that wasn't girlie and that would fit me. "You have your own clothes."

"My clothes are dirty," I said, tugging on some sweatpants and grabbing a sweatshirt.

She ripped the sweatshirt away from me. "You didn't answer my question."

I pulled it back and, in turn, yanked her closer to me. "I told you that it wasn't any of your fucking business."

She sucked in a low breath and stared up at me. "No."

"No what?" I asked, glancing down at how close she was to me. We had never been this close when I was sober. "No, those words didn't just fucking come out of my mouth? Or, no, you're just not going to listen and are hell-bent on being a little brat for me?"

She widened her eyes and pressed her thighs together.

Fuck.

"Maddie," I growled, voice low, "don't fucking do that."

"D-do what?" she whispered, breath hitching.

"Maddie!" Oliver shouted from outside the closet. "Your door is open. You home?"

9

maddie

"MADDIE!" Oliver called, his footsteps approaching my closet door that I slammed shut. "I swear to God, nobody had better be in here. This is my sister's fucking closet. You assholes know this room is off-limits during parties, and if you don't—"

He twisted the doorknob, about to push it open, but Alec sprawled his hand across it and held it closed.

Alec stared down at me, lowered his head until it was inches from my ear, and whispered, "Say something, Maddie."

God, he was so close.

"Open u—"

"Go away, Oliver!" I shouted, heat coursing through me. I pressed my thighs together and stared up into Alec's dark eyes. I placed my hands on his chest, curling my fingers against all his thick muscle. "I-I'm getting changed!"

"Nobody is bothering you, are they?"

Alec twirled me around so I faced the door and then pressed his naked body against my backside. I gulped and placed my hands on the door, my pussy aching to be filled yet again by his huge cock. Part of me didn't even believe that this was happening.

Alec slid his hand down the door to mine, his fingers snuggling between mine. My heart raced. I curled my fingers against the wood, watching as his did the same, locking around my palm. He dropped his head so it rested at the nape of my neck.

"Fuck, Maddie," he groaned. "You don't know how long ..."

"How long what?" I whispered.

"Maddie!" Oliver shouted. "What's going on?"

"I'm getting changed!" I said after gathering my thoughts. "Leave me alone."

"Nobody is bothering you, are they?" he repeated.

He had been so overprotective, almost to the point of overbearing, after Spencer completely crushed our relationship last year. I could barely breathe with Oliver around sometimes ... or maybe that was because the biggest flirt in all of Redwood was holding my hand at this very moment.

"N-no," I whispered.

"Good." Oliver paused. "You haven't seen Alec, have you?"

"You're always looking for him, aren't you?" I asked, remembering last night, when he had almost barged into my room while Alec was thrusting me into my mattress.

Oliver needed to get Alec a damn collar with a bell for how much Alec disappeared on him.

"He's been missing since he slept with that girl last night on the deck."

My entire body froze, my heart shattering.

Wh-what?

Staying quiet, I ripped myself away from Alec and glared at him through tears in my eyes. He shook his head, as if to say it wasn't true, as if to say that he hadn't lied to me this morning when I asked him if he had slept with another girl.

But this fucker ... this dickhead ...

I wanted to scream. *Why am I so stupid? Why am I so naive?*

He had literally said Sandra's name last night before he left, and I'd stupidly thought he wanted me. *Me!* The freaking loser little sister who he probably thought he could bag and dump off—and I had stupidly let him.

Alec walked closer to me with his hands up. "Maddie, I …"

Hot tears burned my eyes, and I continued to move back until I hit the end of my closet. "Stay away from me, you fucking asshole," I growled lowly so if Oliver was still in my room, he wouldn't hear. I didn't need the drama of another Spencer situation right now.

"Maddie, please," he pleaded, brown eyes almost … glistening. "I …"

He couldn't even form a cohesive sentence, not even give me a sappy excuse.

Oh, I was too drunk. Oh, sorry, I thought it was you on the deck.

I gritted my teeth, tears bursting from my eyes. "Get out."

"Maddie," he whispered, pain all over his face.

"Get out!" I screamed, not giving a fuck about Oliver anymore. "Now!"

Tears welled in his eyes. *Fucking tears!* I didn't know what the fuck was wrong with him, but crocodile tears weren't going to work on me. I had seen enough of them from Spencer, and I … I couldn't believe that I had been so damn stupid a second time!

What is wrong with me?

"Please," he begged. "Let me explain."

"Explain?!" I shouted, slamming my hands into his chest when he stepped closer. "Explain what? That you fucked another girl on the deck, then crawled into my bed afterward? And when I asked you if you did it, you looked into my fucking eyes and told me no! What else is there to explain?"

Alec suddenly became quiet.

Usually, he was the loudmouthed hockey star who said whatever shit he was thinking. He didn't know how to be quiet, never had nothing to say. But he was lost for words now, grasping at all the little lies he had told me.

"You're a liar."

"You don't understand," he whispered, dropping his gaze and clenching his jaw.

"No, I don't understand." I was seething. "Especially why you would do something like this to me when you saw me so fucking broken after Spencer. I don't understand why you never talked to me and suddenly wanted to fuck me last night."

He parted his lips, then pressed them back together. "I-I'm sorry."

When those two little words left his mouth, pain shot through my body. It was the admission of guilt. He had really done what Oliver had said he did. He had betrayed me. He felt sorry for it. And what? Did he think I would just forgive him for that?

Tears streamed down my cheeks. "Get out."

He turned around and faced the door, every muscle in his body rippling. For a mere moment, he rested his head and fist against my closet door, muttering something to himself, and then he slammed his fist into the wood and stormed out of my room.

And out of my fucking life.

10

alec

MY BACKSEAT WAS CLUTTERED with hockey gear for practice today at noon, but it was already one p.m., and I hadn't been able to move from my car. I had been sitting here for two and a half hours, staring at the entrance to the Redwood Hospital.

I didn't know if it was too late, but I had driven myself here this morning.

But I couldn't gather the courage to step out of the car. I didn't have any physical injuries from Friday night. I didn't have the clothes I had worn. No weapons or texts. Nothing that would make anyone believe me.

All I wanted was to get tested for STDs.

Gripping the steering wheel with both hands, I gulped. *STDs?! What will happen if I have one that isn't curable?*

I ran a hand through my messy hair, wanting to tear it out. All my chances of playing in the National Hockey League one day would be gone.

Gone!

My breathing quickened, and I rocked back in the seat, hitting my head against the rest. This wasn't supposed to happen. I hadn't even had a choice. I'd wanted to spend the night with Maddie, but my drunk ass had had to ruin it by being myself.

Why the fuck did I mention Sandra's name? What is wrong with me?

Another hour of staring at flashing ambulance lights and sick men and women walking into the ER. And then two o'clock turned to three o'clock. And three turned to six at night.

My phone buzzed on the seat beside me—messages from my teammates, coach, and parents, all wondering why I hadn't shown up for hockey or dinner. Part of me never wanted to set foot on the ice. I wanted to stay in bed forever.

No more parties. No more drinking.

That would never happen to me again.

If I told my coach, he wouldn't believe me. If I told my parents, they wouldn't believe me. If I told my teammates *again*, they wouldn't believe me either. They'd all ask me if I had been drinking, if I had really wanted it, if I didn't remember coming on to the girl.

My memory was shot from that night.

Fucking shot.

Chest tight—almost to the point where I couldn't breathe—I slammed my fist into the steering wheel. Then, I picked up my phone, ignored all the other messages, and scrolled to Maddie's contact. We had each other's numbers—from that one time years ago when I had gotten up the courage to talk to her—but we had never once messaged each other.

Me: Can we talk?

Almost instantly, she read the message.

Little gray bubbles appeared next to her profile picture that I had snapped of her at one of my games, standing in the bleachers, her frizzy red hair curled and a complete mess on top of her head. But I thought she looked cute.

The bubbles disappeared.

Fuck.

After running my hand over my face, I turned on the car and drove out of the hospital lot. I couldn't go in. Not now. I'd do it before I did anything else with Maddie—*if* I did anything else with her—but ... now, it was useless.

I wouldn't be able to deal with the questions.

Once I merged onto the main road, I headed home.

Maddie wanted nothing to do with me, and I didn't blame her. Oliver had made it seem like I had basically cheated on Maddie with whoever the fuck had drugged me the other night. And if I were Maddie, I wouldn't want a sorry excuse for an explanation either.

We barely knew each other, but she was the only person who could calm me down. She didn't even know it either. Every time I looked up into the student section of the bleachers during a hockey game. Every time my thoughts got the worst of me at school in AP Calc. Every time I made an excuse to hang out with Oliver when I really just wanted to see her.

When I pulled into my driveway, I blew out a deep breath, leaned against my seat, and closed my eyes. The door opened, and Dad appeared in front of it with a glass of top-shelf whiskey in his hand.

I cursed to myself and slipped out of the car, grabbing my hockey gear from the back. Walking up the walkway, I could smell the thick scent of ham and pineapple from one of the open windows.

Dad stepped out into the chilly fall night and held the door open for me. "You missed dinner."

You miss dinner every Friday and Saturday with your fucking business meetings.

"Sorry," I forced myself to say instead.

He slung his arm around my shoulders. "How was practice?"

"Good."

He leaned even closer to me. "And the party Friday night?"

I tensed. "It was fine."

"Something happen?" he asked, a small smirk on his lips and a brow arched.

"No."

He grabbed my shoulder and squeezed *playfully*. "Come on. I've been gone all weekend. I want to know what went down." He guided me toward the kitchen. "You score any chicks? When I was your age, I'd get all the—"

Mom pulled out a plate from the microwave, twirled around, and narrowed her gaze at Dad. "You'd better not finish that sentence, Wolfe." She walked over to the kitchen island and placed the plate on the counter. "Here you go, sweetheart."

"I'm not hungry," I said. "I have homework to finish."

"Is there something wrong?" she asked before I could slip out the door. "You're always hungry after practice. Did you eat at Oliver's?"

"Yeah."

"Okay, well, if you want anything to eat, I'll wrap this and put it in the fridge for you," she started, but then her gaze dropped to my neck. Her eyes widened, and she hurried over. "Alec, what's that on your neck?"

I pulled up my collar to hide my body from her. I didn't want her touching me.

Yet she pushed my hand away and rolled my collar down anyway.

"Hives?" she asked, brow furrowed.

"It's not hives." Lie. "Just roughhousing at practice."

Dad swished whiskey around in a glass, one brow arched. "Looks more like a hickey to me."

I dropped my gaze and headed for the stairs, dragging my hockey equipment to my bedroom. Before Mom could ask me more about the fucking hives on my neck or Dad could tell me more about how he used to snag all the girls in high school—like I fucking thought it was cool—I slammed my door closed and pulled out my phone.

I really needed to talk to someone, but Maddie still hadn't texted back.

I doubted that she ever would.

11

maddie

"WHAT'S WRONG?" I asked Oliver after he parked his car next to mine in the student parking lot early Monday morning.

Vera zipped up her thin fall jacket, tugged on her backpack straps, and leaned against my car, watching Oliver with wide eyes. Standing next to her, I crossed my arms and arched a brow at my brother, who tore his backpack out of the passenger seat and gritted his teeth.

"We're going to have a shit game tonight," he said.

"You have another game tonight?" Vera asked. "Didn't you have one on Friday?"

"Yeah, they did," I said to her, then returned to my brother. "Why? You have Alec."

Just his name on my tongue tasted like venom. I hated any and all things that had to do with him, especially after he had fucked some random chick after he fucked me. But that was my fault for stupidly allowing him into my bedroom.

"He skipped practice yesterday. Can't play tonight."

"Alec skipped practice?" I asked. "Why?"

"I don't know," Oliver growled. "I haven't been able to get ahold of him."

I chewed on the inside of my cheek. Well, he had messaged me last night …

"It's too cold!" Vera said, looping her arm around mine and tugging me toward the entrance of Redwood Academy. She bounced up and down on her toes, her teeth chattering. "Why is it always so cold in the fall? I want summer back!"

"So you can wear skimpy little dresses for Blaise?" I hummed, smirking.

She cut her gaze to me. "No … maybe."

When we finally stepped inside the building, a wall of heat hit us. Vera relaxed and tugged off her jacket, scanning the halls and finding Piper at her locker. Vera dragged me down the hallway toward Piper, who met us halfway.

With heavy bags under her tired eyes, Piper swiped a hand across her face to push some pink-blonde hair off her forehead. "God, how are you this bubbly already? It's too damn early for school to start." When she made it to us, she rested her head against my shoulder. "I'm so tired."

"Guess what!" Vera beamed.

"Uh, you have way too much energy for Monday morning?" Piper asked.

"No!" Vera playfully smacked her shoulder, then swung an arm around me. "Maddie slept with Alec on Friday night!"

My eyes widened, and I slapped my hand right across her mouth to shut her up. Why was she screaming this in Redwood's hallway on a Monday freaking morning? Didn't she know that people had nothing better to do than eavesdrop and spread rumors here?

"Can you not scream that?!" I whisper-yelled. "Nobody can find out. My brother would kill both of us!"

Especially after what had happened with Spencer. And besides, nothing would ever happen between Alec and me. I squeezed my hands into fists and gritted my teeth, nostrils flaring. Especially not after what Alec had pulled the other day.

"With Alec, Mads?" Piper scrunched her nose. "Why him?"

That was the damn question I had been asking all weekend. Out of all the people who could've flirted with me in the kitchen, tried to get me to dance with him, then followed me up to my room to fuck me senseless, why Alec?

"Hello?" Piper asked, waving a hand across my face. "Alec Wolfe?"

"He, uh ..." I scratched the back of my neck. "Came on to me?"

I honestly didn't know. It had happened so suddenly.

"Is it serious?" Piper asked, pulling some books out of her locker beside mine.

"God, no," I said. "I want to puke at the sight of him."

"It definitely is," Vera said, grinning like a madwoman from ear to ear.

Piper looked between us, arched her brow, and leaned against the locker beside me, giving me that *I don't believe you, but I'm going to shut my mouth for now* look. And I was glad because if anyone found out, it would spread like wildfire across these halls, and soon, Oliver would know.

"Like I told you on Friday, V, it didn't mean anything," I concluded.

Though I knew my words were just chaotically crafted lies.

It had meant something.

Then, he had ripped my heart out and stomped on it with a muddy boot.

"Suuure," Vera said.

"Speaking of the king of Redwood ..." Piper glanced behind me and bit back a gag.

I followed her gaze to see Sandra and her best friend, Tiffany, standing right next to Alec, staring up at him through mascara-heavy lashes.

"Gross. They're fawning over him like he's a god or something."

I dug my nails into my palms, nearly ripping the skin. I'd bet those texts were from Sandra or Tiffany or both of them at the same time. I gritted my teeth and was seething as he glanced over his shoulder at me. Sandra looped her arm around his, like she always did. And he let her.

That asshole let her.

I wanted to wrap my hands around his throat and—

I blew out a breath. No.

"It wasn't anything serious," I whispered to myself, but my words came out through clenched teeth.

Vera bumped her hip against mine. "Someone sounds jealous ..."

I slammed my locker closed. "I'm not jealous."

Piper gave a dry laugh. "You really like him, don't you?"

"No." I flared my nostrils. "I hate him." I glanced back over my shoulder at him, just to remind myself that he was the biggest player at Redwood Academy and that I, Maddie Weber, didn't like him, not even in the slightest. "He's a dick."

Walking backward down the hallway toward us, Alec raised his hand to wave to Sandra. "See you later, Sandra!" he shouted loud enough for the entire school to hear. And then he bumped into me, shoving me against my locker, purposefully.

"Watch it," Alec said, turning around to face me.

"You watch it." I ground my teeth together but felt those tingles zip across my body when he brushed his hand against mine briefly. He felt like he had on Friday night, but better somehow, and I hated it. Fucking hated it. "You bumped into me."

Alec curled his lips in disgust, but those dark brown eyes were softer than usual.

"What'd you say?" Alec sneered at me.

Gathering all my courage, I stared him right in the eye. "I said, watch it."

Alec had had no reason to walk over to me, to bump into me, to say a word to me. But he had. Which meant that he wanted something from me. And if he wanted to fuck me again, then I would punch him right in the face.

Instead of walking away, he smacked his large hand across my books, shoving them to the ground, our hands grazing against each other again. Then, he leaned closer to me and lowered his voice so only I could hear him. "Can't wait to see you bend over to pick up those books, Cupcake."

I hurled my fist back and slammed it into his jaw. "I hate you, you fucking dickhead."

While Alec didn't stumble back, he grasped his jaw and chuckled, which made me angrier with him. Who the hell did he think he was?! Flirting with Sandra all night at the party, sleeping with me, then another girl, flirting with Sandra again, then with me?! He was giving me a goddamn headache.

"Don't laugh," I scolded quietly. "Pick up my books."

When he leaned down and grabbed my books, I widened my eyes. He was really …

He handed me the stack of books, his fingers lingering on mine, his smirk gone, and his eyes suddenly duller than usual. "Can we talk?"

"No," I snapped.

He drew his tongue across his teeth, walked a few steps backward down the hallway, then turned around and disappeared around a corner. We both had AP Calc first thing this morning, so I had to see his pretty—*ugly*—mug in less than fifteen minutes.

"He means nothing to you, right?" Vera nudged. "Because that punch sure had a lot of passion behind it."

"I'm passionate about how much I hate him," I said, walking down the hallway. "I'll see you guys at lunch."

Flustered and frustrated, I gritted my teeth and turned the corner to head for AP Calc. I didn't want to see him again this morning. I would honestly love to never see that stupid little smirk again because I—

Before I could make it to Calc, someone slapped a hand over my mouth and tugged me into the first dark, empty classroom.

12

alec

I PRESSED Maddie against the shut door and buried my face into her neck. "Cupcake."

While I had been desperately trying to keep up with the whole king of Redwood attitude that everyone expected from me, we had seven minutes until the bell for first period rang, and I was already exhausted with the whole charade.

Maddie tensed and squirmed in my arms, twisting toward me and shoving her hands into my chest. "What are you doing?!" she whisper-yelled, breathing quickly. "Get off me! I never want to see your ugly face again."

I moved back, but I was still inches from her, posting my arms on the door behind her to trap her in. "Is that better?" I asked.

She stared up at me, her cheeks flushed and her nipples poking through her Redwood Academy hockey T-shirt, and she pursed her full lips. She glanced down between us, pressing her thighs together. "No. You're still too close."

I moved back another few inches, watching as she furrowed her brow, as if she hadn't really wanted me to move back at all and she just wanted to be bratty for me this morning. But she didn't say anything, so I stayed put.

"I need to get to class," she finally said.

But I didn't want her to go. Not now. Not when I could finally talk to her. Though … I didn't know how to start. *Will she think less of me? Will she laugh in my face too?*

"Are you jealous?" I asked instead of telling her what I really wanted to.

"Jealous?!" she asked, eyes blazing. "Of who? Sandra? Tiffany? No."

My lips curled into a smirk, and I hummed.

"What?! I'm not!" she cried. "Why would I be jealous? Because you flirt with them?"

"So, you'd be okay if I got back together with Sandra?"

Maddie wet her lips. "Stop it," she said, voice hoarse.

"She's been all over me lately."

"Alec …"

"She even made a pass at me Fri—"

"Fine!" she shouted, throwing her hands into the air. "I'm jealous, but that doesn't mean that I like you." She was seething and pushed me back a few feet. "Is that what you wanted to hear, Alec? Huh?" She shoved me again. "Now, get away from me before I punch you in your nose this time."

I smirked at her, my stomach light. *Maddie's jealous.*

She rolled her eyes. "Enjoy your little ego boost while it lasts because nothing is going to happen between us."

"Oh?" I asked, stepping closer to her again yet still keeping my distance. Because if she didn't want it, then I wasn't going to push her. But, man, I wanted to touch her again. I posted one arm on the wooden door behind her and trailed my nose up the column of her neck without touching her. "Is that right?"

"Yes," she breathed, voice barely above a whisper. "That's right."

I hadn't touched her yet, but she was squirming around,

grinding her thighs together, and staring at my lips. She opened her mouth, then closed it, brow furrowing.

"If my brother finds out ..." she whispered, reaching up to squeeze her nipple.

And, fuck, I nearly lost all control.

"Yeah, I know. I know," I murmured, reaching underneath her skirt and dragging a finger across her soaked panties. "If Oliver finds out that his sister has moaned my name, he'd kill both of us. Wouldn't he?"

"He will!"

"And how do you think he'd react if he knew how wet your panties were for me?"

Her breath caught, and she placed a hand on my chest, but didn't push me away. I moved my fingers around her clit, rubbing the swollen bundle of nerves back and forth. She rested her head against my chest and whimpered.

"What if he found me playing with your pussy?"

When I slipped my fingers under her silky underwear, she moaned. "Alec ..."

I moved my fingers faster, pushing her so close to the edge already. She scrunched my T-shirt up in her fist and bit back another moan. I was desperate for her to feel good because of me again.

"What about you coming on my fingers?"

Her entire body tensed, her legs shaking. She formed an O with her mouth and threw her head back, her skin tinting pink as she held back a loud moan for me. She stared up at me through hazy eyes, coming on my fingers.

Once she finally came down from her orgasm, she leaned against the door and blew out a breath. Her face contorted from one of pleasure to anger. And suddenly, she shoved me away again. "What's going on with you? Why are you acting so weird?"

"What are you talking about?"

She threw her hands into the air. "First off, you never talk to me. Ever." She crossed her arms and tilted her head, those blazing eyes suffocating me. "Second, we slept together on Friday night! Then, Oliver said that you weren't at practice yesterday."

"I wasn't."

"Why not?"

I shrugged. "Because I didn't want to go."

More like I couldn't get myself to leave the hospital.

"What do you mean, you didn't want to go? You have a game tonight, and if you don't go to practice the day before, then you can't play."

"So what?" I asked, grabbing my backpack and turning toward the door. "I don't care."

Honestly, it didn't really fucking matter anymore. If I had gone to practice, all the guys would have done was tease me about the girl who had fucking drugged and raped me. I hadn't wanted to go. None of it fucking mattered, especially if that chick had gotten pregnant.

She snatched my shoulder and turned me around. "What do you mean?"

"I mean that I don't care."

"You love hockey."

"Yeah, I do."

She stared at me like I was completely insane. "Do you hear yourself right now?"

"Loud and clear," I said.

She stepped closer and lowered her voice. "Is it because of what happened between us?"

I stared at her for a few quiet moments, looking from eye to eye. I had fucking asked her to talk, and now that she was here and asking me what was wrong, I didn't want to tell her. I was stalling to get a few minutes alone with her to calm myself down.

Because I couldn't stop thinking about her all night.

"No," I whispered. "It's not that."

She arched a brow. "Then, what is it?"

God, she was too good for me. I had been nothing but a dick-head to her, sleeping around with Sandra just to get her jealous.

She even thought that I had slept with someone else, and she was here, shouting at me for missing a game.

"It's nothing," I said, mouth dry. "Sorry."

She froze, hurt crossing her face as the last word left my mouth. She dropped her gaze to the floor between us and chewed on the inside of her cheek. "What are you apologizing for? Wasting my time or sleeping with another girl?"

Fuck.

I closed my eyes, not wanting to think about it. But honestly, it was the only thing I *had* been thinking about this entire weekend. She just didn't understand how much what happened affected me. How much it hurt me.

My chest tightened, the anxiety quickly building inside me.

I didn't want her to see me like this.

I was toxic Alec Wolfe, not some weak idiot who broke out into panic attacks.

"Leave," I said, ripping myself away from her.

"I'm not going anywhere," she said stubbornly, walking around me so that she stood right in front of me again.

I averted my gaze to anywhere but her.

She placed both hands on her wide hips. "You're the one who brought me here."

"I brought you in here so I could fuck you," I snapped, coming up with any type of excuse for her to leave. I could barely breathe and didn't want her to see the hives on my neck. I clasped my hands together so they wouldn't shake. "But you had to start bitching, so leave."

Instead of stomping out of the room, Maddie stared up at me. I peered down at her, hoping that she'd hit me across the face again rather than be devastated at the words that had just left my stupid mouth. But tears were trembling in her big eyes.

She opened her mouth, lips twitching. "I ... I hate you."

"I'm sorry," I said, grabbing her face with my shaky hands. "I'm sorry. I didn't mean it."

"Yes, you did."

"No, I didn't. Please …" My heart was beating rapidly, only speeding up. "Maddie, don't cry."

Tears raced down her cheeks. "I hate you!" she sobbed, tearing herself away from me and running to the door. "I hate you so much, Alec Wolfe."

13

maddie

AFTER FLYING out of fourth period for lunch, I yanked my phone out of my pocket and scrolled right to my group chat with Vera and Piper. I didn't want to even step foot in the same room as Alec for the rest of the freaking day. Calc had already been too much for me.

Me: Meet me in the library for lunch.

Me: I cannot deal with certain people right now. 😤

I turned the corner, nearly smacking into Jace Harbor, who tossed around a football between his hands. He and some guys from the football team continued walking toward the cafeteria to eat. My phone buzzed.

Vera: 🤐

Me: pls. 🥺

Vera: I'll be there in five.

Once I grabbed my lunchbox from my locker, I slammed it closed and shoved my phone into the back pocket of my jeans. While waiting for Piper to respond, I walked through the hallway toward the library with the sandwich that I had made this morning.

Why'd Alec have to be a total asshole to me? He had been the one to yank me into the dark classroom this morning, all just to touch me? To get me off?! What kind of messed up bullshit was that dickhead on? Then, he'd had the damn audacity to tell me to leave.

My hands balled into fists by my sides. "I hate him."

But mostly, I hated myself because I had punched him straight in the jaw and then easily given in to him while we were alone. Like I had absolutely no control of my body when I most certainly did. I just wanted him to like me.

And, boy, did he like me, but not in the same way that I wanted him to.

Passing the Computer Science classroom, I peered into the door's thin window and spotted the new teacher that Redwood had hired after the last professor had hacked into her students' parents' bank accounts and nearly cleaned them out. Freezing, I widened my eyes when I spotted Piper crawling out from underneath his desk.

Oh shit!

I quickly returned on my hurried walk to the library, noting that I'd have to tell Vera that Piper probably *wouldn't* be spending lunch with us today. My lips curled into a small smirk. Piper had been getting better at coding and hacking, and I guessed *this* was the reason why.

"Like the new glasses, Astrid," Calix said behind me.

I glanced over my shoulder, spotting good-girl Astrid Khatri blushing and pushing up her glasses as one of the billionaire bad boys from The Crew threw a smirk in her direction.

She pulled her books to her chest, muttered a, "Thank you," and scurried to the cafeteria.

Damn, today just keeps getting weirder and weirder. First, Piper. Now, Astrid?

Once I stepped into the library, I spotted Vera by the counter, talking to the librarian.

"Is it okay if we have lunch here today?" she asked, rocking back on her heels and giving Miss Lang huge eyes. "Please."

Miss Lang *never* said no to Vera because Vera also worked at a library. Crazy how females who loved books and immersing themselves into new worlds ... *and smut* ... got along so well despite their age gap.

"Sure, sweetheart," Miss Lang said, nodding to a small room behind the counter.

Usually, only students who had online classes could work back here, but we now had special privileges. I dumped my backpack on one of the couches and collapsed onto the seat, throwing my head back.

"Piper is having the time of her life right now," I said.

Vera arched her brow. "The time of her life?"

"With the new Computer Science teacher."

"Another one?!" Vera asked, eyes wide. "Damn, these teachers must have good—"

"What do you mean, another one?" I asked.

Vera glanced around to make sure nobody was listening in—even Miss Lang—then leaned closer to me and lowered her voice. "Well, Blaise told me that Sakura Sato and Mr. Avery have been sleeping with each other since the beginning of the year."

"What?!" I whisper-yelled. "Sakura with Mr. Avery?!"

"Don't scream," Vera said. "I'm not even supposed to know."

"But Sakura is so sweet," I said, thinking about a few weeks ago, when Sakura had randomly texted me one night and asked me if Mr. Avery had emailed me about the homework. He had never once emailed me about any homework in his classroom, which meant he had been messaging her. Secretly.

"Apparently, she's also dirty to be sleeping with a professor!" Vera said, grinning wickedly. "I'm actually writing a super-smutty story about a professor and his student now too! Ah, this is going to give me so much inspo." Then, she leaned closer and nudged me. "Next, I'll be writing your love story."

"My life is *not* a love story," I said, scrunching my nose. "Don't you ever put Alec in a book either."

Vera widened her smile and returned to her lunch. "We'll see."

"Is it all right if I eat lunch here?" someone said from the counter.

I leaned to the left enough to see Alec fucking Wolfe standing with takeout from Branono's Pizzeria in downtown Redwood, the thick scent of cheese drifting through my nostrils. Usually, students weren't allowed to leave school grounds during the day, but all the popular kids got away with it.

"Mr. Wolfe, what's wrong with the cafeteria?" Miss Lang said.

Thank goodness! Put him in his place, Miss Lang. Tell him he can't—

"It's too crowded," he said to Miss Lang, avoiding all eye contact with her.

After a couple of moments, she nodded to the back room, where Vera and I were supposed to be eating lunch alone. "As long as you stay quiet."

Fuck.

Alec walked into the room, lifted his gaze to me, then pulled it away, and walked toward the couch across the small room. I glared at him, teeth gritted together and nails digging into my palms.

"Awkward," Vera hummed, sipping her water and standing. "Well, I'm going to find a couple of steamy romance books to draw inspiration from for my writing." She glanced over at Alec, then back at me. "I'll leave you two—"

I snatched her wrist and yanked her back down into her seat. "You are not leaving me."

No way would I ever allow myself to be alone in a room with Alec Wolfe again.

14

alec

AT SEVEN P.M., I walked into the hockey arena and pressed my lips together in a tight line. I gazed at Coach and my teammates huddled on our side of the ice, talking gameplay, then scanned the crowd.

Maddie sat with Piper in the stands, immediately pulling her gaze away when we locked eyes. She clenched her jaw, brow furrowed in an angry glare, probably talking shit about all the pain I had caused her this morning.

When my teammates skated out onto the ice, I picked up my heavy feet and walked over to the rest of the guys who had to sit out today. Part of me felt fucking weird because I *never* sat on the bench. I was always pushing, always starting, barely ever hurt.

Until now.

"Wolfe," Coach shouted when I shuffled into the stadium three minutes before the game, dressed in my clothes from school. With his clipboard by his side, he arched a brow at me. "Where the hell have you been?"

"Busy," I mumbled and collapsed down onto the bench next to

him as the team warmed up on the ice for another preseason game. My shoulders slumped forward, my gaze focused on the ground. I hadn't even wanted to come tonight.

"Too busy to message me before practice yesterday to tell me you weren't coming?"

"Sorry, sir."

He paused for a moment, then sat down beside me. "You could've played today if you had shown up for a half hour yesterday. But due to school policy, you're going to have to sit the entire game."

I peered over my shoulder at Maddie again. "I know."

God, I wanted to talk to her so badly, but I didn't want to fucking ruin my relationship with her more than I already had. I was no good for her, had ignored her here and there, barely said anything nice to her, especially lately.

After running a hand through my hair, I placed both forearms on my knees and leaned forward, staring down at the gray piece of gum stuck to the bottom of the bleachers.

Why did my fucking anxiety possess me to be such an asshole to her this morning?

She would never understand it even if I tried to apologize.

"The hell were you at lunch?" Oliver asked, skating up to the sidelines.

"In the library."

All my answers today were so forced, so monotone, so fucking automatic. I didn't have the energy to keep up the facade of being the school flirt, toying with Sandra to piss off Maddie. Especially not after I had made her cry before first period.

"Spending time with that chick?" Frazer nudged me, squeezing a bottle of water through his helmet to rehydrate.

I wrapped a hand over the front of my throat, the heat crawling up my neck. *Fuck.*

Coach glanced over at me as the guys skated back on the ice.

While I didn't want to tell my parents or Maddie, I had known

Coach Leo since I was six years old. He had gone through all the ups and downs with me, had given me extra training sessions when I asked for them, and was preparing me for college hockey.

Plus, he felt more like a father than Dad did at some points.

If I kept this up and didn't show up for practice again, I would have wasted all of his time.

"What's going on?" he asked between plays. "The guys mentioned a party on Friday."

"Yeah," I said quietly, rubbing my hands together until they were raw. "A party ... and a girl."

"A girl?" Coach Leo said with one brow raised. "You're letting a girl get into your head?"

"She ..." I started, a lump forming in my throat. "She ... slept with me."

"Pussy that good?" Jose, an assistant coach in his fifth year of college, asked.

I opened my mouth, then shut it, unsure about what to say. Honestly, I didn't want to say shit in front of Jose, but I had already opened my big mouth. If I didn't tell Coach the entire story, he would think I was throwing my life away for her.

"I didn't want it," I admitted.

Jose clasped his hands over my shoulders and chuckled. "Oh, come on, Wolfe. Who doesn't want a little bit of pussy?" He nodded to Coach Leo. "Bet Leo never turned it down when he was in his prime."

Coach Leo turned away but smirked. "That's enough, Jose."

Between Jose and Coach, my teammates and the sea of parents and students cheering in the bleachers, I ... I couldn't handle it. My stomach twisted, a thin layer of sweat coating my back. There was so much noise, too many people.

I needed to get the hell out of here.

So, while Coach shouted at my teammates a few minutes before the first intermission, I walked toward the exits and slipped out of the stadium. Once the doors closed behind me, I sprinted through the hallway and to the nearest restroom, thrust open a stall, and dropped to my knees, puking up Branono's pizza in the toilet.

I shouldn't have told anyone.

I had known they wouldn't believe me.

15

maddie

FUCK. *Fuck. Fuck. Fuck. Fuck. Fuck. Fuck.*

With my thighs pressed together, I sprinted like a maniac out of the stadium and toward the restrooms. A drip of pee rolled down my inner thigh.

Why did I drink so freaking much before the game?!

After pushing open the women's restroom door, I slammed a stall open, covered the seat with toilet paper, and collapsed down to pee. The pressure subsided in my lower abdomen, and I slumped my shoulders forward, sighing in relief.

Maybe I should've not waited until intermission to use the bathroom.

The person in the stall next to me groaned. I wiped and scrunched my nose, really not wanting to listen to another woman grunt and groan as she shit. I already had enough of that at home when the hockey team came over.

Once I finished my business, I exited the stall and washed my hands. When the grunt came again, I glanced over at the stall to see a man's sweater sticking out from underneath the wall. I furrowed my brow and walked over to it, gently knocking. They were sitting on the *ground* in the restroom.

"Are you okay?" I asked.

"I'm fine."

I pushed the unlocked door open and spotted Alec Wolfe with his head in the toilet. He grasped his stomach, as if he was going to puke, and dry-heaved. A clump of thick brown hair stuck to his sweaty forehead.

"Alec," I whispered, "this is the women's bathroom."

"I want to go home," he cried, clutching on to the toilet seat with his bare hand. "Please."

"It's intermission. Are you sure that your coach would—"

"I want to go home. There're too many people here."

My eyes widened because I had never once seen him like this. He loved hockey, loved training, loved when everyone watched. He put on a fucking performance on the ice. Why had he been acting so weird lately? He looked how I had felt during my entire relationship with Spencer.

I crouched down behind him and gently placed my hand on his shoulder. "Let's go then."

He pulled his head out of the toilet and glanced back at me. "You …"

"What?" I asked.

While I might've been stupid as hell to show him any sympathy after what he had done to me this morning, I didn't want anyone to feel the way I had with Spencer. But I didn't know where this was coming from, didn't know if this was all some sort of twisted game or not.

"What?" I asked. "What is it?"

He stared at me for a few moments, his eyes glossy, but his mouth closed. I wanted him to say something, anything. At least he could tell me what was wrong. But he didn't say a word more.

So, I slipped my hands underneath his arms and pulled him up with all my strength. When he was on both his feet, he turned away from me, like he had this morning, and placed both hands on the white brick wall, smashing his fist into it and splitting the skin.

"Sorry," he gritted out. "You don't have to stay with me."

"Come on," I said, knowing if he apologized once more for Friday night and for this morning, I wouldn't want to be so nice, because I didn't want to feel all these damn emotions that I had for him anymore. "I'm taking you home."

"You don't have to," he said quietly. "Go back to the game."

I crossed my arms. "No."

"Maddie," he growled, "please."

Because I could be a stubborn and stupid bitch sometimes, I wrapped my hand around his bicep, yanked him away from the wall, and dragged him to the exit of the restroom. "No," I said through my teeth. "I'm bringing you home."

To my surprise, he didn't try to argue.

With Alec Wolfe in tow, I marched down the hall and to my car parked in the student lot. I shoved him into the passenger seat, not caring that he was perfectly capable of driving himself home in his own car, and slipped into the car beside him.

"You don't have to do this, Maddie," he said. "I've been a dick to you."

"Yeah," I said, backing out of the spot. "You have been."

He stayed quiet for half the ride, his body becoming tenser and tenser by the second. I glanced over at him to see hives had broken out on his neck, a bead of sweat rolling down his cheek near his hairline.

What the hell is going on with him? I had asked him before, but he wouldn't tell me.

Once I pulled up to his house and shut off my car, he stared with trembling eyes through the windshield. His balled fists were pressed against his thighs, his jaw tight. For a moment, his shoulders bucked forward.

"Sorry," he repeated. "I'm sorry."

"Stop saying that," I said.

"I'm sorry," he sobbed, tears bursting from his eyes. "I didn't mean it."

My eyes widened, my breath catching. Alec Wolfe didn't cry about anything. Rarely showed any emotion other than his flirtatious eyes and smirk, throwing them to any pretty girl he saw in the stadium, in the halls at Redwood.

"What are you talking about?" I asked.

Because there were a couple of incidents I wished he'd apologize for.

He pressed a hand to his mouth to muffle another sob and squeezed his eyes closed. "This is all my fault. I shouldn't have been drinking so much. I shouldn't have come up to your bedroom and left angry. I shouldn't ... I shouldn't have been at the party. I'm sorry." He wrapped his arms around himself. "I'm sorry."

"It's fine, Alec," I whispered. "Please, settle down."

While I had wanted him to be apologetic, this was ... a bit too much. I mean, he was sobbing in my car, had thrown up in the women's restroom, and looked like he was in the middle of a panic attack, all because I had been angry that he—Redwood's player— had slept with another girl after being with me.

"N-no, you don't understand," he whispered, suddenly quiet. "Nobody understands."

16

maddie

I LAY in Alec's bed and stroked his messy brown hair as he slept on my chest. After Alec had calmed down in my car, I had convinced him to let me bring him inside. I hated seeing anyone this way, but especially him.

With his head on my stomach, he clutched my waist and snored softly. I rested my head against his pillow and wished that I had never slept with him on Friday night. Would things be different between us? Would Alec not be acting this ... weird?

"Alec!" Mrs. Wolfe said, opening her son's bedroom door.

I froze in my spot, my fingers deep in his hair, and widened my eyes. *Fuck!*

Halfway through the door, she locked gazes with me and stopped dead in her tracks. We stared at each other for the longest few moments of my life, and then she smiled, dimples forming on her cheeks, just like her son.

She hadn't even been here when I brought him home!

"Mrs. Wolfe," I whispered, careful not to wake Alec. "It-it's not what it looks like."

She smiled even wider and slipped out of the room. "I'll leave you two alone."

When the door closed, I shut my eyes and slapped a hand over my forehead. *Shit.*

Once I set Alec's head on his pillow, I slid off his bed and hurried out of his bedroom. I would have to face Mrs. Wolfe at some point, so I might as well get it over with now so she didn't spill this little secret to Oliver.

Tiptoeing down the hallway, I found my way to the living area, where Mrs. Wolfe was now folding laundry with their maid, as if to busy herself. I lingered at the door, awkwardly playing with my sweaty fingers, until she finally acknowledged me.

"So, um ..." I shifted from foot to foot. "I was just making sure Alec was okay."

Mrs. Wolfe hummed in amusement and continued to fold clothes, her huge ring glimmering underneath the living room light. She placed a pair of Alec's shorts in a pile. "You know, I always thought something was going on between you and him."

My eyes widened. "Wh-what are you talking about? Th-there isn't."

"He always talks about you."

"He does?"

She smiled. "And I always catch him staring up at you during his games."

Warmth exploded through my body, yet I bit back my excitement. Alec always looked up at the student section—not for me, but for Sandra and his other girl groupies. I had nothing to do with those sneaky little peeks.

After rubbing my sweaty palms together, I chewed on my inner lip and rocked forward. "I know it's none of my business, but has anything happened to Alec recently?" I asked, nervous about overstepping. I didn't want to offend her. "Anything?"

"No, sweetheart," she said. "Nothing that I know about, but Alec doesn't tell me much."

"Oh," I hummed. "It's okay. Don't worry about it."

Maybe it was really what had happened between us that threw him off. I had asked him more than once about it, but he continued to either tell me that nothing was wrong or that I wouldn't understand. But he didn't know that.

I had been through hell with Spencer. I could deal with whatever he had going on.

"Thinking about it ..." she started. "His anxiety is back."

"Back?"

She offered a soft smile. "In middle school, he had bad anxiety. Terrible actually. He had it for years until we finally had the doctor prescribe him medication, which he refused to take. I didn't think he'd ever get better until his second hockey game of his eighth-grade season."

My entire body tensed.

She and I remembered that night for completely different reasons.

"Oh yeah?" I whispered.

Oliver had had all his teammates and some popular girls over until late that night, celebrating their win against a team who had completely demolished them the previous year. We were at that age where Truth or Dare and Seven Minutes in Heaven were the thing to do at parties.

I wanted to grab a late-night snack and ignore everyone else, and Alec was retrieving a glass of water from the kitchen for his dare. We both turned the corner at the same time, tripping, and our lips smacked right into each other.

At the time, I had counted it as my first real kiss. Now, I didn't.

It was a simple mistake ... *at first*.

But I had never looked at him as the same annoying kid that my brother called a friend.

Especially with what had happened right after our accidental kiss.

"What're you smiling about?" Mrs. Wolfe laughed.

Quickly, I pushed the thought away and shook my head. "Nothing."

Had *I* helped him through it?

While that wasn't exactly how anxiety worked—I had tried that method of leaning on Vera during my time with Spencer—I couldn't help the butterflies fluttering around inside my stomach. Maybe I hadn't cured his anxiety, but I hoped I made it a bit easier for him.

Or maybe this was all a weird coincidence.

After all, Alec Wolfe didn't *like*, like me. He had only wanted to fuck me, and I wasn't even sure about that when he had called out Sandra's name after we had sex on Friday night, and then he'd—I gritted my teeth—fucked another girl.

She glanced down at her buzzing phone and bit back a smile.

"Sweetheart," she said, peering up for a moment, "your brother just texted me that he's coming over to check on Alec. If you don't want him to catch you, you should probably get out of here. He just left the hockey stadium."

I arched a brow. *Why did my brother have her number? And why was he texting her? Isn't that a bit … weird?*

I shook off the thoughts and retrieved my purse from the front room. I guessed it wasn't *that* weird. I had Ms. Rodriguez's number in case of an emergency. After grabbing my keys, I hollered a thanks and hurried out the front door. I did *not* want Oliver to catch me here.

If I didn't make it back to my house before Oliver did, he would be searching all over Redwood for me, would even probably call Piper's father to ask him to put out a search warrant for me and then put me on house arrest, just for leaving without telling him where the hell I was going.

And I especially didn't want him to think there was anything going on between me and Alec.

17

alec

A BRIGHT LIGHT BLAZED OVERHEAD, jolting me awake.

"The hell did you go, dude?" Oliver asked, walking into my room.

I scrambled in the bed, hurriedly looking around for any sign of Maddie. She had fallen asleep with me here earlier, and if Oliver found us together, he would attempt to kick my fucking ass harder than we had kicked Spencer's a year ago.

When I realized that Maddie wasn't in bed—or even in my room with me—I blew out a low breath and slumped my shoulders forward.

"Can you turn off the light?" I asked, squinting my eyes. "It's too bright in here."

"Get out of bed," Oliver said. "We gotta tal—"

He paused, peered down at the sheets, and gritted his teeth. Maddie's pink Redwood Academy T-shirt lay on my mattress.

My eyes widened. *Fuck. Fuck. Fuck. Fuck. Fuck. Fuck. Fuck.*

He snatched it from me. "You skipped out on watching the game for a fucking girl?" Oliver growled, suddenly cold. He hurled Maddie's sweatshirt at me. "Come on, Alec! What the fuck has gotten into you lately? A girl?!"

I grabbed the sweatshirt that she must've left and swallowed. "No, Oliver."

"Don't lie, Wolfe. You didn't show up to practice, you skipped today's game, and—"

"Shut the fuck up!" I snapped. "You don't know what the fuck I'm going through."

"By the looks of it, you're going through half of the damn pussies in Redwood."

After gritting my teeth, I leaped out of bed and shoved him toward my bedroom door. "Get the fuck out of here."

"So, you're going to fuck around and abandon your teammates like that?" he snapped, nodding like this was my choice, like it had been my choice to get raped at his party. "You're a fucking piece-of-shit friend if you're going to do us like that."

"It's not all about pussy!" I shouted at him. "That's all everyone cares about in this fucking town, isn't it?" I grabbed him by the collar and threw him out of my bedroom and down the hall. "You don't know shit about what's happening."

"Then, why don't you tell me, if it's so much more important than hockey?"

I glared at him, but didn't say a word. How could I? I couldn't even tell Maddie. And Coach ... when I had mentioned it to him, he had just fucking laughed it off. Why would Oliver be any different? All the guys on the team were this way.

"Get out," I said between gritted teeth one last time.

After glaring at me for a couple more moments, he stormed down the hallway. I slammed the door and headed right for my shower. He had no fucking idea what this felt like. I wasn't choosing to feel this way. I didn't want to skip out on hockey.

I wanted to go back to the way things had once been.

After contemplating my life for an hour in the shower, I wrapped a towel around my torso and stepped into the bathroom.

Water droplets dripped off my hair and rolled down my chest. I ran a hand through my hair.

God, I felt like a total idiot.

Breaking down in front of Maddie like that? I gripped the porcelain sink and stared at my heavy eyes in the mirror, wanting to slap the fucking asshole out of me. *Come on, Wolfe. Way to impress her. She probably thinks you're some kind of loser now.*

I snatched my phone from the nightstand and scrolled to her contact.

Me: Sorry about earlier ...

As soon as I sent the message, a phone buzzed on my nightstand. *Maddie left her phone here? Was she in that much of a rush to get out of here that she sprinted out of my bedroom as soon as I fell asleep?*

I eyed the phone and her sweatshirt. She'd probably at least want the phone back before school tomorrow. I tossed the sweatshirt onto my bed, deciding to keep it, and stuffed her phone into my pocket to return it to her.

It'd give me an excuse to get out of a million and one questions with Mom over dinner.

So, I slipped out a side door to head to my car. Instead of heading straight for Maddie's place—because I needed to figure out a way to get in without Oliver spotting me—I stopped at the hospital.

No way would I be able to provide evidence or a case of sexual assault now. But I wanted to at least get tested in case anything did happen between Maddie and me. I doubted that it fucking would, but I didn't want Maddie to get sick because of how stupid I had been for even being at that party.

Once I finished at the hospital, I slipped back into the car. Maddie's phone buzzed.

Because I was a jealous bastard, I peered down at her phone screen.

A couple of messages from Vera. A missed call from Piper. And then ...

Unknown: What did I tell you about staying away from Wolfe?

Unknown: You don't want anything to happen to your friend Vera, do you?

Unknown: What about Piper?

What the fuck is this?

I tapped on the message, typed in her password that I had memorized from being the biggest fucking creep in existence, and opened up the conversation between Maddie and this unknown number.

There had been a series of them throughout this weekend, starting Friday night.

Unknown: Stay away from him.

Unknown: You don't want to know what will happen to you, to your friends and family.

Unknown: I'll make sure you pay for touching him, you little fucking creep.

Unknown: I hate you.

Unknown: Fucking hate you.

Unknown: Bitch.

Unknown: Cunt.

Unknown: Slut.

Pure, disgusting harassment.

I growled through my teeth. Maddie hadn't responded to any of the messages, but she hadn't told me about them either. And I highly doubted she had told Oliver. And that pissed me off because *I* was the reason she had received these texts.

For all I knew, this was Spencer. He was back. And this time ... he might try to kill her.

18

maddie

I PARTED MY LIPS, sat back in my swivel chair, and paused the online horror game on my screen, switching to my favorited hentai tab in Google Chrome. After this weekend and tonight with Alec, I freaking needed it.

Slipping my hand into my underwear, I blew out a low breath and gently rubbed my fingers over my clit. Pressure built higher and higher in my core. I closed my eyes, ignoring everything on the screen, and imagined Alec rubbing my cunt. Not me.

What the hell am I doing, thinking about Alec like this?

"Cupcake," he purred into my ear.

Nearly screaming at the top of my lungs, I yanked my hand from my pants. "Ale—"

Alec slapped a hand over my mouth from behind to stop me from screaming his name and leaned over my chair, his mouth on my ear. "Don't stop," he murmured. "Keep playing with that slutty little pussy for me."

Once I regained my composure, I returned to my relaxed position on the chair and looked over at him, my brow furrowed. "I don't know if this is a good idea, Alec," I whispered. "Oliver is pissed right now."

"Don't. Stop."

I continued rubbing my clit as his hand dropped to my tit. As soon as I had come home earlier, I had ripped off my bra and thrown on an oversized T-shirt. But now, I regretted it as Alec could pull and tug on my nipples as hard as he wanted.

Pressure built higher in my core. He flicked my nipple with his fingers, and I lost it.

After my orgasm, I pulled my fingers away. Alec dropped his from my tit to my pussy and continued rubbing my sensitive clit for me. Back and forth and back and forth, bringing me closer and closer to another orgasm with so much ease.

"A-Alec," I murmured.

"Fuck," he groaned, moving his fingers faster. "I love when you say my name, Cupcake."

Pussy tightening, I threw my head back against my seat and bit back another moan. This was wrong. Oliver was home, right downstairs, pissed off about something. If he found me here with his best friend …

"Keep it coming for me," he ordered. "I want to see you come again." As his fingers drove me higher and higher, he handed me my phone. "Tell me what these are."

"What are wh—" I gazed down at the screen to see messages from that same unknown number. I had been completely ignoring it—even contemplating blocking the number—but I knew they'd just use another one.

But they had sent me more messages since Friday night.

"I-I don't know," I whispered, attempting to find the words between the pleasure.

"Why didn't you tell me?" he growled, his free hand coming around the front of my throat and squeezing gently. He dropped his hand lower and slipped two large fingers into my pussy, the palm of his hand smacking against my clit. "Hmm?"

"B-because," I managed, "it-it's not your problem."

"It is my problem," he said. "Because you're mine. All mine. And I'm going to fucking protect you from anyone. I don't give a fuck who texts you, but when they threaten my girl, then it's my problem."

"Y-your g-girl?" I choked out.

"This pussy"—he twirled me around and fell to his knees, tossing one of my legs over his shoulder and holding the other high in the air, and then he dipped his face, his mouth hovering over my panties—"is mine."

And then he crashed his lips against my sheer underwear and over my clit, kissing me through the thin material. I curled my toes, my legs jerking from the sudden pressure, and I slapped a hand over my mouth to muffle a moan.

"Alec," I whispered through my fingers.

He groaned, the sound sending a wave of pleasure through me, and curled a finger around my panties to pull them to the side. He flicked his tongue across my clit, sucking and licking my juices. "Cupcake ..."

"W-we shouldn't be—" I started, unsure of how to finish. "Oliver is—"

"Right downstairs. I know," he murmured, vibrating my clit. "I had to sneak past him to see you. And I caught you being a dirty little whore for me, rubbing this little pussy without my permission."

Fuck.

I tried to pull my thighs together to stop the immense pressure building between them, but he held them apart and thrust two fingers inside me again, pumping them in and out of me quickly. I squirmed in his strong hold.

"I didn't think I needed your permission to touch myself," I said.

He pushed his fingers into my mouth and stared up at me through dark eyes as he devoured my cunt. "You can rub your pussy anytime, but when you're rubbing it and thinking about me, I'd appreciate a notice so I can watch."

Heat coursed through my body, my core tightening. "Alec ..."

"That's what you were doing, wasn't it? Thinking about me?"

Another moan escaped my lips. "N—"

"Don't lie to me, Cupcake," he mumbled. "Your pussy is quivering on my fingers at the mere mention of it and those cheeks"— he smirked against my clit and stared up at me—"are bright red. No need to be embarrassed about it. I think about you when I jerk off."

Pleasure exploded in my core, and I cried out. Wave after wave of ecstasy rushed through my body. I squeezed my eyes closed, my legs shaking uncontrollably. He flicked my clit one last time, and I fucking lost it.

Alec Wolfe thought about me while stroking his big, fat cock.

Holy f-f-f-f—

"That's my girl," he murmured, sticking his pussy-juice-covered fingers in his mouth as he watched me with those sultry eyes. "That's my good fucking girl."

19

alec

AFTER MADDIE finally came down from her fifth orgasm by only my fingers, I leaned back on her bed and watched her carefully dress into something more comfortable. Her red hair cascaded down her shoulders, shielding her face from me.

"So," she said, fiddling with some sweatpants, "are you feeling better?"

"Somewhat. Why?"

She pulled up her pants and peered over at me. "Your mom told me that you have anxiety."

My entire body froze, and I found myself standing. *My mom told her what?*

"It's okay, Alec. I just wanted to—"

"I should go," I said, turning around because I didn't want to face her.

I didn't even want to look at Maddie. A guy like me wasn't supposed to have anxiety, wasn't supposed to … to have *that* happen to him. I wanted Maddie to think of me as a protector, someone strong that she'd want to spend her life with.

Not a fucking wimp.

"No," Maddie said, her voice soft. She grasped my wrist and pulled me toward her bed. When I sat, she sat in my lap and wrapped her legs around mine, taking my face into her small hands. "I want to know if you're okay."

Okay?

I stifled an ugly chuckle. I would never be okay after what had happened. I was pushing my friends away, skipping games, not wanting to do shit anymore. I felt like absolute garbage, like my world would never get better, like I would never freaking heal.

Before Friday night, I had been on top of the world. Now, I felt like I needed to be out of it.

"I'm fine," I said.

"No, you're not," she whispered, inching closer to me and swooping my hair off my forehead. "You've been acting weirder than usual lately, and I want to know what's going on with you. You can tell me, you know?"

"No," I whispered, "I can't."

"Yes, you can."

"You'll get angry with me." *Or she just won't fucking believe me.*

She had been dead set on thinking that I had wanted to sleep with another woman right after I slept with her—which was partly my fault—but I wouldn't be able to convince her otherwise. And if I tried, I feared I would say something stupid, like I had that night about Sandra.

We sat for a few moments in silence, and when she realized she wasn't getting more out of me than that, she gave me a soft smile and poked me in the chest. "Do you know what I was thinking about earlier?"

"Hmm?" I hummed, watching those full pink lips curl into a smile.

"That night in middle school when you slept over after your hockey game."

My fingers curled around her waist. "You mean the night we made out on your bed?"

"We did not." She giggled.

"I bet that was your first kiss too, huh?"

She blushed. "It was not."

"It was mine."

Her gaze flickered up to me, her eyes widening. "You're lying."

"And I haven't been able to fucking forget how I felt," I whispered, remembering that night like it was yesterday. I leaned back slightly and closed my eyes, sighing softly. "God, I wish we could go back."

"What do you mean?" she asked, voice small.

"When we didn't have to act like we hated each other," I murmured. "Before Spencer."

"Spencer," she repeated.

"Why'd you even date that asshole?"

"Do you want the honest truth? I wanted to make you jealous," she whispered, gaze dropping to the bed between us and her lips curling down. "But things got too out of hand with him, too quickly, and I didn't know how to stop it."

They had gotten more than just out of hand. They had turned violent.

I gently cupped her chin and lifted it so she stared at me. "Well, you succeeded, Cupcake. You've made me a jealous, possessive asshole of a man who would do anything to get closer to you."

She glanced from eye to eye. "Stop it."

Drawing her even closer, I leaned in to whisper into my ear, "You drive me mad." I inhaled the sweet scent of her vanilla shampoo, wanting to be this close to her all the time. Fuck everyone else. "I want you badly, Mads."

She froze and pulled away slightly to stare into my eyes once more.

"No, you don't," she finally said. "Stop whispering things to me that you don't really mean. I'm too weak to stop myself from listening. You don't like me like this, Alec Wolfe. This has to be some sort of joke, a bet, something."

"It's not." I frowned. "Why don't you believe me?"

That was all my life had been lately. People not believing me.

"Because you're the most popular guy in school," she said.

"So?"

"So, why would you want to be with me?" Maddie exclaimed, throwing her arms up. "How don't you get it? Guys like you never date girls like me. You're popular and athletic, and you could score any girl at Redwood without even trying. And I'm just some geek who is obsessed with anime, plays video games, and loves AP Calc."

"So, just because you watch anime, play fucking video games, and love school, I can't have feelings for you?" I asked.

Damn, she didn't think highly of me at all, thought all I cared about was superficial shit.

She stared at me for minutes in silence, as if she was torn, until she finally shook her head and dropped her gaze once more. "We're too different, Alec Wolfe. Too different to be together ever."

I lifted her face again and placed my lips on hers, kissing her softer than I ever had. Very unlike the savage, ruthless hockey star who picked fights whenever I could, the man my father and my coach had attempted to shape me into.

When I finally pulled away, she whimpered against my mouth.

"Don't say that," I whispered, sweeping my thumb across her cheek. "I know you want it too, Maddie. And if you don't, look me in the fucking eye and tell me you don't want this, and I will truly leave you alone."

"I shouldn't," she whispered, balling her hands into fists against my chest. "I shouldn't want you, but I haven't been able to get you out of my head for the past five years. But we can never be together."

"Bullshit."

I had been waiting years to hear this.

"You're my brother's best friend," she said. "He can't know about us."

I rested my forehead against hers. "Then, he won't find out."

20

maddie

"HAVE YOU SEEN THE VIDEO?" Nicole, the head cheerleader, whispered to her friend as I walked into good old Redwood Academy the next morning.

I hummed to myself, wondering what kind of drama they were gossiping about now, and continued to my locker.

Blaise Harleen leaned against my locker, pointing down to Vera's phone. She stared in horror at the screen, then looked back up at him, brow furrowed. He peered over her shoulder at me, then smirked and walked away.

Vera twirled around, holding her phone behind her back. "Oh, um, hi!"

I arched a brow. "What's going on?"

"Nothing."

Vera was a terrible liar.

"Nothing?" I pushed.

Vera chewed on the inside of her cheek, then dropped her hand to her side and clutched her phone tightly. "Maddie," Vera whispered, holding her phone away from me, "you don't want to see it."

"See what?" I asked, curious now. "What is it?"

She reluctantly gave it to me and looped her arm around mine, as if for support, her brows drawn together. "Someone leaked a video of last Friday night with Alec ..." She paused. "Really, Mads, you don't want to see it."

Betrayal rushed through me, tears building in my eyes just from her words. If it was Alec sleeping with that other woman right after he had been in my room, then Vera was right. I didn't want to see it.

But I couldn't stop myself from hitting the play button.

Maybe this was a way that the unknown number was trying to get back at me.

On the screen, Alec sat in a lounge chair by the pool with his head resting back against his shoulder and his eyes closed. A bunch of the hockey athletes were gathered around him, laughing at how his dick—covered in blood and crusting pussy juice—hung out of his pants.

Someone slapped him hard on the cheek. "Dude!"

He lifted his head off his shoulder and slowly opened his eyes, as if he had just woken up from a nap. "What's going on?" he asked groggily, glancing around at his teammates, who laughed at him. "What happened?"

While I wanted to be pissed at Alec, how the fuck could anyone record him in a time like this? He had been asleep, drunk off his ass, but still ... asleep and vulnerable. I wouldn't go around recording Vera half-naked because I thought it was funny.

"Who'd you fuck out here?" Frazer, one of the hockey bros, asked.

"I didn't sleep with anyone," he mumbled.

"Must've been good if you couldn't even stuff it back in your pants," another said.

Eyes widening, he peered down at his jeans and saw his soft cock covered in dried pussy juices and blood hanging between his open zipper. Alec scrambled to quickly stuff himself back into his pants.

He looked around, his eyes widening, as if he was remembering something.

And then, suddenly, his face paled.

He stood and shook his head. "I-I didn't—"

"Dude, come on," someone said. "You're probably too drunk off your ass to remember."

"Y-yeah, you're probably right," Alec said.

But the same desperate, worried expression was written all over his face, like it had been last night in the restroom of the hockey stadium. It looked like he really had no idea of what he had done.

Or maybe … what had been done to him.

My throat dried, my fingers shaking. Tears threatened to spill down my cheeks. I remembered the first time Spencer had raped me, the first time I had begged him not to fucking use me like I meant nothing to him.

I hadn't wanted him to take my virginity. I had wanted Alec to.

But I had … I had felt the exact same goddamn way.

Nobody even knew about it, not even now, except Vera.

After handing her back the phone, I sprinted down the hallway to Alec's locker. He usually didn't show up until right before the bell rang, but lately, he had been getting here earlier. I needed to talk to him before he saw that video.

I didn't want him to do anything rash, anything impulsive.

If he had truly been assaulted that night, then he hadn't told anyone. Or maybe he had, but they just hadn't believed him. Either way, I needed to find him as soon as possible. I wanted to be that person for him that Vera had been to me.

Most importantly, I wanted him to know that he wasn't alone.

When I turned the corner, he stared down at his phone through wide eyes. Red blotches covered his neck, his breathing erratic. He dropped his phone in the middle of the hallway and suddenly took off toward the exit as everyone watched his video on replay.

21

alec

I STUMBLED down the hallway in a blind panic, racing toward the exit. The noise from students seemed to get louder and louder in my ears, becoming overwhelming. And everyone wouldn't stop staring at me. They had all seen it.

The video of that night.

When I reached the exit of Redwood Academy, I shoved the door open and dropped to my knees on the concrete sidewalk. Bile rose in my throat, and I puked up my breakfast. I staggered to my feet once more, wanting to put as much distance between me and the school as possible, and hurried to my car.

I drove and I drove and I fucking drove.

Once I reached the Overlook, I shoved my door open and collapsed down onto the nearest rock. My stomach wouldn't stop twisting tighter and tighter, my throat burning, my eyes filling with tears. Everyone had seen it.

And yet, still, nobody would believe me. Nobody would fucking believe me.

Why had they taken that stupid fucking video of me with my dick hanging out of my jeans while I was fucking drugged the hell out? Why would my fucking teammates, who were supposed to have my back, do that to me? And Mom telling Maddie that I had anxiety?

It was like the world was telling me to fucking off myself.

The thought shook me to my core, but I couldn't get it out of my head. I couldn't stop thinking that the pain would go away, that the constant worrying would finally vanish, that I didn't have to deal with this shit anymore if I just did it.

A car skirted up to the curb behind me, and then a door slammed shut.

"Alec!" Maddie called from behind.

"Go back to fucking Redwood, Maddie," I growled, my voice breaking halfway through.

"Come here," she murmured, pulling me into her arms.

"Go back to fucking Redwood," I repeated, pain shooting through every single inch of my body, every crevice and vessel. I wanted things to go back to the way they fucking had been. "Go back to Redwood and laugh with everyone about me."

"It's okay," she whispered, running her hands through my hair as she pulled me closer and closer to her chest. She tried to grasp me, but we slipped off the rock and onto the ground. Still, she didn't wince. She didn't move. She held me tight. "It's okay, Alec. I'm here."

"Laugh with them all," I cried, finally fucking breaking. "I deserve it for cheating on you."

"Stop it," she whispered. "I know what you're doing—trying to make yourself feel worse for what happened. I used to do that, too, with Spencer. It's not going to make anything any better for you or for us. You can talk to me about what happened, Alec. I'm not going to laugh."

I bit back a cry for the longest time until I physically couldn't anymore.

"I didn't want it, Maddie," I sobbed, grasping on to her like she was the only thing left in this world. "I didn't want it. I didn't want it. I didn't want it. And no-nobody believes me." I opened my mouth to continue, but I could only sob again. "Nobody believes me."

"I believe you," she whispered.

"No."

No matter how many times she said it, I wouldn't believe that she believed me. Nobody had. Not my best friends. Not my coach. Dad wouldn't either. How could a girl who thought that I had cheated on her believe that I had been raped, taken advantage of?

Instead of getting pissed, like I expected, she pulled me even closer and rocked us back and forth. "I'm so sorry this has happened to you, Alec. Nobody deserves this to happen to them. I believe you."

The longer she held me, the weaker my shoulders became. I grasped her as tightly as I could and sobbed into the crook of her shoulder, ugly cries escaping my mouth. Dad, Coach, and all my friends would call me weak if they saw me like this.

But Maddie ...

God, Maddie was holding me tighter than anyone had ever held me before.

I didn't want her to go. I didn't want her to leave me. I needed her.

And when I finally gathered the strength to pull myself together, probably an hour or two later, I lifted my head. She took my face in her hands and drew her thumbs across my cheeks in soothing circles.

"You were passed out that entire time?" she asked, staring at me through teary eyes.

"Y-yes," I sobbed. "I think she drugged me."

"Who?"

"I don't know," I whispered, another wave of pain shooting through me. "I don't know, Maddie, and I'm so sorry. You don't deserve someone like me. What if she ... what if she is pregnant? I don't want to be a fucking dad now, have never wanted to be with anyone but you." The words tumbled out of my mouth before I could stop them.

Maddie froze. "With me?"

And I had to act like I hadn't just said what I said because if I tried to explain it, I might drive her away. I might say something stupid. I couldn't do that. Not now. Not when I had admitted to her my darkest secret and she believed me.

"What am I going to do, Maddie?" I asked, my mind buzzing all over the place. "I don't want to be a fucking father now. All I wanted was to play hockey, and now ... now, that's all over. Nobody believes me."

"We'll figure it out," she whispered. "I promise we will."

22

alec

"YOU PROBABLY THINK LESS of me, huh?" I whispered over breakfast.

We had skipped school and gone back to Maddie's place for the day.

Maddie glanced over her shoulder and pulled some milk out of the fridge. "What?"

I shyly looked back at the pancakes on my plate, feeling guilty and shitty for the way I had reacted earlier, for what I had admitted to her. I wanted her to like me, finally, after all these fucking years, and not feel sorry for me.

"You heard me," I said, twirling a forkful of my pancakes in syrup.

She filled two glasses of milk and set them at the table in front of our plates, and then she sat next to me and placed her small hand on my bicep, squeezing gently, her gaze piercing into me from my side. "Why would you think that?"

After setting down my fork, I sighed and leaned back. "Because I'm fucked up."

"How?" she asked. "Because someone sexually assaulted you?"

I stayed quiet, but so did she. Which confirmed that she thought so too.

"Well, if that's the case"—she pulled her arm away—"then I'm fucked up too."

Snapping my head in her direction, I gritted my teeth. "Who? Who fucking—"

"Spencer did," she said without hesitation. "He didn't just hit me and bully me. He had sexually assaulted me many more times than I could count. I thought it was normal, but I didn't want it either. And I didn't say anything to anyone, except Vera."

My hands balled into fists on the table, and I flung my chair back to stand. "I'll kill him."

She grabbed my bicep and pulled me back down. "No, this isn't about me. Sit down."

"He raped you, Maddie," I said.

"And someone did the same to you too," she said, tugging on my arm. "Please, sit down and eat with me. I didn't tell you because I wanted you to feel sorry for me, just like you didn't tell me so I would feel sorry for you."

Once I let out a soft sigh, I collapsed in my seat and glanced over at Maddie. She offered a smile and then began cutting her pancakes. I grabbed my fork and dipped another piece of pancake into my syrup. But before I could eat it, Maddie stuffed her fork into my mouth and giggled, the sound soft.

I wrapped my lips around the utensil and tore the pancake off with my teeth to eat it. She pulled the fork out of my mouth and grabbed a bite for herself, strands of her red hair falling into her face.

God, she is beautiful.

So fucking beautiful.

I had been waiting to be with her for so long, but the world had screwed me. It sucked that this was what had brought her to me, that I couldn't find the confidence to tell her what I really wanted to on the night of the party. Maybe if I had, that wouldn't have happened.

"I promise I'm not always an utter emotional mess," I said, wanting her to know that I would do anything I could for her.

I would protect her with everything that I had left if Spencer decided to return. She wasn't alone either.

"I know," she hummed, smiling softly. "I've seen you on the ice."

Dropping my gaze, I stared at the pancakes again. "I don't know if I should go back."

"To hockey?" she asked.

"With the guys ... and that video ..."

She stayed silent for a couple of moments, playing with her food. "Don't worry about them."

But I could do nothing but worry. They were the ones who had taken that video of me half-naked after the worst night of my life. They were the only people with access to it. So, one of them must have leaked it.

I balled my hands into fists again, chest tightening. It wasn't fair. I'd trusted them.

Maddie gently cupped my cheek with her free hand. "If you don't want to go back, then you don't have to. They're jealous they can't win a match without you. Don't let them break you. Don't let them win."

"It's hard," I admitted.

Because I had always dreamed of making it into the NHL, marrying my best friend's sister, and having a family with her, staring up at the stands to see her and our family of red-haired girls cheering me on from the sidelines.

Now ... that dream was so much closer ... yet also gone. Because I couldn't find the motivation to step back on the ice. I feared that I wouldn't play as well as I used to, that my teammates would fuck around with me again, that my coaches wouldn't believe me when I needed them the most. And it fucking sucked.

Tears welled up in my eyes. "It's so hard, Maddie."

She brushed some away with her thumbs. "I know it is, but ... you should think about heading to the doctor or the hospital to get tested at the very least. You don't know what that girl might've had, and I … I doubt she used a condom."

"I already have," I said, thinking about the worst-case scenario. "I'm sorry if … if I have an STD or if the girl got pregnant. I don't remember anything from that night. I don't know if she used one or not, what she looked like, anything. I'm sorry."

I wanted to tell her that a thousand times over. I could never make up for this.

"I would never think less of you, Alec Wolfe. Not because you have anxiety or got sexually assaulted, not even if we find out that something is wrong with those test results or that the girl who did it got pregnant."

While I wanted to respond, I could do nothing but let another tear fall.

"I promise that I'll be by your side," she whispered.

"Why?" I asked, partly in disbelief that she would be so supportive after what I had done to her.

"Because I wish I'd had more people on my side when it happened to me."

23

maddie

ALEC LAY on the couch beside me with his head in my lap, his eyes closed, and his breathing even. I gently ran my hand through his messy brown hair and smiled at the ease on his face. All today, he had been so worried. It was nice to finally see him at peace.

My phone buzzed on the side table next to the clock that read one fifty-four p.m.

Vera: Where are you?

Vera: Is it okay if I bring over your backpack and the work you missed today?

Stirring in my lap, Alec turned over to lie on his back and blinked open his eyes. "What time is it?" he said groggily, rubbing his eyes with his fists. He yawned and stared up at me, pushing some hair behind my ear. "Late?"

"The afternoon," I said, tugging at the ends of his hair once more. "School will be out in a couple of minutes, but Oliver won't be home until after hockey practice tonight, so you can sleep a bit longer if you want."

He turned over once more so his head faced my stomach and wrapped an arm around my waist. "I don't want to go to practice tonight," he mumbled against me. "Do you think Coach will punish me for it?"

"No," I said.

Though … I wasn't too sure with Coach Leo. From what I had seen, he was harder on Alec than he was on any of the other athletes because he knew Alec could go far. He wanted that pride of having coached a hockey star more than he cared about his players.

My phone buzzed again.

Vera: Blaise will be with me. I can drop it off out front.

"Who's that?" Alec asked.

"Vera."

"Will you tell me if that number messages you again?"

I chewed on the inside of my cheek. Honestly, I didn't want to bother him or stress him out more than he already was, but if it would give him peace of mind about us, then … "Sure, I'll let you know."

Fifteen minutes later, the motion sensors in the driveway sent me a *motion detected* notification on my phone. I spotted Vera and Blaise walking up the sidewalk out front, and then I headed to the front door while Alec woke up from his second nap of the day.

"Thanks for bringing my stuff," I said to V after opening the door.

She handed me the backpack and smirked at Alec's shoes by the door. "So, are you guys … like, a thing?"

"Sorta, but we're not telling anyone." I peered at Blaise. "So, keep your mouth shut."

"He won't tell anyone," Vera reassured me, grabbing my hand. "But when people do find out … we should go on a double date sometime!"

I stepped closer to her. "A triple date with us and Piper and her guy."

Vera flashed me a smirk, then returned her gaze toward me and glanced into the room at Alec. "Is he okay?"

I shrugged. "Worse than you were when everyone found out that you write smut."

She pressed her lips together and frowned. "Really?"

"Unfortunately."

With his skateboard flipped up onto his shoulder, Blaise leaned against the doorframe and arched his brow at Alec. Vera noticed the uneasiness between the two and grabbed Blaise's hand, scolding him so he wouldn't say anything to him.

Blaise Harleen said what he thought and didn't give a shit how it hurt anyone.

And I'd bet he wanted to comment on Alec's video.

Instead of saying anything, Blaise grabbed Vera's hand back and tugged her down the sidewalk and back toward his father's mansion down the road. He had lived on my street since we had been kids, but that guy had barely ever said two words to anyone.

"See you later, Mads," Vera called over her shoulder, throwing me a wink. "Have fun!"

24

maddie

LATER THAT NIGHT, I slammed the door to hockey practice open and stormed through the empty ice rink to the gym in the back. Less than twenty minutes ago, I had finally taken Alec home for the night and told him that he shouldn't feel bad about missing practice.

Hell, I wouldn't. Not when the people I'd trusted betrayed me like that.

The stench of body odor drifted through my nose as I spotted the guys doing burpees in sync and counting up from seventy-nine. I marched straight into the room, fuming with anger that these fuckheads would do this to their teammate.

"What were you thinking?" I shouted at the guys, not giving a single fuck anymore. When I locked eyes with Oliver, I barreled toward him and slammed my hands into his chest. "You all have to be the stupidest, brattiest fucking asses at Redwood!"

"Miss Weber," Coach Leo said from the other side of the room.

I released my brother and stomped around the group who continued to do burpees, the sweat dripping off their skin, their wet shirts clinging to their bodies. "Which one of your assholes leaked that video?"

"None of us, Maddie," someone said.

My foot twitched, but I stopped myself from kicking him right in the balls. "Bullshit."

"We didn't do it," another said, pausing for a moment to look at his coach. Coach Leo pursed his lips, sending him nothing but a death glare, and the kid continued jumping. "But we're being punished for it."

Still, I didn't believe shit that came from their mouths.

"Alec trusted all of you! And you leaked that video because you were angry that you shitheads can't win a fucking game without him?! You're the most selfish pieces of scum in Redwood by fucking far."

"Miss Weber, that's enough."

"You don't know what they did!"

"I know," Coach Leo said.

"No, you don't know," I shouted, exploding with anger, fury, and annoyance.

How could he be so calm about this? Alec Wolfe was the best player on the Redwood hockey team, already had multiple full scholarships to the best colleges for hockey in the nation, and had scouts from the NHL attending games to watch him play.

A video of him getting sexually assaulted had dropped, and this fucker didn't bat an eye.

The more I thought about him, the angrier I fucking became. "And you," I accused.

This wasn't my place to say anything, but Alec wouldn't. I never spoke out against anyone, especially after what had happened with Spencer, but I couldn't let this pass. Alec had cried out so hard in my lap at the Overlook.

And nobody was in his corner, but me.

"Maddie," Oliver warned, walking over.

"He told you too, didn't he?" I asked Coach Leo and the assistant coach. "And you didn't do shit about it!"

Oliver grabbed me by the elbows and dragged my kicking and screaming ass back through the gym, into the empty stadium, and then out through the back doors to the parking lot where I had parked.

"You can't be saying shit like that to Coach," Oliver said, releasing me.

"And why not?! Because he's an adult? Because he's supposed to be respected?! Do you fucking know what your best friend has been dealing with for the past few days? Do you fucking know that he told your coach about it and he did nothing?!"

"You're blowing this out of proportion, Maddie."

"You're supposed to be his best friend!" I shouted at my idiot brother.

"I am," he said, pushing me toward my car. "Go home."

"No," I growled, snapping myself out of his harsh hold and twirling around so I faced him, the fury building up inside me by the damn second. "If you were his best friend, then you would've believed him when he told you that he didn't want to have sex with her. You would've done something other than take a video and laugh at him!"

"Why the fuck do you care, Maddie?"

He was getting defensive and angry because he knew that he was wrong. He shouldn't have laughed at his best friend and taken that video. He shouldn't be pushing Alec away and becoming angry with him for being assaulted.

"Huh?"

Tears welled up in my eyes, but I pushed them back. "Because I do."

"What, do you like him or something?"

"No."

"Because you know what happened the last time you fell for one of the hockey—"

"You don't have to remind me," I snapped, crossing my arms and turning away from Oliver. "I remember what happened to me when I dated Spencer. Why can't I give a fuck when something shitty happens to someone in Redwood?"

"Because nobody else does."

I twirled back around and shoved him hard in the chest. "You're heartless. Absolutely heartless, Oliver Weber. I can't believe that Alec has ever seen you as a friend. You're one of the most terrible human beings that I've met!"

Oliver glared at me for a couple more moments, and then his jaw twitched the way it always did when he knew he was wrong but didn't want to admit to it. If he kept talking, he'd dig himself into a deeper and deeper hole.

"You might be my sister," Oliver said, "but you don't know shit about me."

I crossed my arms. "I know you're a terrible friend and brother."

"A terrible brother?" Oliver repeated. "Do you remember what I did to Spencer for you?"

"Just because you did one nice thing for me, I'm suddenly expected to treat you like a god?!" I exclaimed, shaking my head and storming to my car. "No. Fuck that, Oliver." I got in and slammed my door. "Fuck every one of your stupid, heartless asshole friends too."

This town was going to shit, and I wanted to see it burn, just like Poison did.

25

alec

AFTER A LONG DAY AT SCHOOL, listening to constant whispering about me and watching my own teammates give me looks that I couldn't quite decipher, I exited my car and walked into the gym for practice.

While I didn't particularly want to work out today, if Mom caught me home again, she would be even more suspicious than she already was. Honestly, I was surprised that she hadn't found out yet with how much Redwood gossiped. And I wouldn't hear the end of it from her.

When I walked into the building, a couple of guys nodded to me, but didn't say a word. I awkwardly headed toward the locker rooms, spotting a couple of men in suits, talking to Coach. They made eye contact with me, smiling.

Fuck, if these were recruiters …

Stepping into the locker room, I spotted Oliver rummaging through his locker with his training shirt thrown over his bare shoulder. I placed my belongings down on the bench beside his and opened my locker.

Like the other guys, he glanced over at me, but didn't say anything.

"Sorry about the other day during your game," I finally said, wanting to get on with him.

I couldn't deal with this shit alone anymore. I had Maddie, but I couldn't talk to her about guy shit. I had known Oliver for fucking years now.

And suddenly, I had missed one game and got the cold shoulder.

"It's fine," he said, slamming his locker closed and walking out of the room.

I sighed to myself, changed into my hockey gear, and headed back to the main area with my stick. The two suited men from earlier sat in the stadium, watching the team run through warm-ups. I was late.

Before I could skate onto the ice, Coach cleared his throat. "Alec, my office."

Double. Fuck.

Once I followed him into his office in the back, I shut the door behind me and hoped that he wouldn't shout too loudly at me for missing another few hours of practice yesterday. *He has to have seen the video, right? Will he even sympathize?*

"There are scouts here from national teams," Coach said. "They're here to watch you practice, and they'll be here throughout the week for your next game. Are you okay enough to train with us today?"

I opened my mouth, then snapped it shut because I always had an expectation to train, to practice, to learn and hone my skills. I was expected to go into the NHL, and I had wanted to since I was a kid.

But lately … that dream had felt so lost.

"I'm fine," I said.

"You can talk to me."

"No, it's fine," I said, staring down at my shoes. "*I'm fine.*"

A long pause.

"I apologize for how I reacted the other day at the game," he said, clearing his throat. "I should've taken what you told us seriously, and instead, I made a joke of it with Coach Jose. Nobody should go through what you have."

My gaze snapped up to his, eyes widening slightly. "Wh-what?"

Did I even hear him correctly? He is apologizing? To me?

He shifted in his seat uncomfortably. "I should've taken it seriously, but it brought back memories of when I was back in high school. Something similar had happened to me, but with a coach. I've spent the past twenty-five years pushing it down, pretending like it didn't happen because, as men, we're … supposed to be strong." His voice cracked. "And I've fallen right into that fucking behavior. I've failed you."

A stray tear slid down my face, and I quickly pushed it away. I didn't want to cry in front of him. I couldn't. I had spent years expecting to be one way, only to come crashing down when something shitty had happened to me.

"You don't have to forgive me, but I will be better."

I stayed quiet because I didn't know what to say. I didn't want to forgive him or anyone else who had laughed at me when I told them that something was wrong. I didn't want to even face anyone ever again, but I had to see all my teammates today, tomorrow, and for the remainder of the season.

"I'm okay to train today," I said.

"Good."

After a long pause, Coach said, "That was a pretty ballsy thing your girl did."

"My girl?"

"Maddie Weber, Oliver's sister."

I stiffened. "What do you mean, my girl? We're not dating."

As much as I would love for all of Redwood to know about us, Maddie didn't want anyone—especially her brother—to know that we were sorta a thing. I mean, we were, weren't we? She wouldn't have skipped school for someone she hated or just merely liked.

"Stormed into practice and gave us all a piece of her mind," he said.

She stormed into practice yesterday after I skipped again? All for me?

Warmth spread through my chest, and I bit back a small smile. I didn't know how I should feel about it because ... nobody had fucking believed me as hard and as much as she had. Nobody had fucking done that for me before. But she was Oliver's little sister.

"She was just being nice," I said, but I knew it was more than that.

"And I suppose that she ran out to the restroom with you during the hockey game because she was just being nice to you too." He chuckled, a smile painted on his face. He stood and gently squeezed my shoulder. "Don't worry; I won't tell Oliver." He nodded to the door. "Now, get out there and make your teammates proud."

26

maddie

"IT'S GETTING LATE," Piper said, yawning. "I gotta go, or my dad will be pissed."

"Already?" Vera sighed. "It's only eight."

"She's going to meet her man," I added with a wink. "Give him a quickie under his desk."

She playfully rolled her eyes and threw a smirk my way. "I am not."

After grabbing her belongings, she slipped out my bedroom door. A couple of moments later, I watched her walk down the front walkway to her car parked in the driveway, and I turned on my desktop computer.

Vera rolled onto her stomach on my bed and put in her earbuds. Vera and I were best friends, but we didn't need to do everything with each other while we were together. It was a certain kinda ease I had with her compared to everyone else.

I opened Vapor, an online marketplace for video games, and scrolled through the games I had bought but hadn't played much yet. When I spotted Alec Wolfe online in my friends list, I clicked on the game he was playing.

"So," Vera asked, turning down the pop-punk music blasting through her headphones that bad-boy Blaise Harleen must've turned her on to the past couple of months that they'd been a thing, "I kinda wanna open a bookstore one day."

"What're you gonna call it?" I giggled. "The Smut Shoppe?"

"Um, excuse me!" Vera said, her hand over her heart, as if she were offended. A smile crossed her face, and then she continued typing on her laptop. "You know, maybe. That's a good one."

"You're welcome," I said, loading into the game Raid of Durnbone with my half-succubus, half-wolf avatar. "Now, I'd like fifty-one percent of the business for coming up with such a stellar name for you."

"How about no?" Vera said, laughing. "But I'm serious though. I would love to open a bookstore and write all day long. I just don't think I would be able to do it alone. Do you think Sakura would want to join me?"

I paused my game and scoffed. "What about me?"

She waved dismissively in my direction. "You'll be off in new cities every night with your future husband, Mads. You won't have time to run an entire bookshop with me. I was thinking of Sakura because she likes literature and is probably going to stay in the New England area because … Mr. Avery works here."

"Yeah, but does she like smut though?" I asked.

"Who doesn't?"

"True."

"You know, it's funny that you didn't comment on the fact that you're going to marry Alec."

"What?"

She giggled. "I said that you'll be at hockey games with your future husband, and it completely passed over your head, like you expect that to be in your future too, Miss Maddie Weber-Wolfe. MWW."

I rolled my eyes, cheeks tinting red, and returned to my game. "I just misheard you."

I didn't even want anyone to know about Alec and me. How

the hell would we ever marry? Besides, I liked him, but this was more of a high school crush, a fling that probably wouldn't last through college. Not many relationships did.

But the mere thought of that made my stomach turn.

Once Vera turned on her music and continued typing out her latest smutty novel on her laptop, I invited Alec to join my party in Raid of Durnbone, hoping that I didn't look *too* desperate. I hadn't talked to him much today, mainly because I didn't want anyone to become suspicious that I liked him after my episode at hockey practice.

He sent me an invite to join his Discord call.

"Hey," he said, his deep voice drifting through my headset.

"Hi," I said softly so Vera wouldn't hear me.

Because if she did … God, I wouldn't hear the end of it. She'd be gushing to me all damn night about how I was now playing video games with Alec Wolfe. How I was destined to marry him and have his babies.

"Uh, I just wanted to let you know that my test results came back a couple of hours ago," he said, nervousness building in his voice. "And I'm negative for everything that they tested me for. So …"

"So we can have sex." I giggled. "Is that why you called me?"

"No, it wasn't. I was just …" He paused. "I thought you might want to know."

"Well, thank you."

"And I wanted to ask you something else … about hockey."

"What is it?" I asked, running around the map with my avatar.

"You coming to the game tomorrow night?"

"I don't think I've missed a hockey game for the past five years, Wolfe. I'll be there." I followed his avatar through the creature-filled town to the trinket shop to buy goods. "Are you going to play?"

"Probably."

I paused. "Are you okay enough to play?"

"I think so."

"Nobody is pressuring you, are they?"

"Damn, you sound like my mom."

"Sorry," I whispered. "I just ..." *Care about you.*

"Don't be sorry," he said quickly. "I know that you ..."

We were the most awkward couple—were we a couple? I still wasn't clear on that—in existence. We both stayed silent for a few moments until he cleared his throat.

"I, um, talked to my coach today."

"You did?"

"He said that you ... talked to the guys during practice yesterday."

My cheeks warmed, my words catching in the back of my throat. "Oh, um, about that ..." I chewed on the inside of my cheek, attempting to find an excuse that I could use to get me out of this one.

I mean, I hadn't done anything wrong, but I couldn't hold myself back last night. I was fuming with anger that every one of those assholes had laughed at him and taken a damn *video* of that shit, then leaked it!

"Listen, I didn't mean to flip out on them," I said, chest tightening. "I'm sorry if I got you in trouble. I just ... God, I care about you so much, Alec. I don't want anyone hurting you right now. It's hard after ... something like that happens."

He stayed quiet for a long time, and then I could *hear* the smile on his face. "Why are you apologizing to me, Cupcake? That was ... the most caring thing anyone has ever done for me. I don't know how to repay you."

"How to repay me?" I repeated. "You don't have to do that."

"What if I take you out on a date this weekend?"

"A date?" I whispered, heart racing at the thought.

"A date."

27

maddie

"THREE SECONDS LEFT IN OVERTIME. Oliver Weber steals the puck. A pass to Alec Wolfe!"

The cheering crowd suddenly quieted down for the last three seconds of the game, excitingly watching Alec skate down the ice with the puck. He snapped his wrist, sending it flying across the ice and straight into the net.

"SCORE!" the announcer shouted over the intercom. "Alec Wolfe scores the winning goal for Redwood Academy!"

The mob of students roared in excitement, waving their arms and cheering for their favorite players. Even I screamed until my throat hurt, watching Alec from the stands and actually smiling genuinely for the first time since last Friday.

Once the game was over, Piper pulled Vera and me out of the stadium and into the hallway to wait for the team. "I don't know how Alec does it," Piper said. "But he always comes out on top."

"He's not *that* good," I said.

Well, he was, but I didn't want to boost his ego too much. That man knew he was a god, but if he thought that *I thought* he was a god, then he would make me treat him like one in the bedroom.

"He literally scored every goal tonight," Piper fired back.

Vera scoffed playfully at me and rolled her brown eyes. "You're so full of it, Maddie. You love him, and we all know it."

Love?

I did not love Alec. But … maybe I did like him a bit more than I'd been putting on.

"There he is!" Vera shouted once the rest of Redwood Academy and the hockey team spilled out into the Redwood hallways.

Vera looped her arm around mine and jumped up and down excitedly for me as Blaise stood off to the side, leaning against the exit door, crossing his arms, and raising a suspicious brow at his girlfriend.

I glanced over my shoulder to see Alec walk through the crowd, giving people small smiles. But his eyes didn't really light up until he saw me standing across from him in the packed corridor.

Before I even had a chance to turn around and run far away—because everyone was around—Sandra curled her arm around his and smirked.

"I can't believe you scored the winning goal in overtime, Alec!" She touched him like she owned him, and I hated it. "You were so awesome tonight."

Alec stiffened, an uncomfortable expression crossing his face. Everyone at school watched him like a hawk, wondering how he would react to Sandra after they had seen the video.

"What are you waiting for, Maddie?" Vera whisper-yelled at me.

After swallowing hard, I shook my head. "Vera …"

"Why can't you forget about what people think for once?" Vera pushed.

"I … I can't," I whispered, glancing at Alec.

Oliver was right there with him, watching me watch him. After the other night, he probably had his suspicions about my feelings toward Alec, but I didn't think Oliver knew that Alec liked me too.

When Sandra pulled him closer, he stiffened even more and

pulled himself out of her hold. Sandra wrapped her arm around his again—that bitch *loathed* rejection—and tried to tug him closer to her.

"Get off me, Sandra," he said, his voice weak. "I have somewhere to be."

"Somewhere to be?" she asked, hands on her hips.

Oliver slung his arm around Alec's shoulders. "The party at my place."

I gritted my teeth together, wanting to grab Oliver by his big ears, throw him out into the cold, and stomp on his little pea brain. All day today, he had barely *looked* at Alec during school, and now, he was inviting him to another party after what had happened last time!

Sure, Alec could go if he wanted, but come on!

Oliver and the team didn't give a fuck about Alec unless Alec helped them win games against other teams, show off to recruiters, and secure their victories on and off the ice. And I fucking hated it.

Alec walked backward down the hallway in the opposite direction as the exit, hurling his thumb back. "Actually, I have something else to do," he said, his face turning white with fear as he nearly tripped backward over his own two feet.

"I'll catch up with you later," Alec said, taking one quick look at me.

I stared at the back of Alec's head as he walked down the hallway. Right before he turned the corner, he looked back at me again, as if he wanted me to follow him. But I couldn't do that with Oliver still here. No way in hell.

"You should stay at Vera's tonight, Maddie," Oliver said, shrugging on his winter coat and staring out the glass door windows at Redwood going insane outside. "The guys are going to go crazy. I don't want any of them coming on to you."

Vera slung an arm over my shoulders. "Don't worry about that."

I cut my gaze to Vera, who snickered to herself.

Oliver raised a brow. "What is it? Did one of them already—"

"No!" I shouted too quickly. "Vera was just kidding. She, uh, thinks I like someone in my Stats class, but I don't."

"Who?" Oliver asked.

"Jace Harbor," I said, nearly puking in my mouth at the sound of his name on my tongue.

I'd never liked him, but Jace's name got the job done because Oliver scrunched his nose.

"Jace Harbor? Isn't he dating his stepsister or something? They were a thing a couple of months ago. Why would you like—"

"*Like I said*, I don't like him. So, no need to worry."

"You'd better not," Oliver said. "He's bad news."

"I don't," I said through gritted teeth.

This was why Oliver couldn't find out about Alec. If he was this protective over someone I didn't even like, then he would flip out once he knew I was seeing his best friend, who was also Redwood's biggest player.

"All right," Oliver said, sighing softly to himself. He stuffed his hands into his pockets. "Well, I'll see ya."

When Oliver left, Vera hooked her arm around Piper's and walked toward the exit, saying to me, "See you! Go find Alec!"

After they disappeared out the door, I cursed at myself and slipped down the same hallway Alec had gone down and turned the corner, glancing in rooms that Alec could be in, the scent of his cologne heavy in the air.

"Always following me, Maddie ..." His arms came around my waist from behind. "I heard that you have a little crush on Jace Harbor."

"You know that's not true, Alec," I said, the words coming out low and throaty.

"Of course I do, Cupcake." Alec drew his nose up the column of my neck. "Do you want to know how I know?"

"How?"

"Because every part of you is mine." He kissed my neck, right out in the open. "All mine."

28

maddie

"ARE you sure nobody is in here?" I asked, following Alec into the Redwood hockey team locker room after all the guys and Coach had turned the showers off, gotten dressed, and cleared out for the night.

He flicked on a light, illuminating the dark room, and gently pulled my hips toward his body, his mouth finding the crook of my neck again. "Stop worrying, Cupcake. Nobody's in here. We just watched everyone leave."

"But ..."

"I'd love to take you back to my place, but you don't want anyone finding out about us, right?" he asked, throwing those words back at me. "My parents are home tonight, and my father will do nothing but run his mouth to his rich friends anyway. If they see you with me, all of Redwood will know about us by the morning."

I stared at Alec and gulped. Something inside me told me that we really shouldn't be in public together like this. It was bad enough Alec had snuck me into a classroom on Monday. If we kept sneaking around at school, someone was bound to find out.

Still … I didn't really want to sneak around with him anymore.

"Unless you want me to bring you home," Alec said.

Hell no.

Oliver was throwing another party. If I showed up with Alec …

"No," I said, shaking my head. "You can't."

"We need to talk here then."

"About what?"

Alec pulled himself away from me for the first time since I had snuck down the hallway to find him, then looked down at his feet, suddenly quiet. An unreadable expression crossed his face, and his lips pulled into a frown.

"After the game, all the guys get to celebrate with their girlfriends." He paused. "And I want that too. I want more than this." He gestured to the locker room we were hiding in so nobody would find us. "I want to be able to hug you …"

In a moment, he wrapped his strong arms around my waist and pulled me closer until our chests met. I inhaled sharply at our closeness, but this time, it wasn't sexual. This touch, this moment … it was so intimate.

"I want to be able to kiss you," he said. He shoved one hand into my hair to tug it back, then grasped my chin in the other. Dipping his head, he kissed me on the lips, his tongue making no move to slip inside my mouth, like our usual heated kisses.

This kiss meant something.

Not just to him, but to me too.

"People at Redwood are ruthless, Alec," I said in a breathy whisper, my stomach twisting into knots. "Do you remember what happened to Jace and Allie? People have been whispering about them for weeks now … and they're not even *official*, official yet again."

Alec rested his forehead against mine. "Don't you want us?" he asked, his voice so soft, so much more vulnerable than usual.

And I freaking hated it so much. If my brother wasn't such an ass, then this could've been different.

"All this week at school, I ..." I stared into his big brown eyes, my chest tightening. "I wanted this too."

I liked Alec Wolfe. Maybe even loved him—not that I would ever tell him that to his face anytime soon. And I didn't know how much longer I could just sneak around with him, didn't know how much longer we could keep us a secret.

Unable to stop myself, I wrapped my arms around his torso and pulled him closer. "And, God, I want to be with you."

Alec cupped my face. "Then, be with me."

Still, it hurt so badly. We weren't supposed to be together. After what Spencer had done, I hated the thought of going public with anyone. Especially a player like Alec. *What if he does the same thing to me?*

"Give me a couple of weeks, Alec," I finally said, watching his eyes widen. "I need to ... figure out how I'm going to tell Oliver. Please ..."

"Okay ..." he agreed. "A couple of weeks."

When Alec grasped my hands to pull them to his lips, a sound echoed through the boys' locker room. I didn't know what it was, but it seemed like someone was nearby. Either just outside of the locker room or worse ... here with us.

"Did you hear that?" I asked, glancing around as my heart pounded in my ears.

"Mads, you're getting in your head again."

"No, I definitely heard something," I said.

"There's nobody else here. I made sure of it before bringing you in." Alec grasped the sides of my face and pulled me closer again until our lips touched. "You worry too much."

When he pulled away, I glanced around the locker room and gnawed on the inside of my cheek. "I guess you're right," I whispered, but still feeling uneasy. Maybe it was because I had been waiting for that random number to text me back all week, but they hadn't. Or maybe it was because I had been thinking about Spencer again.

And he always gave me the creeps.

"Come on," Alec murmured. "Let's get out of here."

"Where are we going?" I asked, eyes wide as he pulled me along.

"On a date."

29

alec

WITH HER JACKET zipped up to her chin, Maddie waddled next to me to the movie theater. It was lame to take her to the movies on a first date, but nobody that we knew would be here tonight since Oliver was throwing another fucking party. And besides, she had wanted to come.

"There's anime playing!" She giggled, her curly hair blowing in the breeze.

I stifled a chuckle because this was the fifth time she had said that since the ride over from the stadium. It was amusing how excited she was about it, and I didn't want to take that away from her.

"Can we see it?" she asked once we stepped in line to get tickets.

"Sure."

"Are you *sure*, sure?"

"Yes, I'm *sure*, sure."

She bit back a smile, wrapped her arm around mine, and peered at the ground, not speaking another word until we purchased tickets to the movie that she wanted to watch. Then, she grinned even wider.

"You really got them," she said in disbelief.

"Of course I did," I said. "You said you wanted to go."

"Yeah." She paused. "But … when I was with Spencer, he never let me watch anime."

I clenched my jaw. *That bastard.* "Why not?"

She shrugged. "He used to say it was for kids."

"He hasn't watched enough then."

"You've watched anime?" she asked, eyes wide.

"Yeah," I said, stepping in line to grab drinks and popcorn. "I've been watching *Attack on Titan*."

She beamed at me. "That's, like, one of my favorites! I used to watch some slice-of-life stuff, but Vera's brother watches AOT almost every time I go over there, so I kinda got hooked on it." She pulled me closer, craning her head to look up at me. "Do you want to watch it with me sometime?"

My lips curled into a smile. "I'd love to."

"Next!" the lady at the register called.

Once we ordered two slushies and a large popcorn, I walked with Maddie to auditorium 3. There were only a couple of people scattered in the room. We walked all the way up to the fourth row to our seats, and I placed the popcorn on Maddie's lap.

———

"I don't want to go home," Maddie said, half-asleep after the movie ended. She desperately attempted to keep her eyes open. "Oliver is going to be there, and I want to spend the night with you."

"Why don't we head to the Overlook? Sound good?"

With her head resting against the seat belt, she yawned and nodded. "Sounds good."

Once we made it to the Overlook, Maddie was passed out in the passenger seat with her mouth half-opened and strands of her red hair in her face. I tucked some behind her ear, admiring how the moonlight bounced off her face.

My lips curled into a soft smile, my heart swelling. Why had I been such a dick to her for the longest time? Why had I let Spencer take her away from me, treat her like shit behind closed doors? If I had known what he was doing to her, I would've fucking killed him at the time.

I still wanted to, but I wanted to be better for her. Stronger. Because she was strong for me. She was my fucking rock, my only friend when everyone had turned their backs on me, when everyone had laughed at that stupid video that I wished I could erase from existence.

Hand sprawling out on her thigh, I lightly dug my fingers into her leg and closed my eyes. The dream, the need, the *fire* that had once burned inside me wasn't as bright—and I didn't know if it would ever be—but I still imagined how my life would be in five or ten years. How I would be skating on the rink in the NHL, grinning as our daughter cheered me on with her mom.

I took her hand and brought her knuckles to my lips. "I'm going to get better—*be better*—for you, Cupcake." I gently kissed her knuckles and closed my eyes, vowing that I would do whatever it took to be the man she needed me to be. "I promise."

30

maddie

SUNLIGHT FLOODED into the car through the windows. I squinted my eyes and slowly blinked them open, shielding myself from the light with my arm. I lay in the backseat of Alec's smallish car, squished up onto his chest.

He stirred next to me, his muscular arm around my waist and his fingers lightly moving back and forth on my hip while he still slept. Warmth exploded through my chest, and I bit back a giggle.

Alec does this in his sleep?

Is it soothing for him? Is it me?

Once he tugged me closer until I basically sat in his lap with my head on his shoulder, I glanced up at those full lips and watched him smile.

"What time is it?" I mumbled, closing my eyes and laying my head back down on his chest. I didn't want to wake up yet, didn't want to go home to more red Solo cups and piss all over our floor.

It was bad enough that Mom and Dad were rarely home to scold Oliver for being such a dick. They left our poor housekeeper to clean it all up. I always felt bad for her, so I offered to help out, but I was just so sick of it all.

One way or another, Oliver needed to learn a lesson.

Not like that would ever happen though.

"Too early," he said. "Go back to sleep."

I relaxed on his chest again, my breathing evening out and my mind becoming empty. Since Spencer, my mind had been a complete wreck. I worried constantly, throwing myself into my friends' love lives just to occupy my brain. I hadn't felt this calm, this … easy for a while.

"I wish we could live together, like Vera and Blaise do," I hummed softly.

Spending time in that house with Oliver was taking a damn toll on my mental health. I completely understood why he was so protective—I would be like that with him if a girl treated him the same way that Spencer had treated me—but it was suffocating.

And it wasn't like Mom and Dad cared. They were on a yacht in the Mediterranean right about now, hadn't called in almost a month, failed to check in even with our housekeepers to ensure that their *lovely* children weren't trashing their billion-dollar house.

"Me too," Alec said sleepily, gently scratching my head. "You know, we could."

"Oliver would never let that happen."

"Fuck him."

My eyes widened, and I sat up and stared down at him, my brow furrowed as panic ran through my veins. Alec had never once said anything bad about my brother. They had been best friends for years, but …

"Alec," I whispered, running my fingers through his messy hair.

After slowly blinking his tired eyes open, he clutched my waist and frowned. "He's rude to you too," Alec said. "He throws parties while you're home and trying to study, doesn't give a fuck what you think or what you say."

I frowned. "He's your best friend."

"A *great* one, huh?" he asked, his voice filled with nothing but distaste.

When I went to respond, I caught sight of Kai Koh from Poison dumping something off the rocks and into the Atlantic Ocean. Alec followed my gaze and froze alongside me.

Kai turned to head back to his bike parked near the bushes and eyed us. "What?"

I rolled down the window. "What are you doing?"

"You didn't see anything," Kai said, leaning against the window and looking in at Alec.

Alec sat back and blew out a breath. "I don't give a fuck what you do, Kai."

Before Kai could walk away, I snatched his wrist through the open window. "Wait."

He stiffened, pulled himself out of my grip, and peered over his shoulder at me. "What?"

"When Poison killed Principal Vaughn last m—"

"We didn't kill the principal," Kai said, his face void of any emotion.

But I knew that they had. Hell, the entire school knew it. The Poison boys weren't to be messed with. They were the only gang in Redwood who cared enough to watch the rich burn in the fire that they had created themselves.

"Well," I said, clearing my throat, "whoever did do it said that they wanted Redwood to burn." I lowered my voice so if anyone was in those bushes or behind those rocks or in the nearest houses, they wouldn't be able to hear. "I want in."

"Maddie," Alec said.

"I want in," I said to Kai again. "I'm sick of this town."

Alec grabbed my arm. "Maddie, you don't want to get messed up in Poison's business."

"Spencer should've been thrown in jail for what he did to me," I said. "Someone raped you and got away with it. Shit is happening every single day in Redwood, and nobody gives a fuck about it. I want to do something about it."

Kai turned around with a smirk painted on his lips. "I like the attitude, but João would never allow that. He's barely allowed

Imani to get involved in our business. He wouldn't want a rich girl and her rich boyfriend to be added to the mix too."

"But—"

Instead of letting me finish, Kai walked toward his bike, started it up, and disappeared down the street, leaving me alone with Alec Wolfe. I swallowed hard and glanced over at him, hoping he wouldn't be mad at what I had said to Kai.

I wanted this town to burn for what it had done to us.

"Maddie," Alec said, pushing some hair behind my ear, "you don't have to do that for me."

"Yes, I do," I said, gently cupping his chin. "Because you would've done it for me if you had known what Spencer did when he did it. You would've burned this entire town to the fucking ground. And I promise to do whatever I have to do in order to get whoever did that to you thrown in jail, no matter how corrupt the police force is or the connections that she might have to the rich."

We stared at each other for a few moments until he drew me in for a kiss.

"Don't get yourself into trouble, Cupcake. Not for me." He leaned his forehead against mine, his lips barely brushing on mine. "We have a life that we're going to build together."

Warmth exploded through my chest. "A life?"

"Eighty years together," he murmured. "And I can't have that cut short. I've waited too long."

My cheeks tingled, my breath quickening. Had he really just said that? Part of me didn't want to believe it. I couldn't. Alec Wolfe—more than once—had admitted to having feelings for me, to wanting to spend forever with me. How could that be?

"Promise me," he murmured, "that you won't get caught up in their business."

I curled my fingers into his chest, desperately wanting to fix this for him, to get back at all the people who had hurt him, hurt Vera, hurt all my friends. But I ... I wanted exactly what Alec wanted. I wanted to be together with him.

"Okay," I whispered, "I promise."

After pecking me on the lips again, Alec started the car. "Good."

He drove us the long way back toward the stadium so I could get my car. I stared out the window at the dead and desolate winter beaches and stopped humming to myself when I spotted a black Jeep Wrangler with tinted windows parked near the Overlook.

My breath caught in the back of my throat, my body stiffening. *Fuck.*

I only caught a glimpse of the man's back as he slipped into the driver's seat, the tattoo on the back of his neck of a black snake, drifting around his shoulder and slipping down to his biceps. One that I had seen too many times.

Spencer Katz.

31

maddie

ON MONDAY MORNING, I walked toward Redwood with a smile on my face. I had spent all weekend talking to Alec Wolfe, and, God, it felt so good. I felt like I had been on top of the world since Friday night, like nothing could stop the feeling of warmth spreading through my body.

Not even Spencer.

Wind seared my cheeks, so I pulled the hood of my coat up and trudged toward the front doors. It had been an odd occurrence, seeing Spencer in Redwood, but I had pushed it to the back of my mind. He wouldn't dare fuck with me again after what the hockey team did to him.

At least, that was what I told myself. That was what I forced myself to believe.

Everything is fine.

And while I hoped that everything really was fine, as soon as I stepped through the front doors of Redwood Academy, Tiffany— one of Sandra's best friends—shoved herself into my shoulder. It was almost as if she had been waiting for me.

My books fell, and I hurried to pick them up.

"Watch it, slut," Tiffany said.

Sandra smirked down at me and kicked one of my books down the hall with her heel. "A desperate little slut too."

They laughed together and walked off into another hallway, leaving me scrambling to pick up my books. After gathering my belongings, I stood and saw everyone staring. At me. Nobody pulled their gaze away, not even when I made eye contact with them.

"Maddie!" Vera shouted, rushing down the hallway toward me with Piper.

"What's going on? Why's everyone staring at me?" I asked stupidly.

Vera grabbed my hand and tugged me to my locker, shoving people out of the way, which was very unlike Vera unless something was terribly wrong. It only meant that … something bad had happened between the time I had gone to sleep last night and this morning.

"Have you even been on social media today?" she asked me.

I furrowed my brow. "No. Why?"

Vera whipped out her phone and thrust it in front of my face.

My eyes widened. "Oh. My. God."

On her screen was a video. Of Alec and me. Friday night. In the freaking locker room!

"No." I shook my head. "Tell me it's not true."

Tears welled up in my eyes. The videos were posted from Alec's account. Worst of all was his caption—**Finally snagged my best friend's little sister**—which tipped me over the edge and made me a sobbing mess.

"He told me that nobody was watching us!" I said, placing a hand over my mouth to muffle my cries.

I hated being the center of attention, and now, everyone was staring at me with their judgmental eyes.

"We'll figure this out, Maddie," Piper said, rubbing my shoulder.

"He lied to me!" I cried because it was the only logical reason.

Spencer had … posted videos of us—of me—that I hadn't even known that he had taken. He had sent them in a mass email to every single person at Redwood Academy a year ago, and now, this was happening again.

After I'd trusted Alec.

And part of me still did, but … h-how?

Vera flared her nostrils and crossed her arms. "I'll get Blaise to cut off his balls."

Suddenly, the crowd parted for Alec, who hurried into the hallway. He made eye contact with me, eyes filled with sorrow. Unable to hold my anger back, I rushed toward him and slammed my hands into his chest.

"How dare you!" I shoved him. "I told you I wanted to keep it a secret." Another shove. "And instead, you make me look like a desperate slut!"

Alec took every one of my shoves. "Maddie, stop it. You have it all wrong."

"No!" I shouted. "You're a piece of shit. I should've never trusted you."

Part of me knew that he hadn't done this, that I wasn't thinking clearly because Spencer was on my mind. I wanted to scream at Spencer for fucking me up, not Alec. Still, right now, I couldn't tell the difference.

"I swear, I didn't do it."

"All the videos are from your account!"

"I was hacked, Maddie. I swear."

"Don't believe him, Maddie," Piper said, hooking her arm around mine. "He hurt you."

Alec handed me his phone. "I'm locked out of all my accounts. Look."

I grabbed the phone from him and scrolled from app to app. He was locked out of everything. Instagram. Facebook. TikTok. Even his school emails. Stupid him must've used the same password for all his accounts.

"You have to believe me," Alec said desperately, stepping closer to me.

But I stepped back.

All I felt was hurt and betrayal, and all I could remember was what Spender had done to me. Pain like that didn't just go away out of nowhere. It lingered like a quiet beast, readying for when it happened again.

When my back hit the lockers, I stared up at Alec with tears in my eyes. "Alec …" My voice was nothing but a trembling whisper.

He pushed some hair behind my ear, eyes filled with just as much hurt as I felt. "I wouldn't do that to you, Cupcake."

I wanted to believe him so badly. Deep down, I knew he wouldn't do that. He had kept it a secret all this time. But still … it was hard to believe him after seeing Spencer in Redwood. Maybe he was doing this. Maybe he had locked Alec out of his accounts.

"Okay," I whispered. "I believe you."

Though … I wasn't sure I did.

I was scared as fuck that I was being stupid again and falling for a man who'd hurt me.

Alec slumped his taut shoulders forward and wrapped his arms around me, pulling me into the tightest hug that he had ever given me. "I swear, I'll find out whoever did this. I'll make their life hell for you."

When he pulled away, I let a tear fall down my cheek. All this time, I had been so worried about what people would think of me. And all this time, someone had been plotting to make sure Redwood thought I was an easy slut.

Behind Alec, Oliver stormed down the hallway toward us.

My eyes widened at the rage in his eyes.

"I'm going to fix—"Alec started.

Before he could finish the sentence, Oliver slammed his fist into the side of Alec's face.

32

maddie

OLIVER SHOVED Alec against the lockers, hurling his fist at Alec's jaw again.

"Oliver, stop it!" I screamed.

Alec struck him back in the nose, the force pushing Oliver to the other side of the hall. Blood covered Alec's pearly-white teeth, spurt out of Oliver's nose, and drenched the front of both of their shirts.

"Please, stop it!"

Before he could hit Alec again, I desperately tugged on Oliver's arm to try to pull him away. But it was no use. He was too strong, especially for someone like me. And while I tried to pull, a crowd formed around us.

"What is wrong with you all?" I screamed at them when my fingers slipped from Oliver's arm and I fell onto the ground, ass first. "Help me break it up!"

Still, nobody moved in my direction.

Jace Harbor, billionaire football star, grabbed his stepsister and pulled her away from the rowdy group. Poison, Redwood's most cutthroat gang, smoked a blunt and watched from the other side of the hallway. And Carter, our asshole quarterback, cheered on Oliver.

"Get out of the way, Maddie," Vera said, pulling me back. "You're going to get hurt."

"What the fuck are you doing to my sister?" Oliver was seething, hurling another fist at Alec. It collided with his cheek. "This is for putting your hands on her." Another fist to the eye socket this time. "And this is for that fucking post."

Fists began flying between the best friends. They fought like I had only seen them do in hockey. Desperate to hurt each other. Desperate to knock the other to the ground, to gain the advantage, without caring about the consequences.

After a couple of moments, four guys from the hockey team pushed through the crowd. And all four of them finally pulled Oliver and Alec away from each other, holding them back by their arms.

"How could you do this?" Oliver asked, finally calming down slightly and looking at me for an answer, upper lip curled in disgust.

"I ... we ..." I nervously licked my lips. "It happened, Oliver. I don't know what you want me to say."

"Why didn't you tell me that this was happening? He is my best fucking friend!"

Alec growled, "Don't shout at her."

"Why don't you shut the fuck up, Wolfe? I'm talking to my sister."

"You're talking down to my girl," Alec said. "I'm not fucking cool with that."

"You don't need to be cool with it. She's not yours."

"The fuck she isn't."

Oliver turned back to me. "Guys like him will do nothing but hurt you. He sleeps around. Remember what happened with Spencer?"

"I can date anyone I want to, Oliver," I cried, crossing my arms, glaring at him, and vowing that I wouldn't burst out into tears *again* in Redwood's halls. That had happened one too many times this past year. "As much as you think you do, you don't own me."

"If I don't look out for you, who will?"

"What don't you understand about this?! I don't want you to look out for me! I can make my own decisions. Stop acting like our parents because you aren't! If I want to date Alec, then I can date him!"

"Don't come crying to me when he breaks your heart," he said.

After ripping himself away from the guys, Oliver stormed through the crowd and left me there, not even able to mutter another word.

Alec hurried over to me and grasped my face again. "Are you okay?"

"I'm fine, Alec." I wiped some blood off the corner of his lip with my sleeve and glanced down the hallway toward a departing Oliver. My stomach tightened. "I just hope he'll come around."

But honestly, I didn't think he would. When Spencer had broken up with me, Oliver had beaten the shit out of him every day until Spencer transferred out of Redwood. Now, I was dating his best friend. Or at least his former best friend.

"He will," Alec said, following my gaze. "Hopefully."

The crowd erupted into murmurs around us.

Alec grabbed my hand and looked around. "I don't care who is angry about it. Maddie Weber is mine. And if you have a problem with that, you will deal with me. And when I fucking find out which one of you hacked my accounts, I'll personally fuck you up."

After a few moments, the quiet crowd parted again. Dean Sanatora—dean of students and acting principal—stood before us with her hands on her hips. "Alec Wolfe, come with me."

Alec grumbled to himself and kissed my forehead, then left with the dean. Slowly, the students dispersed through the hall. Sandra sent me a dirty look. Piper wished me good luck for the rest of the day and headed off to class. Vera brought me to the parking lot and told me that I should take the day off.

When she finally left to head to class, I leaned against my car and stared at the video posted on Alec's account. My heart hammered against my chest. I couldn't believe that this had happened, that it *was* happening.

My phone buzzed, and an unknown number popped up again.

Unknown: I warned you to stay away from Alec.

Unknown: This isn't the only dirt I have on you and your family.

Unknown: Watch your back, Maddie. I'm coming for him.

Unknown: Alec Wolfe is mine.

33

alec

"YOU'RE STARTING fights in school now, Alec?" Mom cried in Principal Vaughn's old office.

Dean Sanatora sat in the large, cushioned chair across from us, gently tapping her fingers on the wooden desk and probably wondering how she had gotten stuck with this job after Vaughn *passed away unexpectedly.*

I ran a hand through my hair and stood up to pace the room. I had told her more than once in the past fifteen minutes that I hadn't started the fight, that Oliver had come at *me* while I attempted to calm Maddie down.

"Mom, stop!" I shouted, causing them both to jump in their chairs. "Listen to me."

Tears lay heavily in her eyes, and she shook her head. "I am listening to you, but how can I believe you? I love Maddie, but since you've been seeing her—"

My entire body froze. Maddie hadn't wanted anyone to know about our relationship, and as much as I wanted to tell everyone, I wouldn't have opened my mouth about it to anyone. So, how the hell did she know?

"How do you know I've been seeing her?" I asked.

She arched her brow. "Come on. It's obvious. I'm surprised Oliver didn't see it sooner."

I crossed my arms and pressed my lips together. "Did you see us?"

"She was at our home," Mom said. "Stop trying to trying to—"

"I didn't start the fight with him, Mom," I said again, knowing that she was about to bring the conversation back to where it had been since she had arrived at the principal's office.

Oliver had gotten off with a detention, but I couldn't afford that.

"You've been acting so differently," Mom said. "Maddie has been changing you. If your father finds out that you've been skipping games and now fighting, what the hell is he going to think? We've worked so hard for you to be seen by professional hock—"

"*I* have worked so hard," I growled, gritting my teeth. "I'm the one going to multiple practices a day, working out in the gym for hours, even in the off-season, making sure my grades exceed all expectations. You've done nothing but have the money for me to buy my equipment. You act like you've done all the work, but you don't even know about what's happening in my life! You haven't even asked."

Which was a lie. I realized it as I spoke it.

She had asked if something was wrong, but I had been—and still was—too nervous and felt too guilty to tell her. Still, if she had really wanted to know and if she had really cared, then she would've asked Coach or Maddie.

Mom stared at me with tears in her eyes. "I've tried hard to get you to talk to me, Alec."

I wanted to tell her so badly, but I couldn't get myself to do it. I didn't know how she would react, especially because I didn't know the first thing about who it was. I expected her to react worse than Coach because he had been more of a parent figure to me throughout the years. Mom was so much closer to me than Dad was, but still …

They both felt so distant.

Someone knocked on the door, and I collapsed back into my seat and rubbed a hand over my face. If this was Dad, I was about to get chewed out, grounded, forced to practice nonstop for the next twenty-four hours.

"You called Dad?" I asked Mom with venom in my voice.

"No, I didn't."

Dean Sanatora peered at us, blew out a low breath, then said, "Come in!"

Coach opened the door and walked into the room, peering briefly at Mom, then at me. He shut the door behind himself and leaned against the desk with his arms crossed over his chest. "I heard you and Oliver got into a—"

"I didn't start it," I said.

"I know."

When the words left his mouth, I finally relaxed against the chair and slumped my shoulders forward. Even if it was something as small as a fight, I was so relieved that someone besides Maddie believed me without me having to explain myself.

Mom stiffened. "But he—"

"He didn't start the fight," Coach said. "Why would he?"

I forced myself *not* to roll my eyes at Mom, but, damn, she really was attempting to defend Oliver in any way that she could, huh? I let out a low breath, blowing some hair off my forehead, and slumped even lower in my seat.

"If you're going to give me detention too, just assign it, so I can find Maddie," I said.

It would look shitty as hell with the recruiters sitting in on practice and games this week, but if that was what it took to get me out of this damn principal's office and to find Maddie—because she was a fucking wreck—then I would take it.

Dean Sanatora and Coach shared a glance, and then she finally sat up and cleared her throat. "You have a clean record, Mr. Wolfe. You will not be assigned detention today, but I expect that you will be on your best behavior for the rest of the year, which means no fighting on school grounds."

I stood up and nodded. "Thank you."

Once she finally dismissed me while Mom fumed inside the room for some reason or another, I hurried into the hallway and headed straight for the parking lot. I needed to get to Maddie's place—or at least find her.

I didn't know if she would be home, but I—

When I turned the corner, I slammed right into Piper. Her books scattered everywhere, and she bent down to pick them up.

"Sorry," she muttered, then peered up at me, brow furrowed. "Oh, hey."

After picking up some books, I handed them to her and grimaced. "Sorry about that."

She tucked some hair behind her ear. "Have you seen Maddie?"

"I've been stuck in the principal's office. Have you?"

"Yeah, she left about fifteen minutes ago," Piper said, frowning. "Sobbing."

"Where'd she go?"

"Probably her house," Piper said. "But I hope she got in safely. When I last saw her, she was a mess. Vera left her with me while she grabbed some tissues from the restroom, and Maddie just ran off to her car. She was in no shape to drive—"

"Fuck," I growled, rushing through the exit door and heading straight for my car.

"Wait up!" Piper shouted, hurrying after me. "I can—"

But before she could finish her sentence, I slipped into my car, slammed the door closed, and sped out of the parking lot to find my girl.

34

maddie

CURLED up into a tight ball underneath my blankets, I stared emptily at some anime playing on my TV screen. My phone lay in my lap, the screen lighting up with about a hundred notifications from social media.

And I wasn't exaggerating.

Since the last time I had been on Instagram, which was half an hour ago, my social media tab on my iPhone had had ninety-eight notifications. Ninety-freaking-eight notifications from Sandra, Tiffany, and about every other girl at Redwood.

I pulled my gaze away from the TV and looked down at my phone with tears in my eyes, finally succumbing to the pressure. Unable to stop myself, I tapped on one of the Instagram notifications, where a girl I didn't even know had tagged me in a porn star's post.

There were fifteen comments from fifteen bitches at Redwood, all tagging me and gossiping about how slutty I must've been to snag Alec Wolfe because Alec didn't go for girls like me. He went for those like Sandra, who threw themselves at him every chance they got.

My phone vibrated, jolting me out of my teary-eyed trance.

Vera: I'll be over as soon as school ends. xx

Quickly, I pushed her notification away and continued to scroll through the hundreds of negative comments. I just wanted to wallow in my own self-pity and disappear so I wouldn't have to go back and face everyone at Redwood, even the teachers.

They were just as bad as the students and spread gossip to people who didn't even go to Redwood Academy and didn't even know Alec and me.

Tears streamed down my face, and I held back a hiccup behind my hand. The comments got worse and worse as I scrolled, calling me an easy slut, a Redwood whore, asking me how much it'd cost for a night.

Everything.

Vera: You'd better not be all over social media.

Vera: I swear to God ... I see you on Insta.

Vera: GET OFF NOW! YOU DON'T NEED THAT NEGATIVITY.

Deciding that it wasn't worth it, I clicked on Vera's messages and stared at them. I didn't know what to say to my own best friend. This was my worst fucking fear. This shit was happening for a second time. After Spencer ...

Spencer had fucking destroyed me. He had done the same thing, but on purpose. And while Alec hadn't done anything, it still hurt. Whoever had hacked into his social media knew that this would put me in a world full of pain.

It wasn't only that, but now, I was dealing with this chick messaging me constantly about Alec being hers. Not many people had my number, only my close friends and a couple of people who I'd had to do school projects with in class.

I had to find a way to figure this out. I needed to do something.

I didn't know if I could deal with any more negativity.

And almost as if my life couldn't get any worse, my phone buzzed in my hand, and Oliver's name flashed on the screen.

Oliver: I got fucking detention, which means I'll sit out at the next game.

Oliver: We're talking when I get home.

With anger rushing through me, I hurled my phone to the other side of the room, watched it smack against the wall, then fall to the floor with a thud. I pulled my blankets over my head and sank down into the mattress, screaming into my pillow.

This wasn't my fault, but Redwood would blame me.

Because if Oliver had detention, then Alec probably did too.

Alec and Oliver were Redwood's two strongest hockey players. Our team would collapse without them in the next game. All chances of going to the playoffs would go straight out the door. If I thought people talking shit about me now was bad, it was about to get so much fucking worse.

"Why?" I cried out and stared up at the ceiling through teary eyes.

I didn't even believe in a god, definitely not one who had created this shitty town, but why was this happening?! To me? I had tried to do everything right in my life, tried to stay out of the drama. But I fucking hated Redwood with a passion now.

I wanted it to burn.

Someone banged on the front door, jerking me out of my furious trance.

I glared at my bedroom door and hoped that they would go away. But it was probably Alec or Vera, who might have skipped school after I didn't respond to her, or even Oliver, who might have lost his house key again.

The knock came again, and I trudged out of bed and toward my front door with my blankets cocooned around my body. After pushing away my tears, I blew out a deep breath, pulled open the door, and stared wide-eyed into the heartless eyes of Spencer Katz.

35

maddie

"MADDIE WEBER," Spencer cooed at me, stepping into my house, uninvited.

I stepped back farther into the foyer, keeping space between us, and cursed myself for being so stupid and opening the front door without checking who it was first. This was exactly how white girls like me died in horror movies.

"What are you doing here, Spencer?" I asked, frantically racking my brain as to why he could be here.

He hadn't dared to show up since Oliver had beaten up his ass until he was broken and bleeding all over our foyer last year.

My stomach twisted into tight knots, and I glanced around for something to protect me.

Because Oliver had always been here to protect me. Because I didn't trust Spencer in the slightest. Because I guessed that I had always been an easy target for people like him to take advantage of and embarrass for entertainment.

"I wanted to talk," Spencer said, taking another threatening step toward me.

When my back hit the wall, I quickly scooted away from it and tried to steer myself toward the open door that led to the living room. He was blocking my exit to leave the house, and if I turned around and sprinted toward it, Spencer could snatch me up quickly in his arms.

"We don't need to talk about anything."

"Yes, we do."

"Then, what?" I asked through gritted teeth. "What do you want?"

Spencer smirked. "You're dating Redwood's new player. Guess you didn't have anyone new to fawn over after I left Redwood to go on to bigger and better things, Weber. Hmm? You're missing me so much that you decided to go for Alec Wolfe?"

"I don't miss you."

Only he would come up with some shit like that.

Balling my hands into fists, I hardened my glare, tired of being mentally thrown around by him. I was drained from school today, and I didn't have the patience right now. "I'm having a bad day. Leave."

"Oh," he said, dragging out the word, just like he used to do. "You know I can't do that."

After hardening my glare, I sank my nails into my palms. "You're the one who fucked with me, huh? Are you the one who's been texting me to scare me too? Did you release that shit on Alec's accounts?"

"As much as I wish I could take credit for that, I didn't do it."

Spencer gave me that shit-eating grin, and I so desperately wanted to hurl my fist into his assholey face. I hated him so much.

Crossing his arms, he moved toward me. "But you know I love to see you squirm. I'll have to find out who did it and thank them."

"I hate you," I said through gritted teeth. "So damn much!"

"Come on, Maddie." Spencer stepped closer to me. "I know you really miss me."

"I don't miss you. I have *never* missed you. You're the most delusional man I have ever met!"

Before I could stop him, he shoved me against the wall and

trapped me between his arms. "You don't miss this, darling? You don't miss me touching *every fucking inch* of your body, my lips on your cunt, your legs trembling, even in Redwood's classrooms?"

I shoved my hands into his chest. "Get away from me!"

Instead of budging, he moved closer to me and dipped his head, his nose on my neck. I slammed my hands against his body again, grabbing fistfuls of his shirt and banging my fists against his muscle.

"Please, Spencer!"

"I'm not going anywhere, Maddie," Spencer said. "We were dating, and your fucking brother couldn't handle that fucking shit and broke us up. I'm not letting you fuck that loser, who'd much rather sleep with half the cheer team."

My chest tightened, but I knew he was just trying to make me angry.

"Stop it." I was seething. "Stop it now."

"You don't know what he did after the first night you were together, huh?"

"We weren't even a couple yet," I growled, crossing my arms. He was pulling shit out of his ass now, and I needed to stop listening to him before he got into my head. "I don't care about what Alec did back then."

Alec Wolfe was mine now.

Spencer grinned. "Not even if it involved Sandra?"

Just hearing her name, I dropped my hands and searched his eyes for any sort of deceit. He was a known liar, a known cheater, a known asshole to Redwood that I had fallen for a couple of years ago. Now, he was back and successfully messing with my head.

"Get out of here," I snarled. "Now!"

"Come on, M—"

"Maddie ..." Alec called from the front door. "You home? The door's wide open."

When I heard his voice, I froze and glanced over Spencer's shoulder at Alec Wolfe standing in the open doorway with his eyes wide and his lips turned into a frown. He stepped into the house, and Spencer didn't even fucking move.

"What the fuck is going on?" Alec asked.

"What does it look like, Wolfe?" Spencer said, finally pulling away from me and looking over his shoulder. "I'm taking back what's mine."

36

maddie

"GET THE FUCK OUT OF HERE." Alec seized Spencer by his shirt and threw him out the front door. "You'll never get Maddie Weber again, you fucking asshole. Next time you come back and harass her, I'll kick your fucking ass."

"Is that right, Wolfe?" Spencer taunted. "Just like you *kicked* Oliver's ass this morning?"

I clenched my jaw and grabbed Alec's hand to pull him back into the house before Spencer could tease and taunt him anymore. This was exactly what Spencer did all the time, even when we were together. He would either spin things around or bully people relentlessly.

"Don't listen to him, Alec," I said. "He's trying to make you angry."

Alec growled lowly, jaw clenched hard and his heated gaze on Spencer. "I said to get the fuck out of here."

"Alec, come on," I pleaded.

If I didn't settle him down now, then things would surely get out of hand. Spencer was too good at shit like this and even better than

Alec at fighting. Sure, he had gotten beaten up by Oliver last year. But deep down, I knew that he had let Oliver kick his ass. Spencer knew how much Oliver meant to me and hadn't wanted to fuck him up.

After stepping between Alec and Spencer, I swallowed hard and placed my hand on each of their chests, glancing toward Spencer. He might've still had a thing for me—even if that thing was wanting to control me again—but I had grown these past few weeks.

He wouldn't run all over me again. If I didn't stand up to him now, he would keep pushing me. But ... maybe he would do that to me anyway.

"Leave," I said, making sure that I left no sympathy or softness in my voice. "Now."

Spencer tried to step closer to me, but I shoved him back.

"I mean it, Spencer. We're over."

A couple of moments passed, and his smirk turned into a full scowl. He showed me his pearly-white teeth that his daddy must've paid for and turned quickly on his heel, pulling himself away from me and storming down the sidewalk to his car parked down the street.

Once he drove off in a fury, I turned toward Alec and wrapped my arms around his shoulders, pulling him down into a tight hug. The whole weight of what had happened today at Redwood Academy laid on my shoulders, and I didn't know how to handle it.

"Thank you for coming," I whispered into the crook of his neck, tears piling in my eyes.

Alec tensed for a moment, his arms slowly coming around my waist. "You didn't invite him over, right, Maddie?" he asked, voice actually sounding a bit ... vulnerable.

I had never heard him sound so soft and scared.

Alec Wolfe never showed his soft side.

"No," I said, shaking my head and pulling back to look him in the eyes. "I would *never* do that. I don't even like him anymore. He hurt me so much in the past. You saw it firsthand, the hell that he put me through."

Swallowing hard, Alec glanced down between us and nodded. "I know."

I grasped his face to force him to look at me and frowned. "You don't believe me."

"I do, Maddie," he said with a sigh. "I just … you might think I'm good with this relationship stuff, but I refuse to lose you. I've liked you for years now. I saw what he put you through, and I had seen the way you used to look at him, like he was your world."

Gently stroking his face with my fingers, I stared into his eyes. "I don't look at him like that, now do I?"

"No, but …" He paused for a long time and ran a hand through his hair. "Never mind."

"What is it?"

"It's stupid."

"What is it, Alec? Tell me."

"You don't look at me like that," he whispered, eyes becoming glossy. "Through all the girls at Redwood and all the years I've known you, I've only wanted you to look at me the way you used to look at him. I've dreamed of that for so fucking long."

My eyes widened slightly, and I had the urge to slap that boy. He didn't know that he had been the only one getting me through those years, the only guy who I'd kept hoping would make a move while I was with Spencer.

All those eyes I had made at Spencer meant nothing.

They were fake. They were what Spencer had forced me to do if I didn't want to be screamed at and controlled as badly later on in the night. They weren't real; they were never real. The only time I had felt something real was with …

Alec Wolfe.

"You might think that you want me to look at you the way I did with Spencer, but I don't want our relationship to be anything like mine was with him," I whispered, resting my forehead against the center of his chest. "I can't allow that. I can't be controlled like that again. You didn't see what he did to me outside of school. I didn't look at him like that then."

Alec picked up my face. "He hurt you, worse than what he did at school."

I balled my hands into tight fists, all those suppressed memories flooding through my head. Months ago, I had buried them and vowed to never reopen that part of my life, but today, at school and seeing Spencer again ... it fucked with me.

Part of me wanted to believe that Spencer was the man behind the videos today, just to mess with me more, but I knew that it wasn't him. I knew that it was whoever the hell had been sending me those text messages—probably that bitch Sandra.

And right now, I just wanted to forget it all, especially this pain.

"Yes," I whispered. "But I can't talk about it now. It brings back too many nightmares." I grasped his hands, then my house keys, and walked out of the house toward Alec's car. "Let's go on a drive. I don't want to be here when Oliver gets home either."

If Oliver found out that Spencer had paid me a visit today too, he would pack me up himself and send me to another school where Spencer would never be able to find me. Or he would do something much, much worse.

After all, this was Redwood.

37

alec

GRIPPING the steering wheel until my knuckles turned white, I slammed my foot on the gas and drove through Redwood's brightly lit streets in the heart of the rich neighborhoods. Every so often, I peered into the rearview mirror to make sure Spencer—or anyone else from Redwood—wasn't following us.

My thoughts were scattered, my mind racing. I should've done something to Spencer back at the house, but all I could think about was getting Maddie out of there. After she had told me what he did to her and that look on her face when I walked into the house …

She was terrified.

And if I hadn't shown up, what would've happened? The same thing that had happened to me at Oliver's bash a couple of weeks ago? Fuck that. I wouldn't ever let Maddie be in that situation. Never fucking ever.

Once we had driven down every last street, I gritted my teeth and turned onto the main road that led toward the beach. One of these fucking days, I would kill Spencer Katz myself for ever messing with Maddie the way he had.

"Are you okay?" Maddie asked softly.

"I want to kill them," I growled.

Her eyes widened. "Who?"

"Spencer, for what he did to you, and whoever the fuck posted those pictures," I said.

For all I knew, Spencer had posted those pictures. But that dickhead wasn't that smart. He could've taken the pictures, but he couldn't hack into someone else's accounts without help. And I planned to figure out who had done it.

I pulled up to the Overlook and parked the car in an empty space that overlooked the ocean. Waves crashed hard against the rocks, the tide high tonight. Moonlight glimmered against the water and glinted into Maddie's eyes.

"Don't kill him," she said.

"Why not?"

"Because if you do and someone finds out, all your chances at hockey are done for."

"Then, what do you want me to do, Maddie?" I snapped, my voice louder than it should be, but I was so fucking frustrated.

I wanted a life for us, but Spencer deserved to be dead after what he had done to her.

"Don't worry about it," she whispered. "I'll take care of it."

"No."

"You don't even know—"

"You want to get Poison involved," I said.

She swallowed hard and pressed her lips together, staying quiet, which meant that I was right. She wanted Poison involved, but those three assholes would make things incredibly worse, and they would charge her for it.

After sighing, I pushed back my seat, took off her seat belt, and pulled her into my lap. I held her close to my chest and buried my face into her messy red hair. I didn't know what to do anymore. The only time I fought was on the ice.

But I wanted to protect my girl.

I pressed my chest against hers and hummed softly. "I'm sorry this happened to you. I feel like this shit is my fault. I should've noticed that someone had hacked into my accounts. I should've changed my passwords. I should've done something."

"It's not your fault."

"It fucking feels like it."

Maddie interlaced her fingers into my hair and tugged lightly until I stared at her. "Don't blame yourself. You didn't know. You can't do anything about it, except try to get back into your accounts. Have you?"

I grunted lowly and ran a hand through my hair, stressed the fuck out. "I've tried to contact customer support on social media, and nobody is helpful. They won't do shit about it. Whoever hacked my phone even has double authentication activated on their device now. Customer service wouldn't even give me their full number."

"It's probably a cheap knockoff phone anyway," Maddie murmured with a frown.

She grabbed her phone from the passenger seat and swiped to Piper's contact.

"What are you doing?" I asked.

"Piper is learning how to code," she said. "She might be able to help."

I gazed over her shoulder as she typed out her message.

Maddie: Can you help us get Alec's accounts back?

Piper: I can try, but I'm not that good yet. 😟

Piper: I've been working with our new coding teacher and my dad, but it's kinda hard, doing it myself right now. You will probably have better luck with Kai Koh, if you can convince him to help you.

Maddie: Do you know his number?

Piper: No, but Vera might have João's because she babysits for his family. Or if you feel comfortable texting Imani, she'll probably have it. I know you and Vera hang out with her sometimes.

Maddie: Thanks!

Maddie glanced up at me and chewed on the inside of her lip. "It's the only way, Alec."

I didn't want Poison involved at all, but we had no other choice. Still, she needed to understand what she was getting into and how much they charged. Poison didn't do shit for free unless there was something in it for them.

"I don't want them fucking with us more."

She placed her hands on my chest. "It's our only option. And, come on, it's not like our parents will notice a couple thousand dollars missing."

"I heard they forced Jace Harbor to pay two million dollars for a job," I said.

Her eyes widened. "Two million?!"

"Yep."

She ran a hand through her hair. "I know Imani, their ... girl-friend. She's in my Biology class, and we hung out a few times after Vera's incident at school a while ago. I can try to talk to her about it. The least we can do is try to ask Kai. If he asks for too much, then we'll find someone else. Deal?"

"Deal."

38

maddie

HEART THUMPING, I gulped. "Do you think there are more videos?"

"I'm not sure," he said honestly, jaw clenching. "There could be."

"Do you think ... Sandra did it?"

"Sandra?" he asked, brows raised. "Sandra's a bitch, but she didn't do this."

"How do you know?"

"Because," Alec said tensely, "she didn't."

I sat back and furrowed my brow at him, reading him like a damn book. He was hiding something from me, something about his ex-girlfriend that he didn't want me to know about, something damn important.

"Why are you lying to me?"

"I'm not lying to you."

"Then, what aren't you telling me?"

My chest tightened, and I was afraid of his answer. I feared that all those remarks from Sandra—that I wasn't suited for Alec—

hadn't just come out of anywhere. She still liked him, and what if he liked her too?

"How do you know she didn't do this?" I asked, scrambling off his lap.

He went to hold my hips down against his, but I pushed myself away and sat in the passenger seat. Anger and fury rushed through me, and I wanted so desperately to cry my eyes out. This wasn't fair. My day had already been fucked up. I didn't want this to make it worse, but deep down, I knew that it would.

Alec rubbed his hand over his face. "It's not my place to tell you."

"I'm your girlfriend," I said between gritted teeth as I crossed my arms over my chest in an attempt to hold myself together. "Or at least ... that's what you told me you wanted me to be to you. I deserve to know."

"Because, Maddie ..." he said after a long sigh.

"Because why?"

"Because she was at my house by the time we left the locker room. I got a notification from our security system. My house is thirty minutes from the school. She never would've made it there."

I gritted my teeth, hurt rushing through me. "And why the fuck was she at your house?"

"Because she's crazy," he said. "My mom threw her out."

Deciding that *I* couldn't go batshit crazy on him right now, I sat back in my seat and stared through the windshield, taking deep breaths before I blew up at him. While I desperately wanted to see the best in Alec and think the best of this situation, my day had gone to shit hours ago. Nothing positive could come out of this.

"Please, don't be angry. I didn't want to tell you because I didn't want you to get angry—"

Unable to listen to another damn second of this, I slammed open the car door and stepped onto the icy road. I didn't give a fuck about how chillingly bitter it was outside. I refused to sit here and be talked at. This was how it had been with Spencer.

I wanted some silence.

As I stormed down the street, Alec got out of the car and followed after me. "Maddie, wait, please." He ran toward me, but I picked up my pace. "Please, let me continue. If you would just listen—"

"Don't take me for a fool, Alec."

Maybe I was a fool, but I was a mess too right now. I needed time to myself, which was why I had been at home, cuddled up in my blankets, crying my eyes out. Now, I was walking back home in the freezing cold and wishing I had never opened up that door.

He snatched my wrist and pulled me back in the middle of the damn street. I stopped, but refused to look over my shoulder at him or turn around. Tears were already streaming down my face, and I felt like shit.

Maybe Oliver was right all those years ago. *Don't trust any boys, especially those on the hockey team.*

"I don't think you're a fool," he said softly from behind me.

He went to move around me, and I stood my ground and stared at him through the tears.

"Nothing has happened between Sandra and me since we broke up a year ago," he said, no trace of hesitation or lie in his voice. "I swear to God on my parents' lives, I haven't done shit with her."

"She's always fucking hanging around you, and then she shows up at your house while we're together, and you don't even tell me?!" I cried out, bile rising in my throat at the memories of me screaming at Spencer for the same thing.

And while I knew that Alec wasn't Spencer, that Alec was different, I couldn't help it.

I was broken.

"I swear, Maddie," he said, running a hand through his hair. "Listen, I'm not supposed to tell you this, but when I dated her, she realized that she ..." He blew out a breath. "That she doesn't like guys as much as she likes girls, but she is nervous to come out."

I rolled my teary eyes. "Alec, she's all over you all the time."

"She's faking it," he said. "And I'm the only person she's told."

"Still, Alec, if she was into girls only, why does she dance all over you at every party my brother has thrown? It's not like she's making out with girls or even flirting with them. She's obsessed with *you*."

He shook his head. "I don't know, Maddie. All she tells me is that it's hard to express herself, especially with her parents and their conservative views. But you have to believe me. I would never fucking do the shit that Spencer did to you. I haven't even talked to her since we started dating."

"Then, why didn't you tell me?" I asked, crossing my arms.

"Because I knew you wouldn't believe me."

My stomach twisted and turned. I wiped my tears away from my cheeks with the back of my hand and stared emptily at him. I wanted to believe him so badly, but after what Spencer had done to me and the lies he had told me, it was so hard.

"You don't believe me," he said.

"Do you expect me to?"

"Yes. I haven't done anything to make you distrust me, have I?"

"This is pretty sketchy, Alec."

After staring at me for a couple of moments, Alec pulled out his phone and scrolled to his messages with Sandra. He went through the texts from a couple of weeks ago—the night of the party—and handed me the phone, letting me see what he and Sandra really talked about.

Sandra: I'm so scared.

Sandra: What if people at school bully me? You know how people at Redwood are, Alec. And my parents … they're not going to accept me when I tell them I don't like guys. They expect me to get married, be a trophy wife for some doctor. If they find out … my life will be over. They'll disown me.

Sandra: Will you please go to my family's winter party with me to …

Sandra: You know … make it at least seem like we're dating

so they don't get suspicious? If my dad finds out what I've been doing with Tiffany, I'm so afraid he'll hurt her.

The more I scrolled through the messages, the harder and harder they became to read. I stared at the screen with so much pain inside me because this was exactly how I felt about Redwood Academy. So many people judged others here for the stupidest things. It wasn't fair.

But Sandra was one of the people who had made it worse for me.

Bully so you don't get bullied must have been her motto.

"Do you believe me now?" Alec said, watching me with hopeful eyes. "I'm sorry I didn't tell you. That wasn't fair to you, but I haven't been with her since we stopped dating. You can ask her yourself if you want confirmation."

I handed him back the phone and frowned. I didn't know if I was stupid for freaking out or stupid for actually sorta, kinda feeling bad for Sandra now. Still, what if this was all some scheme to get closer to him? Someone had sent those texts to me and hacked his accounts.

Since they had dated, she might've known his passwords.

Headlights shone on us from a distance. Alec took my hand and led me to the side of the road and back toward his car. My body was trembling from the frigid air, the tearstains left on my face frozen.

After sitting down in the car, I rested my head on his shoulder and stared through the window at the raging sea. This town was fucked up, so fucked up that I couldn't even trust the one guy who had been nothing but honest with me this entire time.

"I believe you," I whispered. "I'm just hurt."

Alec pulled me back into his arms and gently rocked me from side to side. "I know."

Again, headlights shone in the rearview mirror, blinding me. The car pulled up beside Alec's car on the side of the road. I glanced over at it with Alec and frowned. Someone rolled down the window, and Imani Abara and Allie Hall looked over at us.

What are they doing here?

I rolled down the window.

"Sorry for interrupting," Imani shouted. "We've been texting you all night. I even got Kai to find your street address. We knocked on your front door, but nobody answered, so we decided to come and find you."

They're worried about me?

Alec tightened his grasp on me. "You gonna answer them?"

"Thank you," I whispered, voice hoarse. "I'm good."

"Redwood is shit," Imani said. "If you ever need anything, we're here."

"Actually," I said, sitting up straighter, "there is something you can help with. We need a favor from Kai Koh."

39

maddie

"IF YOU WANT us to hack back into your accounts and delete all that shit from the internet"—João, Poison's ruthless leader, stood in the middle of Poison's basement as he lit a cigarette and gently pushed on Alec's chest—"then it's going to cost you."

I stood next to Alec, Allie, and Imani and crossed my arms, feeling very uncomfortable. Usually, I didn't come to the slums side of Redwood unless I was visiting Vera, and even she lived in a somewhat better neighborhood.

Imani rolled her eyes, as if she didn't fear Poison at all. "Please, can you just do this one thing for me? You know how shitty Maddie and Alec have had it today. All Maddie wants is to have her life back."

João raised a brow and glared harder at Imani. His mere stare gave me the fucking chills, but didn't seem to affect Imani in the slightest. In fact, she glared back just as hard and crossed her arms over her chest, refusing to back down.

"Please."

"No," João said.

"It's fine," Kai said from the couch, scrolling on his computer.

He was the techie of the group and could hack into any software, even the scoreboard at the football game. Everyone at Redwood had seen his work after Poison declared war on Redwood a few weeks ago. "I'm already in." He looked up at Imani. "But just this one time."

Grinning wickedly at João, Imani nodded and walked to the couch beside Kai. She patted beside her for one of us to sit, but I didn't move. Alec didn't let me either. Who knew what these guys did on these couches?

Imani stared over Kai's shoulder, leaning her head onto him. Then, she looked back over at us. "Do you know who did it?"

"No," I said, finally relaxing when João stopped glaring at Imani and disappeared up the stairs with Landon, the brawn of Poison. I grabbed Alec's hand and walked over to her, leaning against the opposite wall and glancing around. "We have no idea."

"What about Sandra?" Imani asked. "She hates you."

My eyes widened. "You think so too?"

She nodded. "It's obvious."

I looked at Alec, who scratched the back of his head.

"I'll talk to her about that."

"It wasn't her," I said, though I still wasn't a hundred percent on that.

I refused to believe her after a couple of text messages.

"Do you think it was a teacher?" she asked.

"A teacher?" I asked, confusion building up inside me. "Why would it be a teacher?"

Imani and Kai shared a long and tense look, and then Imani scrunched her nose. "You have no idea how corrupt some of the teachers at Redwood are. They flirt with students, watch them in the locker room—*cough, cough, our last principal*—and, you know, are just bad people, like most of the Redwood rich."

Alec took my hand and finally sat on the couch, pulling me down next to him. "I don't think it's a teacher. It's someone close to us. It has to be. They knew exactly where we'd be and when we'd be there."

"Well, if you find them, let me know." Imani jumped up and hiked her thumb back to the stairs, where the other two members of Poison had disappeared. "I'll get those two on them to kick their ass. Nobody should go through what you did. Students at Redwood are nasty."

My lips curled into a small smile. Imani was so much nicer than I'd expected her to be. She had always been nice to me during class, but she was actually like best-friend material, like Vera and Piper were. I'd never really had that many friends, only a select few, but girls like us needed to stay together, especially in a town like Redwood.

"Thank you," I said honestly. "This means so much to me."

"Anytime, girl," she said.

"Got it," Kai said, looking up at Alec. "I changed your password for all your social media accounts and took down what I could of the videos left up online of you and Maddie in the locker room."

I was so happy that I could burst into tears, but I held them back.

"Make sure you change your passwords once more to something that you will remember," Kai said. "And don't make them all the same thing. That's how you get hacked and locked out of your accounts."

After Alec thanked Kai and changed his passwords, he pulled Kai over to the side and talked quietly to him about something that I couldn't quite hear. Imani slumped on the couch next to me.

"I know this week at school is probably going to be hell for you," she said. "You, Vera, and Piper are welcome to sit with me and Allie at lunch. We usually sit with the football team or Poison. If you sit with us, people will know to back off you."

"I'll have to take you up on that," I said. "Vera would like that."

Alec scooped up my hand and nodded toward the other door. "Let's get you back home."

I stood up and thanked Kai again. "I'll see you at lunch tomorrow, Imani."

"See you then!" she called.

Once we were outside, I blew out a breath and felt so much better now that the images and videos were off the internet and Alec had all his accounts back. Now, the only thing bothering me and making my chest tight was the thought of heading back home for tonight.

Oliver had to be home, waiting for me, *waiting to scream at me* for what had happened today.

And I didn't want to deal with the drama.

Because once Oliver found out that Spencer had been there, he'd be out for blood.

40

maddie

"PLEASE," I asked, desperate for Alec to stay out all night with me.

I didn't want to go home to face Oliver because he was surely back by now and he would scream at me for the next three hours about where I had been and about how I couldn't be so stupid to let another Redwood athlete into my fucking heart.

Spencer had utterly destroyed me, ripped me to pieces, thrown daggers right into my heart. How could I let another one of Oliver's close friends get with me? How could I be *that* sister, who listened to her brother's warnings and continued to defy him?

"He'll kill me if I don't bring you home tonight," Alec said, pulling up my driveway and cutting the lights. When he shut off the car, he curled an arm around the back of my seat and turned toward me, then pushed some hair off my face. "You need to talk to him anyway."

Swallowing hard, I stared through the windshield. My heart was beating so hard against my chest, my mouth drying. I didn't want to even think about what had happened today, but Oliver would bring it up without any sympathy.

"Okay," I whispered. "I'll go."

"Promise me you'll be at school tomorrow," Alec said, resting his forehead against mine. "I know you didn't want this ... us ... to be public, but I want to finally be able to be with you. I don't want you to be ashamed of us. I'm not going to hurt you."

That was what Spencer had said too, but he'd fucking annihilated me.

But Alec wasn't Spencer, and I had to keep reminding myself of that. It was wrong to ever compare the two of them, but still ... I couldn't seem to help it. Spencer had been my only boyfriend before Alec, and he had fucked me up.

"I promise that I'll be there," I said, finally able to get the words past my lips.

After Alec planted a fat, wet kiss on my mouth, I said good-bye and dragged my feet all the way up to the front door. I pulled my key out of my purse and prayed that Oliver was sleeping because I didn't want to talk to him right now.

Once I took a deep breath, I stepped inside the house. Almost as if he had been waiting for me, Oliver stood in the foyer with his arms crossed over his chest and a grim look in his eyes—a look that I only saw during hockey matches.

"Who were you with?" he asked.

"None of your business." I pushed past him and headed toward the kitchen to grab something to eat before I retired to my bedroom for tonight.

It had been such a long night, and I didn't know if I would be able to handle another moment of it.

Oliver grabbed my elbow just as I entered the kitchen. "Who were you with?"

I ripped myself away from him. "None of your business, Oliver."

"You can't date Alec," he said to me, ignoring everything I had said earlier about not wanting him to baby me anymore.

Mom and Dad might not have been around as much as normal parents, but that didn't mean he needed to become a parent to me.

I had enough problems, and it wasn't like he was actually grown up enough to handle me. He still partied endlessly with his friends.

"I will date whoever the hell I want."

"Not Alec," he said again through gritted teeth. "That's who you were out with tonight, wasn't it?"

"Why ask if you already know the answer?" I said, finally glaring at him now. "You will never be Mom and Dad! I know that they're off doing God knows what, but you will never be able to be them for me! Stop acting like you control every aspect of my life!"

"I'm not trying to—"

"Yes, you are! And I'm sick of it. God, stop trying!"

Suddenly, Oliver got quiet.

Quieter than he had ever been.

He was the loudest, most annoying guy I knew, but he had never been one to get this terrifyingly quiet. Not even when Spencer had broken my heart. He had gone on nothing but a rage back then.

"I'm just trying to look out for you," he said. "Redwood is—"

"Fucked up?" I interrupted. "Yeah, I know it is."

"Maddie," Oliver said, "I—"

"Stop it!" I found myself yelling. "I don't want to listen to it anymore. I'm so done with this. I'm so done with everything. All I want is a normal life, where I can date whoever I want to date without feeling so bad about myself."

Instead of facing my brother and having a civil conversation with him, I ran up to my bedroom and slammed my door, then locked it so he wouldn't be able to come in at all. I just wanted to be alone tonight, to think through everything that had happened.

Tears were streaming down my face. Part of me felt like I was overreacting. Oliver was just being a big brother. But so much of my life had been controlled by him and by Spencer when I had been dating him. Alec made me feel so free, and that was what I wanted.

Freedom.

41

alec

AFTER DRIVING around Redwood in an attempt to find scumbag Spencer, I headed back to my place. Finding him was one of the two reasons that I had wanted to bring Maddie home and why I hadn't wanted to stay the night.

She didn't want me to hurt him, but he was going to get everything he fucking deserved.

When I opened the garage, only Dad's car was parked inside, which was better than facing Mom, but I didn't want to deal with him either. Though if I hadn't come home, I would have been screwed. Mom would have thrown a hissy fit, like she had at Redwood today, and I would have been grounded for weeks without the option of playing hockey.

Slumping my shoulders forward, I walked into the house.

She pissed me off too. Why had she wanted me to sit through the next few hockey games? I didn't even do anything other than protect myself and protect Maddie today. Oliver had come at me, swinging his fists and screaming at me for dating his sister.

I gritted my teeth. "Fucking Spencer."

He had caused all of this drama. If he hadn't dated Maddie—If

I had had the courage to ask her out freshman *and* sophomore year, like I had wanted—then none of this would be happening right now.

And that damn hacker would pay.

Shit kept getting worse in this fucking town, and I couldn't wait to leave. Only a few more months, and I would whisk Maddie away to a faraway city, where I could play hockey and all she had to do was carry our children.

"Dad!" I shouted, wanting to get his yelling over with tonight so I could relax.

I had no doubt in my mind that Mom had told Dad what happened, and *that* was why he was home tonight. He rarely ever showed up during the week, having meetings and conferences all over the States, and didn't give a shit about me unless it was about hockey.

When he didn't answer, I grumbled to myself and headed toward his office. I would rather turn in for the night, crawl into my bed, and FaceTime Maddie, but I didn't want him to barge in and have her listen to him scream at me.

Seizing the office door handle, I blew out a low breath and shoved the door open.

"Listen, I know that—"

"Alec!" Dad shouted.

I snapped my gaze up from the ground to him.

Dad had Jamal Simmons, football player and Jace Harbor's best friend, bent over his desk with his cock buried in—

Bile rose in my throat. God, I didn't want to know where my own father's dick was.

They both snapped their gazes up to mine, eyes wide. Dad pulled out of Jamal, yanked up his pants, and began shuffling himself together. He stepped toward me, but I stepped back toward the door.

"You're cheating on Mom?" I asked, mouth dry.

"Alec, I can explain," Dad stuttered, extending one arm. "We're—"

"You're cheating on Mom," I repeated. "On our family?"

My throat closed, my thoughts racing. I wrapped my arms around my body and tried hard to calm myself down, but my stomach was twisting, and I had the urge to ... to—

I grabbed the trash bin near the door and hurled into it.

While I had never taken our family and my parents' money for granted before, I never thought that this could happen. I never thought that either one of my parents could cheat on the other, especially with anyone at my school.

Hands shaking, I stumbled back into the doorframe. My heart pounded against my chest, as I was on the brink of another anxiety attack. I could feel it coming, but I couldn't stop it. No matter how hard I tried to look away, push the feelings away.

"Wh-what is goin—"

Carter, quarterback of the football team, walked into the room from Dad's connected bathroom with his shirt thrown over his shoulder, sweat rolling down his chest, and his pants hanging loosely around his waist. "Mr. Wolfe, you have the—"

Dad cursed under his breath and shook his head. "Alec, it's not what—"

Before he could mutter another word, I sprinted out of the office, out of the house, and into my car. I gripped the steering wheel and stared straight through the windshield, not moving. I couldn't see straight. My mind was pounding. I ... our family ...

With trembling fingers, I pulled out my phone and dialed Maddie's number.

She answered on the second ring. "Alec, I thought—"

"Please, come get me," I pleaded. "I need you."

42

maddie

AFTER SWIPING some mascara over my lashes and caking on the makeup to cover up my flushed cheeks, I stared at Alec sleeping through the mirror and frowned.

Last night, I'd had to ask him a gazillion times what had happened before he finally told me that he caught his father cheating. He didn't tell me with whom, but I didn't want to push it. We both had a long night, and I had to sneak a sobbing Alec into my house without Oliver hearing. Thankfully, I had been able to calm him down, but still ...

I shook my head and continued to prepare for the day. This morning, Mom had called from a boat somewhere far, far away and left me a voice mail, asking if I was okay, but I decided not to call her back. If they ever even cared, then they would come back every now and then. They might have been able to retire early with all the money they had, but I still needed them.

They were just gone. Always.

"Get your ass out of bed," Vera said from my bedroom door, holding a Boston cream doughnut and an iced coffee. She widened her eyes. "Oh, you are." She handed me the breakfast and glanced over at a groggy Alec. "Sorry if I woke you."

"It's okay," I said, answering for him. I sipped the coffee. "Thanks, Vera. You're the best."

Vera collapsed on my couch and tossed some hair over her shoulder. "I know."

There was shuffling out in the hallway, and then I heard the front door close, which meant that Oliver was finally gone. I hadn't talked to him since last night, and it was driving me crazy. He was the only damn family that I had here in this fucking enormous house. I wanted to be on good terms with him, but I wasn't going to drop Alec.

I refused to drop Alec.

Not when he was a precious, vulnerable little babe. I glanced over my shoulder at his messy hair, and his eyes were barely open. And, God, was he adorable when he first woke up. I couldn't wait until we could spend every morning like this.

Minus the drama.

After a few moments, Vera frowned. "Are you okay? Seriously, Mads?"

"I'm fine," I said, voice strong until the very end, when it trembled.

I stared blankly in the mirror at myself and watched the tears build in my eyes. All night, I had told myself that I was fine when I had been pushing the thoughts and feelings from yesterday back.

Even though Alec hadn't done anything, I felt so betrayed by Redwood itself. Everyone had seen me naked and begging for Alec, like some desperate little whore. I hated it so fucking much and could only imagine what people would say to me today.

"You're not fine," Vera said, wrapping her arms around me from behind and resting her chin on my shoulder to stare into the mirror at me. "And it's okay not to be okay sometimes, Maddie. I know you try to act as if nothing is wrong, but what you experienced isn't something that can be brushed off."

But still, I felt so bad about complaining. My problems were nothing compared to what happened in the slums of Redwood. Hell, I looked at Poison and the shitty place they lived and couldn't help but think how small my problems were compared to theirs.

Even Vera … she didn't live in the rich part of town. She lived in the slums too. Ms. Rodriguez worked her ass off so Vera and her brother could have a better life. My problems weren't even problems to them.

"I shouldn't be complaining," I said, guilt washing over me. "I have a good life here."

"Problems are problems," Vera said. "We all have them. No matter how rich you are."

Still, it felt so wrong.

The bed creaked behind us, and Alec tumbled out of the bed and landed flat on the rug, belly first. "Fuck, that hurt," he grunted, turning over onto his back and covering his eyes with his forearm. "Why is it so bright?"

"Because it's school time!" Vera chimed. "I've got to go. Blaise is outside, waiting for me."

As if on cue, a horn beeped outside. I peered out the window to see Blaise Harleen, eating a Boston cream doughnut in the driver's side of his sports car. I thanked Vera again for bringing over a coffee and told her that we'd see her at school.

Once she left, Alec climbed up from the floor and sat on the edge of the bed, running a hand through his hair and cursing. He hadn't showered since yesterday. His hair was a greasy mess, and he honestly looked like shit.

But I wasn't going to tell him that after the night he had.

"Do you want to talk about it?" I asked quietly, sitting beside him.

"He was fucking two guys from our school," Alec said.

"What?"

"Two guys in our senior class."

My eyes widened, and I opened my big mouth to respond, but

I didn't know what the hell to say to him. Did Mrs. Wolfe know? They both seemed so happy together, but his father wasn't home a lot due to work …

He wrapped his arms around my waist, pulled me into his lap, and buried his face into the crook of my neck. "What the fuck am I going to do? Do I tell my mom? What will happen at school today if I see them?"

"Maybe you won't run into them," I offered.

"And Spencer," he said, running another hand through his hair. "I'm so fucking stressed."

"It's okay," I murmured, taking his face in my hands.

When he looked up at me, he sighed softly and grabbed my waist tighter. "I'm a terrible fucking boyfriend, huh?" He barely let out a laugh. "Can't even ask my girl how she is doing after the worst day of her life. How are you?"

"I'm fine."

"Maddie."

"I just don't want anyone to look at me differently today, but I know that it will happen."

"If anyone tries to fuck with you, I'll kick their ass."

"No," I said, shaking my head. "I don't want you getting in any more trouble. You have so much on your shoulders as it is. And if you do, you might be out for the rest of the hockey season. This is your senior year."

"I don't give a fuck. I'd do it for you."

"You would risk your own hockey career for me?"

"Yes."

It was one simple word, but it meant everything to me.

While I would never let him even *think* about doing that, it sorta … kinda … felt nice for someone to be devoted to me because they liked me rather than because they wanted something from me, like Spencer had.

"Why don't we shower together?" I hummed, running my hands through his hair.

I had already put makeup on and done my hair, but I didn't mind.

He pulled me in for a kiss. "I stink that badly?"

A giggle escaped my lips. "Maybe."

He tossed me over his shoulder and headed toward the bathroom. "A shower then."

43

alec

"YOU'RE SO DIRTY," I hummed against Maddie's shoulder in the shower.

She whimpered softly and arched her back, grinding herself against me. My dick hardened against her backside, twitching and aching to be inside her already. So, I slipped my hand around her waist and rubbed her clit as the shower water ran down our bodies.

"Alec," she murmured, placing her hands on the wall, "we're going to be late."

I moved my fingers faster until her body stiffened underneath my touch. "We'll get out once I've fucked your pretty little pussy, Maddie," I mumbled against the back of her neck, chuckling when her clit quivered.

"B-but—" she started, grabbing my hand.

"You're so desperate for me to touch your body," I said, thrusting my hips back and forth so my cock would rub against her sopping little entrance. And once it did, she arched her back harder and moaned.

"Tell me you want it," I said, resting my forehead against the back of her neck.

"Alec …" she whimpered, wiggling her ass against my dick.

"Tell me, Maddie. Or I'll stop."

She gazed back at me with her lips parted and her eyes glazed over. "P-please."

With the rain pouring around us, I grasped her wide hips and lined myself up with her entrance, her pussy drooling all over me already.

"That's a good girl," I cooed, then slammed myself into her. "*My* good girl."

Throwing her head back, she cried out in pleasure, "Alec!"

I dipped my head and kissed her shoulder from behind, all my stress melting away. She clenched around me, her pussy walls tightening. I grunted into her ear and placed my hands over hers, intertwining our fingers and pumping into her.

She curled her fingers around mine and pushed back against me with every thrust, her wet red hair plastered against her body. I moved closer to her, wanting more and more and more of her. Anything I could get.

Legs trembling, she leaned back against me and cried out in pleasure. As her pussy exploded around me, I pounded into her faster, pushing myself closer and closer. My balls smacked against her clit, feeling so heavy and warm, the way they did right before—

"Alec," she moaned.

After pumping one last time into her, I stilled.

"God, I love you," I murmured.

The words had tumbled out of my mouth before I could stop them, and Maddie tightened around me almost instantly.

She leaned against the wall and glanced back at me, breathing heavily. "D-did you mean to say that?"

"Y-yes," I whispered, wrapping my arms around her torso and drawing her closer.

No more hiding the fact that I had been in love with her for years.

"I love you, Maddie Weber," I murmured. "I've loved you for so long."

She twisted in the shower so she faced me, the water still pounding around us. And then she smiled softly at me and moved her hands up my arms and around my shoulders, pulling me down for a kiss. "I love you too, Wolfe."

44

maddie

AFTER FIRST PERIOD, I marched through the science wing toward Sandra's locker. I had to go through it to get to Biology anyway, so I might as well stop by to see if Sandra had actually come to school today. I didn't know what the hell I was going to say to her, but I wanted to start standing up for myself.

People walked all over me at Redwood. It was time for a change.

A *big* change.

Shy Maddie Weber needed to step out of her fucking shell at some point. I couldn't let Oliver baby me forever, and I wanted to prove to him that I didn't need his protection anymore. He didn't need to be another parent.

Besides, I officially had Alec Wolfe as mine.

I pressed my hands to my chest and tried to stop the butterflies because I wanted to be serious with Sandra. But I couldn't stop thinking about what had happened in the shower this morning. Alec Wolfe had told me he loved me.

Me!

Once I made it halfway down the hallway, I spotted Sandra

standing at her locker with a bunch of her friends, shoving in some textbooks. I approached them cautiously, nerves zipping through my body at the mere thought of talking to her because *I hated her.*

"Sandra?" I said, stopping feet away.

She glanced over her shoulder at me and scrunched her nose. "What?"

"Can I talk to you?"

Her friends giggled, one of them stepping forward.

"*You* talk to *her* after you slept with her ex-boyfriend?" She scoffed, earning a laugh from all the other girls besides Sandra. "Gross. Get lost, you whore."

Instead of paying them any attention, I stared at Sandra and hoped that she'd get them to go away. She might've been pissed at me for being with Alec, but she was over him, right? At least, if what Alec had said was the truth.

"Go," Sandra said.

"See," her friend continued. "Run off somewhere—"

"I was talking to you," Sandra said to her friend.

The girls around her snapped their heads in Sandra's direction, then scurried away, as if Sandra would explode on them if they didn't do as she said.

When they were gone, Sandra turned toward me. "Make it quick."

"I wanted to ask about Alec."

"What about him? How you stole him from me?"

"Alec said that … that you don't like him like that," I said, glancing around to make sure nobody was listening. When I was sure, I leaned forward just in case and lowered my voice. "That you like girls too."

It wasn't really my place to tell her. She hadn't come out to me yet, and I felt so bad … but I couldn't help it. I needed to know the truth or else my jealousy would just get worse. And after seeing how widely Alec had smiled after I kissed him in front of everyone, I didn't want to lose him. Besides, I still didn't trust her yet.

And—as bad as it was—if I could hang this over her head to

get her to stop bullying me, then I would. She had tortured me for years, and if I was going to stand up for myself and claim Alec as mine, then I had to push back.

Sandra's face paled. "He didn't tell you that. You're lying."

"He didn't tell anyone else. I just need to know that you don't like him like that anymore, that you will never like him like that, no matter how much you make it seem like you do." I glanced down at the dirty tiled floor. "Please."

After a few moments of lethal silence, Sandra grabbed my arm hard and yanked me into an empty classroom. She slammed the door closed and shoved me against it. "I swear to God, if you tell anyone, I will kick your ass. I don't give a fuck. Don't say that shit out loud again."

"So, it is true?"

Another moment passed, and Sandra released me and paced the room. "Yes," she snapped. "It's true, okay?"

My shoulders fell forward, and weight seemed to roll off them. It felt so good to hear it confirmed by someone other than Alec. I knew that I could trust him, but Spencer had really just destroyed my trust for everyone and everything.

"So, you didn't send me those messages?"

"What messages?" Sandra asked, brow furrowed.

"I keep getting nasty messages from someone who likes Alec. I'm assuming it's the same person who hacked his accounts and fucked my entire life up," I said, opening the messages from the unknown number.

When Sandra looked over my shoulder at it, another message suddenly popped up.

Unknown: You think kissing Alec in front of the entire school makes you better than me? You have another thing coming, bitch.

She scrunched her nose. "Ew. Who the fuck is that?"

"I don't know."

"What are you going to do about it?" she asked. "Because it's obviously not me."

I arched a brow, still not trusting her. "Why do you care?"

She let out a breath. "Because Alec cares about you and he's one of my best friends."

I literally scoffed *because* if Alec was her best friend, then she didn't have *any* true friends.

"Mmhmm," I hummed suspiciously.

"Okay, fine." Sandra shrugged. "Looks like you don't need my help."

When she went to walk through the door, I grabbed her wrist. "Wait. I'm sorry. I need help. I just ... I don't know who it is. I can't really ask Poison for another favor, and Alec doesn't want me getting involved in too much trouble, but I want ... to sock this girl's face in."

Sandra grinned. "Finally growing a backbone, Weber." She tossed her hair over her shoulder and headed to the exit. "If you want me to kick anyone's ass for you"—she wiped the grin off her face and sighed like I was wasting her time—"then you can ask me."

"Thanks, I guess."

I didn't know what I would get if I asked for her help, but I wanted these messages to stop.

She stopped at the door, then walked back over to me, and grabbed the phone from my hand. And before I could stop her, she blocked the unknown number and slammed it back into my hand. "You're welcome."

45

alec

WHEN LUNCHTIME ROLLED AROUND, I slung my
backpack over my right shoulder and exited the Health class that I
had with Oliver. He had been shooting me a glare filled with
daggers all throughout class, and I had tried to ignore him. I had
bigger problems than him hating me.

I slowed to a stroll, not caring about getting to my usual table
right away because I wasn't sitting there today with Oliver or any
of the guys on the hockey team. They could go fuck themselves for
all I cared.

Today, I would sit with my girl for the first time. And I didn't
give a fuck about what Oliver thought about it. If he wanted to
fight me again, then I would be happy to do so *off* of school
grounds, when I couldn't get in trouble.

And where, apparently, Mom wouldn't get angry because I
didn't get detention.

Butterflies fluttered in my stomach as I thought about this
morning. I had admitted to Maddie that I loved her, and she had
… said it back. I hadn't been planning to say anything to her until
all this drama died down. But I couldn't help it.

Once I made it to the first floor, I pulled out my phone.

Me: You'd better be at lunch today, Cupcake.

Maddie: I will be. 🩶

Maddie: I talked to Sandra today.

My eyes widened slightly. *She talked to Sandra? About what I told her?* I balled my hands into fists and hoped that Sandra had actually been honest with her and hadn't lied to get underneath Maddie's skin.

Me: And?

Maddie: I still don't trust her, but she admitted to what you'd told me.

After blowing out a breath, I relaxed my shoulders and turned down the hallway to the cafeteria.

Before I could even walk into the cafeteria, someone grabbed the back of my jacket from behind and slammed me up against the lockers.

"You like to take it from the back, like your daddy?" Carter, the asshole, asked.

I shoved myself off the lockers and turned around, catching a glimpse of the dean standing down the hallway. *Fuck.*

She had her arms crossed, waiting—just fucking *waiting*—for me to fight back so she could give me the detention that I had gotten out of yesterday. I didn't know why the entire world was against me this year.

Balling my hands into fists, I stepped toward him. "Stay the fuck away from me."

"Or what're you going to do? Go tell your daddy?" He curled his lips into a menacing scowl. "He'll take my side, just like your mommy took Oliver's yesterday after you got sent to the office for fighting him."

My fists ached to plow right into that shit-eating grin. "The fuck does that mean?"

"Come on," he taunted. "You're smart, right? You can figure it out."

"Did Oliver—*that fucking asshole*—put you up to this?" I growled.

It wouldn't surprise me if Oliver had fed Carter all these fucking lies, hoping that I'd slam my fist into Carter's face and get suspended for it, hoping that Coach would sit me out these next few games and that my career would be over before it even started.

"Didn't have to." He chuckled. "I don't need his parents' money."

"Then, why the fuck are you here?"

"Because if you tell anyone what you saw last night, I'm going to rip *you* a new one."

Standing inches from me, the quarterback of the football team crossed his arms. It took everything inside me not to shove my hands into his chest and push him away, but I could still fucking see the dean watching us.

"Get the fuck out of my face, Carter," I said between gritted teeth.

The dean and Coach had said not to fight on school property, but if I saw this asshole anywhere else in Redwood, then it would be fair game. I would shove my foot so deep into his ass that he *wouldn't* enjoy it.

After glaring at me for another moment, he knocked me against the lockers once more and headed into the cafeteria. I pushed myself off the lockers and readjusted my jacket, glancing toward the dean. She grimaced and walked into her office.

A low growl escaped my throat, and I balled my hands into fists.

The fuck was he even trying to insinuate about my mother defending Oliver yesterday?

My stomach twisted into a knot, fury building even higher inside me.

It'd better not mean what I think it means.

Or all hell would break loose.

46

maddie

AFTER SCHOOL, while Alec was at hockey practice, I sat in Beans 'n' Cream Café with Vera, Imani, Allie, Nicole, and Piper. We had spent time with Imani and Allie regularly outside of school, but Nicole was another story.

She had been a bitch to basically all of us, up until a couple of months ago. I especially didn't understand why Allie kept inviting her to hang out with us since Nicole had tried to steal Allie's man multiple times throughout high school, but I couldn't complain. Nicole wasn't *that* bad.

"Listen," Nicole said, leaning closer to me, "if you ever need me to kick anyone's ass, just say the word. I saw you coming out of a classroom with Sandra this morning, and you looked pissed."

"Thanks," I said, sipping my hot chocolate. "But I think I can handle myself for now."

"Yeah, I can get Poison on her ass too," Imani said. "Say the word."

"Poison will make her pay," Allie said. "Like an astronomical amount."

"I doubt that she is as desperate as Jace." Imani giggled, referring to Allie's stepbrother boyfriend. "Or as dumb."

A laugh escaped my mouth. "I heard that they made Jace pay two million for a file."

"Two million," Imani corrected, grinning and giggling at Allie.

Allie shushed her. "Okay, okay. He was a bit desperate, but for good reason."

When we quieted down, Piper nudged me. "Is that Sakura Sato with Mr. Avery?"

All the girls glanced over at the register, watching Sakura Sato, the school's valedictorian, and Mr. Avery, our Literature professor, order coffee together and ... being way too handsy to be coincidentally spotting each other in public.

"Don't be mean," Vera said in a hushed tone.

"I'm not," Piper said. "Just curious."

"I think they're seeing each other," Vera hummed to the girls. "Blaise told me."

Everyone at the table snapped their heads toward Vera.

"What do you mean, they're seeing each other?" Imani asked. "As in fucking?"

"Well, yes ..." Vera started. "But I think they're actually in a relationship."

"Sakura?" Nicole asked, jaw hanging down. "Sakura Sato? She's so sweet and quiet."

I frowned. "I don't think she has that many friends."

"Well, let's change that! Besides, I want the tea," Imani said, leaping up and waving her arms across the Beans 'n' Cream Café in an *attempt* to get their attention. "Hey, Sakura!"

Sakura leaped back from Mr. Avery and twirled around, her cheeks flushed. "Oh, hi!"

Mr. Avery and Sakura exchanged a glance and some hushed words, and then Sakura took her jasmine tea and walked over to us.

She smiled softly. "Hi." Her voice was so quiet that I was sure she'd win a yearbook superlative for it.

"Wanna have coffee with us?" Imani asked.

"Oh, um"—she glanced over her shoulder at Mr. Avery—"I actually have plans tonight."

"With Mr. Avery?" Nicole asked.

Sakura's cheeks flushed, and she nervously tapped her fingers on the hot cup. "N-no."

"It's okay." Vera grinned. "Piper is fucking a teacher too."

"Vera!" Piper exclaimed, slapping her playfully.

Sakura's cheeks darkened even more, and she shook her head. "It is nothing like—"

"I've slept with a few teachers in Redwood myself," Nicole said. "Imani gets fucked by three gangsters every day. Allie sucks her stepbrother's dick in the locker room. Vera has done it on school property. And Maddie is screwing around with her brother's bestie. We don't judge."

"Sit with us," I said, scooting over so Sakura could sit down.

While she hesitated, she eventually placed her drink down on the table. "Give me a sec."

After she hurried back over to Mr. Avery, they exchanged another few words, and then he kissed her. My mouth dropped open, and I slapped Vera in excitement underneath the table. She stiffened and peered over her shoulder at us, her hair in her face. Then, once he left, she walked back to us.

"It's not what it looks like," she whispered.

"Mmhmm," the girls said in unison.

"Really," she said. "He's a lot sweeter than he is in class."

"Mr. Avery is a grump in class most days," Allie said.

"He's great in our class," I said, smirking at Sakura. "Now, I know why."

She giggled nervously and sipped on her tea. "I don't want to bother you girls."

"Stop it," Imani said. "You're not a bother. We were just talking about how stupid Jace Harbor could be sometimes."

Allie shot her a look. "More like how Poison takes advantage of everyone they can."

"Hey." Imani laughed. "Take that up with Poison. Not with me."

"They charge way too much for some of their stuff," Allie said.

The door clattered, and I glanced over my shoulder to see Carter—the damn asshole quarterback who messed with literally everyone and their parents. After I had finally gotten it out of Alec at lunch what had happened and with whom, I had been in shock all day, especially about Jamal Simmons. But I could definitely believe that Carter was stirring up shit at Redwood.

Like usual.

"Why don't we start our own gang?" I offered. "Hurt all the people who have wronged us."

Alec would literally kill me if he knew that I'd even suggested the idea, but I was so tired of all this shit. Every day, something happened in the shitty town of Redwood, and everyone else at this table was sick of it too.

"A gang?" Vera giggled. "I'm not sure I'm fit to be in a gang."

"Poison won't like having competition." Imani chuckled. "I'm in."

"Me too," Nicole said. "I've been wanting to take care of a few people."

Allie grinned at Imani. "I guess I'm in too. I really want to sock Carter in the face."

I glanced over at Carter, who stood in line. "You're not the only one."

"Looks like we've found our first …" Nicole said.

"Our first what?" Allie asked.

"You know …" Nicole paused, then looked over at Imani. "I don't know what they call it."

"What's Poison call it?" Allie asked her best friend.

"Piece of business?" Imani offered.

I watched Carter exit the café with two coffees and grabbed my keys. "Come on, girls. We have business to take care of."

47

maddie

"MADDIE and the girls want to start a gang," Vera whispered into the phone.

I arched a brow at her, wondering why the hell she was whispering when we all could hear her *and* when she had put Blaise on speaker so—in Vera's words—he could convince us that it was a bad idea.

"A gang?" he repeated. "What kind of gang?"

"Like one where we beat people up."

"We're planning to kick Carter's ass!" I added while following behind Carter's car.

"Damn, sounds like fun." Blaise chuckled. "Does Poison know that you're competing with them for business? Because if you're not careful, Sunshine, they'll wipe you off the board. Anyway, let me know how it goes. I'm proud of you."

"Blaise?!" she exclaimed. "Did you not hear Maddie?! We're going to beat up Carter."

"Heard her loud and clear. Make sure you punch him real hard, like I showed you."

Vera's cheeks flushed, and she mumbled a good-bye to Blaise and shut off the phone. She slipped her phone into her purse and pursed her lips. "I still don't think this is a good idea. What if we get into trouble?"

"Don't worry about that," I said. "My parents have money."

"Mine too," Allie, Imani, and Nicole said in unison from the backseat.

"Where do you think he's going?" Nicole said, glancing out the windshield from the backseat of my car.

Vera sat up front with me, but the other girls were cramped in the back, wondering where the hell we were going.

Carter lived on the good side of town, but not in Alec's neighborhood.

My stomach twisted as I watched Carter park three houses down from the Wolfes'. He flipped up his hoodie and walked with the coffees on the side of the road to Alec's house. If this asshole was planning to visit Mr. Wolfe *again*, I swore to fucking God ...

That was definitely something that I didn't want Alec to walk in on again. Carter and Mr. Wolfe had some nerve, meeting up after what had happened last night, and this close to hockey practice ending too?!

"Let's go!" I said, grabbing something from my glove box. "And be quiet."

"Grab the duct tape!" Nicole whisper-yelled to Imani.

All the girls crawled out of the car and shut the doors quietly behind themselves. We hid behind some bushes on the neighbor's property as Carter walked closer to the Wolfe residence, completely oblivious to us.

"Maddie," Nicole whispered, "what is that in your hand?"

"You'll see."

"Shh!" Allie whispered. "He's coming."

I glanced around the corner to see him feet from us now. And just before he could walk onto the Wolfes' property, I leaped out of the darkness.

"Now!" I said, watching as the girls mobbed him, our hands pushing and shoving and gripping on to him.

Hot coffee spilled all over Carter, hopefully burning off his dick.

Once we tackled him to the ground, we taped his mouth with the duct tape that Imani had had in her car, probably from a job that she had done with Poison at some point. I wasn't going to question it.

"Wait!" I said, ripping the tape off his mouth and shoving the dildo from my glove box into his mouth. I snapped it shut with the tape so he couldn't spit it back out. "Choke on a fucking dick, you prick."

Allie straddled his waist to keep him relatively still as she twirled the tape roll around his wrist so he couldn't fight back. And then she slammed her fist into his pretty-boy face as hard as she could, breaking his nose in three places.

"Kick his ass!" Nicole said, slamming her heel into his abdomen.

We kicked, hit, and punched the helpless asshole, who flopped around like a worm on the ground, covering his head and shielding his face. And while he was on the football team, he was no match for seven women he'd pissed off.

Sakura even got a couple of punches in on him too, which surprised me because she was a good girl who barely said a few words. But between this and Mr. Avery, that girl had a wild side that I wanted to see more of.

Ah, peer pressure at its finest.

At some point, one of the girls pulled out a stick of Sin lipstick and used it to write all over his skin with the words *piece of shit, asshole, dickhead,* and more expletives that anyone at Redwood would agree with.

If Alec found out about this, he'd be so angry with me, but I couldn't stop beating the shit out of Carter. I wanted the world—especially Redwood—to burn for what they had done to all of us because it wasn't fair. None of this was fair.

But after a few moments, Carter stopped grunting and stopped protecting himself altogether.

I pushed myself off him and stood up with the rest of the girls, mouth parting slightly.

Vera stepped back, blood dripping from her fist. "I-is he dead?"

48

maddie

IMANI NUDGED Carter's unmoving body with her sneaker. "I'll call Poison."

Tears welled up in Vera's eyes, and she backed up. "Maddie, we killed someone!"

"He's not dead," I said. Well, I hoped not because that'd be bad.

"I can call Callan too," Sakura whispered.

Allie arched a brow. "What will he do?"

Sakura sucked in her inner cheek and rocked back on her heels. "You'd be surprised."

"Isn't Mr. Avery in the Redwood mob?" Nicole asked.

Sakura blushed. "Not anymore."

"Not after I killed—" Imani started.

"Killed who?" João, the leader of Poison, said through the phone.

Imani walked down the street, pacing by my car to talk to João. Thankfully, we were able to drag Carter behind some dark bushes so nobody could see him—or us—standing over his heavy body.

Vera grabbed my arm. "Why did we do this?! We're going to be in so much trouble!"

"It'll be fine, Vera," I whispered. "Poison will take care of it."

"What if they don't?" she said. "I don't want to go to jail."

"Then, you'd better wipe his blood off your knuckles," I said.

After a couple of moments, Imani walked back over. "They'll be here in five."

Allie crouched over Carter, brow furrowed. "Do you think he's really—"

Before she could finish her sentence, Carter somehow suddenly woke back up, ripped the duct tape on his hands apart, and grabbed Allie by the throat. Vera screamed and stomped right on his head with her new designer boots that Blaise had bought her.

Carter's head bounced off the ground, and he was knocked out cold again.

Five minutes later, a car without headlights rolled up to the curb behind my car. João, Landon, and Kai stepped out of it and walked over, eyeing us up and then gazing down at Carter, who hadn't woken back up from Vera's attack.

"Damn," João said. "Which one of you cracked his skull?"

We all pointed to Vera, who pressed her lips together.

"He was attacking Allie, okay?!"

"And the duct tape?" Kai asked, glancing over at Imani with a prideful smirk on his face. "Impressive."

"Is that a dildo in his mouth?" Landon asked, crouching down in front of Carter.

"Maybe," I said.

Imani moved closer to João, toyed with the ends of his hair, and batted her lashes at him. "Can you please make sure he doesn't go to the police? Maybe embarrass him a bit more since we did all the dirty work for you?"

"The dirty work?" João scoffed. "You beat him up and called me for help."

Imani pressed herself against him. "Pleeeease."

João threw her a pissed look, then nodded to Landon. "Throw him in the trunk."

As Landon picked up Carter, another car with its headlights on pulled up behind João's Mercedes.

Mr. Avery exited the car and slammed the door behind himself, walking over to us with his arms crossed. "What's going on here?"

"Who the fuck called Avery?" João scowled.

Mr. Avery grabbed Sakura's hand and pulled her behind him. "What's going on?"

"We formed a gang," Imani said, smirking at João.

"Is that right?" João growled, staring her down and snatching her chin. "A gang? You think you're tough enough to start your own girl group who kicks the shit out of people and then calls for help?"

Vera shook her head. "I told you guys this was a bad idea!"

"Nobody speaks a word about this to anyone," Mr. Avery said, guiding Sakura to his car.

She gazed back at us with a smile. "I had fun!"

"Come hang out with us anytime," Nicole said. "We'll do more of this."

"No, you won't," João said. "Because I'm not cleaning up your mess again."

Imani rolled her eyes, then grabbed his hand. "I'll see you all later!"

Once Sakura and Imani disappeared with their lovers, I grabbed the duct tape from the bushes and walked back to my car with Vera, Allie, Nicole, and Piper. We slipped into the warm car, and I started the engine.

"That was fun," Nicole said.

"Yeah, I especially liked the part where we thought Carter was almost dead," Allie said.

"You guys are actually insane," Vera said, sniffling from the passenger seat. "I want to go home."

"Okay, okay," I hummed, turning the car around in the middle of the street and heading toward the main road.

I stopped at the Stop sign and blew out a low breath, hoping that Carter wouldn't mess with any of us anymore.

And as I turned the corner to pull onto the next street, I spotted my brother's car turning onto the road. Since he had fought with Alec the other day, he wasn't allowed to go to practice, which meant that he was lounging around, doing some shit with …

My jaw dropped open when I saw Mrs. Wolfe in the passenger seat of his car.

49

maddie

"DID YOU SEE THAT?" Vera asked when I pulled up to her house.

I had dropped the rest of the girls off at their respective cars at Redwood Academy and nearly sped to Vera's house because I wanted to catch Oliver with Mrs. Wolfe before he left so I could scream at them both.

What the fuck were they thinking?!

"Who, Oliver and Alec's mom?" I said between gritted teeth. "Yeah."

"I didn't want to say anything with the other girls in the car," Vera said.

"I hate that bastard," I growled, pulling to the curb. "He is such a fucking hypocrite."

Vera's brother, Mateo, and Blaise Harleen both stood near the front door, holding skateboards.

Blaise dropped his, hopped on it, and rode over to us, pulling open the door. "Kick some ass, Sunshine?"

Once Vera said good-bye, she slipped out of the car and scolded Blaise for ever thinking that she would do something like that. But my girl, V, had some anger in her the way she had completely decked Carter.

I sped down the road toward the Wolfe residence. After a ten-minute drive, I turned onto their road and hit the accelerator to drive faster. Oliver was probably long gone by now, but I wanted to at least try to catch him in the act because that asshole had pissed me the fuck off.

Who the hell was he to tell me I couldn't see Alec when he was driving around Redwood with Alec's own mother?! And his father was sleeping with two other classmates of ours?! His parents had never seemed weird as fuck until now. What kind of fetish did they both have, sleeping with eighteen-year-olds?

When I finally pulled up their driveway, Oliver's car was still parked, which surprised me because Mr. Wolfe was home too. If I walked in on some type of orgy, I would force Alec to move away from here with me for good.

Storming right through the open garage and into the house without invitation, I rushed into the living room.

"Oliver!" I shouted, hands balled into tight fists. "Where are you? And what the fuck are you doing here?!"

Oliver walked out of a back room on the second floor and glanced over the wooden balcony, brow furrowed and the most confused expression written across his stupid face. "Maddie, what're you doing here?"

"What the fuck is wrong with you?!" I shouted, storming up the stairs. "Really, Oliver?"

Mrs. Wolfe and Mr. Wolfe walked out from the back room, looking just as confused. I grabbed Oliver by his ear, pinching it as hard as I could between my fingers and yanking him back down the stairs.

"Maddie, let go! What are you doing?"

"What the fuck are *you* doing here?" I asked. "You still haven't answered my question!"

"I'm helping Mr. and Mrs. Wolfe out with something," Oliver said, yanking himself away from me and clutching his ear. "The fuck is wrong with you? I'm bleeding now because of you." He looked up at Mrs. Wolfe. "Do you have any Band—"

I snapped my hand around his wrist. "We're going home."

"Oh, of course I do, dear," she said, scurrying to the bathroom.

Again, Oliver yanked himself away from me and stood his ground, refusing to move anymore. I tried harder and harder, but he continued to stand stoically in the middle of the living room with the smallest amount of blood dripping from his ear.

What a fucking baby.

If he was hurt because of me pinching his stupid ear, how did he think Alec had felt after he kicked the shit out of him during school? I balled my hands into fists, wanting to hurl one right at my stupid brother's face.

As Mr. and Mrs. Wolfe descended the stairs, I crossed my arms over my chest. "You both should feel ashamed of yourselves."

I didn't know what was going on with Oliver in this; I could make my best guess, but I hadn't seen anything.

But Mr. Wolfe … I turned toward him. "You're about the biggest piece of trash that I have ever met."

"Don't talk about my husband that way," Mrs. Wolfe said, handing Oliver the Band-Aid and turning toward me. Her lovely, caring expression that she always had with me was suddenly gone, and she crossed her arms.

"Your husband is cheating on you," I growled. "With two of my classmates." I stepped closer to her, refusing to back down to a grown-ass woman. "And Alec walked in on them last night, if you even fucking care." Not giving anyone any time to speak, I turned toward Oliver. "And you're sleeping with his mom."

Oliver scrunched his nose. "I'm not sleeping with Mrs. Wolfe."

"Then, why the fuck are you here, on your night off from hockey?!" I shouted, throwing my hands up in the air. "I highly doubt that Alec knows you're hanging out with his mother behind his back! You're the biggest—argh, forget it!"

Deciding that I wouldn't surrender this time, I snapped both hands around his wrist and pulled him out to the garage and to his car. I didn't give a fuck if he was sleeping with her or not. It didn't matter to me.

But what did matter was that he had been doing this behind Alec's back.

Alec already felt betrayed because of his father and mother. If he found out that his best friend could possibly be banging one— or both—of them too, he would be devastated.

Although Alec and I had kinda done the same thing, this was far different.

This was Alec's parents. His parents!

"Get in your fucking car, Oliver," I growled. "We're going home."

"Maybe you're going home, sis." Oliver crossed his arms. "But I'm not going anywhere with you."

50

alec

"ALEC WOLFE?" a recruiter dressed in a suit said, extending his hand to me after practice. Usually, college recruiters came alone or with another person, but there were a handful of them behind this guy. "Salvador Larsen. We work for the Glaciers."

My eyes widened. The Glaciers?! They were a team in the NHL. I shook his hand. "It's nice to meet you, sir."

"Very impressive out on the ice tonight," he complimented. "We've attended a couple of your games, and we wanted to extend an invitation for you and your family to visit our stadium and watch training for a national league."

"I would love that," I said, hiking my training gear up my shoulder.

He placed a hand on another man's shoulder behind him. "I'll have Jeremy send you the information via email. You're welcome to bring both of your parents and siblings, if you have any, for a couple of days in the spring."

Lips curled into a smile, I nodded. "That'd be great, but can I bring someone else instead?" I paused because I didn't want to overstep, but I didn't want my parents coming with me. "Someone who has supported me even more?"

"Sure." He nodded and extended his hand once more for me to shake. "It was nice meeting you, Alec. And we look forward to seeing you at the training, and hopefully, we'll see you at the draft in June too."

I bit back a grin and shook his hand to say good-bye. Once they headed out the back door, I glanced over at Coach, who was leaning against his office door and smiling at me.

"Congratulations, son."

"Thank you," I said, rushing over and enveloping him in a hug. "Thank you. Thank you."

He chuckled and slung his arm around my shoulder. "You've put in all the hard work."

"But I couldn't have done it without you," I said.

"Don't discredit your achievements, Alec. Why don't you go celebrate with Maddie?"

"That's what I'm going to do, sir." I squeezed him one last time and headed out the doors, jogging to my car. I could barely hold in my excitement, so as soon as I slipped into the car, I called her.

No answer.

I called again as I drove to my house to dump my belongings and shower before seeing her.

Nothing.

When I pulled up my driveway, both Maddie and Oliver stood there, yelling at each other, while my parents stared at them from the open garage. They all stopped and glanced over at me as I parked.

I grabbed my hockey gear and hopped out of the car. "What's going on here?"

Nobody said a word.

"Maddie?" I said, dragging a hand around her waist.

She pulled me in for a long, hard kiss in front of my parents and her brother. She had been so against kissing in front of anyone, especially her brother, so why was she doing this? Right here and right now?

After kissing her, I pulled away and looked between them. "What happened?"

"I think that—" Maddie started.

"Nothing happened," Oliver growled.

"Shut the fuck up, Oliver," she said, snapping her gaze toward him.

My eyes widened slightly. Maddie had sworn in front of me many times before, but she usually stayed quiet in front of parents and teachers. Something terrible must've happened tonight. Maybe I could tell if I looked at the security cameras.

"I need to talk to Oliver alone," Maddie said. "I have had a long night."

I grabbed her hands and forced her to stare at me. "What happened?"

"Carter happened, and then ..." She looked over at my parents and brother. "Them."

"Carter happened?" I repeated, balling my hands into fists. "What the fuck did he do?"

If he had laid a damn hand on Maddie tonight, I would show up at his house and kick the living shit out of him. He had threatened me during school, and I couldn't fight back. But he couldn't threaten my girl. No fucking way would I let that slide.

"Oh"—she laughed emptily—"more like what happened to him."

My gaze drifted to my dad. *Did he do something to Carter? Did someone find out?*

"What happened?" I asked again.

"Redwood's Girl Gang happened," she said, ushering me into the garage. "Go rest."

Redwood's Girl Gang? Who the hell is—

I dropped my gaze to Maddie's knuckles to see the bruises. "Maddie, are you serious?"

"Alec," she said, snapping her hands around Oliver's wrist, "I don't have time to explain."

Oliver yanked himself away from her, sending her to the ground.

I dropped all my hockey gear and ran over to her, standing in front of her and slamming my hands into his chest. "Don't touch her, you fucking prick."

"She was the one touching me," he said.

Maddie scrambled to her feet. "Because you're fucking Alec's mom!"

51

maddie

EVERYONE SUDDENLY WENT QUIET. I glared at my brother and swallowed, my heart racing harder than it should. I hadn't meant to scream the words, but I couldn't stop them from tumbling from my mouth.

Alec deserved to know.

"Wh-what?" Alec whispered.

"We didn't do shit together," Oliver said, looking at his car.

"You're a liar," I growled at him. "You can never keep eye contact when you lie."

Alec peered over at his mom. "Is it true?"

"No," she said, but then dropped her gaze and her voice. "Of course not."

I crossed my arms, not wanting to be part of this, but already too deep. Alec wasn't going to stand up for himself—at least, I wouldn't be able to if I had gotten raped, then had everyone bully me for it, then found out my dad was sleeping with two male classmates and my best friend was banging my mother.

"Then, what were you doing with her, Oliver?" I asked as calmly as I could.

"She wanted help with a gift for Alec's birthday," he said.

"Where's the gift then?" I asked.

"In my car."

"Get it."

Oliver stormed to his car, slipped into the driver's seat, and threw the car in reverse, speeding down the driveway and then onto the road. I slammed my foot into my own tire because I was pissed.

"I'll be back," I said to Alec.

Because I was about to follow my idiot brother wherever he went and beat his ass for being such a dickhead to his own best friend. Alec was going through more than Oliver could wrap his tiny mind around, and he needed someone.

Not a lousy friend who'd sleep with his mother!

"Wait," Alec said, catching my wrist and pulling me back.

Midway through opening the driver's door, I paused and gazed back at him, worried that I shouldn't leave him alone here, all by himself. Maybe we should just find a place together, like Blaise and Vera, and live there for the rest of the semester until college.

"I got some good news tonight," he whispered.

Anger slowly dissipating, I released my grip on the door handle and gently took his face into my hands. "That's great, Alec," I whispered, warmth flooding through my chest for him. "What happened?"

"A group of people who work for Glacier showed up at practice tonight," he said, keeping his voice quiet. "They want me to come watch a couple of their practices in the spring, and he said that I could bring you."

My eyes widened, and I threw my arms around his shoulders. "That's amazing!"

He pulled me closer and relaxed in my embrace, his shoulders slumping forward and a low breath escaping his mouth. I held him tightly for as long as he needed, and after another moment, he pulled away.

"Are you going to be all right?" I asked.

"As fine as I can be," he mumbled. "I should just expect this shit."

I grabbed his hands. "We're going to get out of this town. I promise."

Tears welled up in his eyes. "Soon?"

"Soon."

After he pulled me closer once more, he kissed me on the forehead. "Be careful."

"I will," I said, sliding into the driver's seat. "And then I'll come pick you up."

Once I sped down the Wolfes' driveway, I gripped the steering wheel and headed to my house. I hoped that Alec would be okay for a few hours, but I wanted to rip Oliver a new one. He was such a fucking hypocrite and probably only did it to get back at Alec.

I fucking hate him. Hate him!

After speeding up my driveway and *not* finding Oliver, I headed toward town and hoped to the fucking gods that he hadn't run away like the little asshole he was. He had to be here somewhere. Maybe with one of the guys from the hockey team or finding another mom to bend over.

My hand tightened around the steering wheel, nails digging into the leather. "Fuck!"

I stopped at a light, nostrils flared, and glared through the windshield down the street. Oliver's car was parked in the middle of the road, diagonal across both lanes, with the driver's door open.

When the light turned green, I hit the accelerator and slammed on the brakes once I made it feet from his car. I jumped out, wondering where the fuck he was, and screamed his name so loudly that everyone in the houses around us could probably hear it.

And when nobody responded, I stormed to his driver's door to pull his car out of the road, but found a note sitting on the seat. I picked it up and unfolded it.

Baby,
I'll take good care of your brother.
Love,
Spencer <3

52

alec

"THAT GIRL IS NO GOOD," Mom said.

"That girl's name is Maddie," I snarled, stomping up the stairs. "And I love her."

"All she does is make up lies to make us look bad," Mom said.

Dad stood next to her, rubbing the lines in his forehead. "Just stop."

"No!" Mom exclaimed. "She's turning our son against us."

"I don't want to hear your fucking excuses," I growled, slamming my bedroom door and locking it so that my parents—who had been trying to calm me down for the past half hour—wouldn't barge into the room.

After slumping down on the bed, I pulled out my phone and opened an email from the Glaciers.

Dear Alec,

It was great meeting you at practice. We spoke about bringing you out to watch practice this spring, but we chatted about it on our way to the airport and would love to invite you and your

family out to watch practice and a game next weekend. All expenses paid.

What do you think?

- **Jeremy**

I grinned and stared at the email, typing a response that I would love to bring Maddie this weekend. It would be great for us to get away from Redwood Academy a bit. Between everything going on, we both needed it.

As soon as I sent the message, Maddie's name popped up on my phone.

"Alec!" Maddie sobbed on the other end, screaming and crying.

"Maddie, what's going on?" I asked, hopping off my bed and grabbing my keys.

"S-S-Spencer ..."

My stomach dropped, and I sprinted out of my bedroom, down the stairs, and to my car without informing those stupid idiots about where I was headed. They didn't deserve it. I slammed my door shut and started the car.

"What happened?" I asked, squealing out the driveway. "Where are you?"

"He took Oliver!" she sobbed. "He took him."

"Where are you?" I repeated, heading in the direction of her house.

She had been on her way home to find Oliver, right?

"B-by the school."

After speeding through nearly every Stop sign, I hit the brakes and parked the car when I saw flashing police lights. I grabbed my keys and sprinted to the scene, where Maddie paced on the phone with someone, bursting out into tears.

"Maddie!" I called.

She snapped her gaze to mine and ran over, throwing her arms around my shoulders and sobbing into the crook of my neck. "Alec"—she sniffled, snot everywhere—"h-h-he's g-g-gone. He's gone!"

"What happened?" I asked, glancing past her at the police checking out Oliver's car.

It had been parked diagonally in the middle of the street with the car door wide open. Officers walked back and forth from their cars to the Oliver's, chatting quietly with one another and shaking their heads.

"Oliver wasn't home, so I drove around Redwood to find him. I s-saw his car p-parked here, and I got out to move it off the road. A-and he was nowhere to be found." Tears streamed down her face, and she gripped my jacket in her fists. "Alec ..."

"How do you know it was Spencer?"

"B-because he left a note," she said. "I gave it to the police chief."

A couple officers walked over to us. "Ma'am ..."

"Yes," Maddie said, picking her head up from my shoulder. "What's wrong? How can—"

"Unfortunately, it doesn't look like your brother has been kidnapped," he started.

"What do you mean?" I asked. "He wouldn't just park his car in the middle of the road."

The other officer shook his head. "That's what it seems like to us. We're going to move it off the road and give you the keys, but there is nothing else we can do at the moment for you. We apologize—"

"What the fuck do you mean?!" Maddie exclaimed. "You have the note that Spencer left!"

"Ma'am, you didn't provide us with any note."

"I gave it to your boss," she said.

"He doesn't have one," the officer said, walking back to Oliver's car.

"You can't do this!" she screamed at the officers. "My brother has been taken by a psychotic piece of shit, and you're just leaving?! Do your fucking job and help him! Find him! Stop being the dickhead Redwood officers you are and be useful for once!"

"Maddie," I whispered, holding her back.

"How much did he pay you?" Maddie screamed.

"Maddie," I scolded quietly, "stop it."

"We all know you fuckers don't do anything without getting pai—"

I slapped my hand over her mouth to keep her quiet. Everyone knew that the Redwood Police were corrupt. We had seen instances of it about a million times in the past four months of school, but nobody dared say it out loud.

"Do you want to be next?" I whisper-yelled, dragging her back to her car and smiling at the officers so they wouldn't hurt her. "Don't worry, Officers. She knows you're just doing your job to the best of your abilities."

Maddie slithered out of my hold and sprinted at them. "You are fucking li—"

Before she could get halfway there, I seized her waist and threw her over my shoulder, holding on to her body as tightly as I could so she wouldn't escape again. And then I walked all the way to the football field at Redwood Academy, a few blocks away, with her in my arms.

"Let me down!" she shouted, banging on my back. "They took my brother!"

"I know," I whispered.

"They took my brother," she cried, her voice beginning to tremble. "They took him."

"I know," I repeated. "I know they did."

"Why didn't you say anything?" she sobbed, her body shaking violently now.

"Because I don't want them to take you too," I said, holding on to her tighter because I fucking loved her and I never wanted to see her cry.

She had held me this tightly when I needed it the most, and I had promised myself that I would be there when she needed me.

"Alec"—she sniffled—"what if ... what if Spencer kills him?"

"Spencer isn't going to kill him."

Though, as the words left my mouth, they sounded like one big, fat lie. Spencer was unhinged and would do whatever it took to take Maddie back. If he had to kill Oliver to get Maddie in a vulnerable state, then he would.

He knew that Maddie would do anything to find Oliver.

Anything.

Even drive to his house in a rage, all by herself, to rescue him.

"We'll find him," I murmured. "I promise."

53

maddie

"THE POLICE ARE IN ON THIS!" I cried, falling to my knees and running my hands through my unruly hair. I shook my head from side to side, sobbing as Alec picked me up. "They're fucking in on this, and they ... they don't care that my brother is gone!"

As annoying as that asshole was, he was the only family that I had left who cared. I wanted to kick his ass myself and not let Spencer do it because Spencer ... Spencer might fucking kill him. And if Oliver died in my ex-boyfriend's hands ...

I would never forgive myself. Tears streamed down my cheeks.

Every single officer left the scene. Like nothing had happened. Like my brother wasn't missing. Like my psycho ex wasn't taunting me and threatening to kill my brother.

When the last one drove away, Alec released his grip on me. I dropped to the grass in the middle of the football field and slammed my fist against the ground over and over until my skin split open and my knuckles began bleeding.

"Maddie, stop it," Alec said, sitting behind me and pulling me into his lap.

"They don't care," I sobbed. "Oliver is going to die."

"He won't die."

"That's a lie," I said, snotting everywhere and curling into his lap. "And you know it."

"Maddie!" someone shouted behind us.

We glanced over our shoulders to see Vera running onto the field from Blaise's sports car parked on the side of the road. He slammed the door closed behind her and walked toward Oliver's car, which the police hadn't actually moved.

Vera dropped to her knees in front of me and wrapped me up into a hug. I collapsed into her lap, sobbing uncontrollably and grasping on to her.

"They're all in on it, V. Spencer took him, and I don't think I'll ever see him again."

"Shh. Shh. Shh," she cooed, rocking us back and forth. "We'll figure this out."

"D-did you call Piper?" I asked. "Can you see if her father—"

"Already done," Vera said. "She's checking with her dad to see if he can look at the security cameras around here. If Spencer was here, we should be able to prove that it was him. And then ... you can press charges."

"But I can't," I said, feeling so hopeless. "Redwood Police aren't going to do shit for me."

"Then, we can—"

More tears poured from my eyes. "They're working with him."

Vera pulled me closer. "Even if they're working with him, we'll find Oliver. Spencer isn't that smart. He's not working alone. We just have to find out who he is working with. The police, sure. But who else? Why would the police want your brother dead?"

"If it were me ..." Blaise said, tossing Vera the keys to Oliver's car, which he had moved out of the road. He sat down beside us and looked over at Alec. "I would grow a fucking pair and take care of Spencer myself."

"No," I said. "Alec can't."

"Why not?" Blaise said. "I'd do it if some psycho maniac was—"

"Stop it," Vera scolded. "Alec has recruiters watching him."

"He's right," Alec said.

I grabbed his chin and shook my head. "No."

"Maddie, it's—"

"No," I growled, my voice final. "I'm not going to lose both of you."

My chest tightened at the thought of watching Spencer torture and kill both my brother and my boyfriend, all at once. I squeezed my stinging eyes closed and shook my head, another cry escaping my lips.

"You can't," I said. "So, get that out of your head."

"Then, the only thing left to do is call Poison," Blaise said.

"We're not getting involved with them," Alec said.

But I was already on my feet. "It's the only way."

54

alec

AFTER WE KNOCKED on his door, João opened it, peered out at us, then almost immediately slammed it shut. Before he could close it all the way, Vera placed her foot between the door and the frame and shoved her shoulder against it.

"We need your help."

"No," João said.

"Please, João," Vera said, pushing the door open.

"Vera, is that you?" a little girl said from the couch, dressed in princess pajamas with her eyes half-opened. She staggered out from the small living room to the door, standing next to João, and reached her small arms up for Vera. "Why are you here so late?"

"To talk to your brother," Vera said. "Will you ask him to talk to me, Ana?"

With her head resting on Vera's shoulder and her eyes closed, Ana pointed at João. "Talk to Vera. She's my best friend. If you're mean to her, then I'm not going to talk to you for an entire week."

João rolled his eyes and hiked his thumb back to the hallway. "Put her to bed."

Vera smiled at João—which made Blaise growl—and then

hurried into the back hallway. When Vera disappeared, Maddie stepped forward.

"I need your help, and I'm willing to pay for it." She poked a finger into his chest. "But you're not screwing me over like you did with Jace."

"We didn't screw Jace Harbor," João said, leaning against the back of his couch. "Jace paid for a service. We delivered. He valued that information at the price we provided him."

"Well, I'm not paying two million."

"You're right. You're going to pay more," João said. "If you want your brother back."

Maddie stared at him through bewildered eyes. "H-how'd you know he's gone?"

"Kai saw Spencer take him on the town's security cameras."

Maddie balled her hands into fists and screamed, "I hate him!"

"We'll do it for four," João offered.

"Two," Maddie countered.

Nerves built up inside me, making my chest tight. I didn't like Poison—hated them actually—and I loathed the way this conversation was going. Working with them could hurt us—badly—in the end.

"Four."

With flared nostrils, Maddie glared at João. "Two, and we'll help you."

João snorted. "You'll help me like you helped with Carter earlier?"

Maddie tensed and glanced over at me.

"What happened tonight?" I asked.

"The girls beat the shit out of Carter. Almost killed him," João said.

She had mentioned it briefly earlier, but ...

I seized Maddie's hand and squeezed it, heart breaking. "You did?"

Blaise chuckled next to me and leaned against the door, his lips curled into a smirk, as Vera walked back into the room, tucking some hair behind her ears.

"Asshole deserved it. He's been a dickhead since elementary school."

"Vera knocked him out," Maddie said.

"That's my girl," Blaise said.

"Maddie," I said, pulling her toward me, "you should not be kicking anyone's ass."

Maddie pressed her lips together. "He deserved it for what he did to you."

"What he did to you?" João asked, rubbing his hands together. "Getting interesting now."

"He didn't do anything," I said between my teeth. I tugged Maddie. "We're leaving."

"No," she said.

"Maddie," I said, grabbing her elbow, "working with Poison is a bad idea."

Maddie turned to me with tears in her eyes and shook her head. "This is the only chance that we have of getting him back, Alec. I don't care what happens to me as long as Spencer doesn't kill my brother. I-I wouldn't be able to live with myself."

"This isn't the only chance we have," I said. "I can do something."

"No," she said immediately. "You have hockey. You can't risk it. This is the only way."

João cleared his throat. "We'll do it for three, but then you work for us."

"No," I said.

"Deal," Maddie said. "But if you don't bring my brother back alive, then the deal's off."

I released Maddie's hand and rubbed my forehead, wondering when I'd get wrinkles like my father had. Because I couldn't deal with all this stress. I didn't want Maddie working with Poison. What would they force her to do?

"You're not working with them," I said.

"If they find him alive, then I will," Maddie said.

"What're you going to make her do?" I asked João.

"Whatever she is useful for."

After blowing out a heavy breath, I shook my head and paced around the room. Maddie, João, and Vera talked quietly about what had happened and what Poison would do, but I couldn't stand it. Maddie was putting herself in danger with the worst gang in Redwood.

I wouldn't let her get in trouble. I refused.

So, I slipped out the front door and shut it behind me.

"I don't blame you," Blaise said, leaning against the side of the house.

I jumped back in surprise. "When the hell did you come out here?"

"When you started pacing inside," he said. "You looked like an idiot."

"Fuck you," I spit. "I don't give a fuck what you think. I'm only here for Maddie."

Blaise chuckled and kicked himself off the house. "And I'm only here for Vera, and I don't like her working with Poison either. João's messing around with Imani, but he's too close with Vera for my liking."

"I have bigger problems than listening to you bitch about João," I said, walking to my car.

"You want to stop Spencer without getting Poison involved," Blaise said. "Let me help."

"How—and why—would you do that?" I asked, pausing at the curb.

"Because he screwed me over two years ago," Blaise said. "I'm not going to explain shit to you, but I've been wanting to kick his ass ever since. I'll help you without getting Poison involved."

"And what do you want out of the deal?" I asked.

"Nothing."

"Bullshit."

"If Vera found out that I forced you to pay me for some shit like this, she'd have my dick." Blaise drew his tongue across his teeth. "All I want is to stick my foot so deep up his ass that he can't shit again."

I twisted my head and stared over my shoulder at him, pressing my lips together. I didn't know if I trusted him, but it was better to work with him than associate ourselves with Poison. Though ... somehow, I still felt like Poison would insert themselves into our situation.

After clenching my jaw, I pulled my phone out of my pocket and scrolled to my Contacts. Blaise arched a brow and gazed down at the phone. I waited and waited and waited as it rang repeatedly, driving me higher and higher into an anxious mess. And then someone answered.

"Alec Wolfe," Spencer hummed over the phone. "I was hoping you'd call me."

55

alec

"I CAN'T BELIEVE we just left the girls at João's," I mumbled, turning down a road.

We had been driving for the past thirty minutes to Spencer's house, which wasn't in Redwood anymore. And the longer I drove, the tighter my stomach twisted into knots. Maybe I should've let Poison do this shit. Maybe we had gotten a little ahead of ourselves.

Blaise was tough and could kick anyone's ass, but he wasn't Poison. He was one guy who had mostly kept to himself, and for some reason, he wanted to hurt Spencer. He didn't have the experience that Poison did.

"They'll be fine," Blaise said. "As much as I don't like that asshole, he'll protect Vera and Maddie if something happens. Besides, we have more important shit to do than listen to them talk about giving Poison millions of dollars."

After turning onto Franklin Street, I ran a hand through my hair. I had to go see the Glaciers this weekend, and I didn't want us to miss it. Maddie wouldn't even think about going if Spencer still had her brother hostage. We needed to find him.

And while Blaise might've been right, I had acted on pure emotion. I should've waited a bit—or at least told Maddie that we were going out on a drive. Instead, I had gotten too psyched up to kick Spencer's ass and find Oliver for her that I just left.

"You gonna chicken out on me?" Blaise asked from the passenger seat.

My palms were sweating against the leather steering wheel. "No."

"Good," Blaise said, staring out his window and nodding. "It's right up here."

Bile rose in my throat, but I swallowed it down and parked on the street a couple of houses down from Spencer's new place, which was more luxurious than his old home in Redwood. But his parents were broke as shit after they had to move, so I wasn't sure why he lived *here*.

"What'd Spencer do to you?" I asked, mouth dry.

"Pulled Vera's hair in freshman year."

Nearly choking on my own spit, I peered over at him. "You want to kick his ass for pulling her hair, even when you weren't dating, when *you* used to make fun of her? That's why you wanted to come out with me?!"

While I really didn't know Vera, I had seen her many times with Maddie, growing up. And I had heard more than one story about Blaise being a dick to both of them. I had been a dick too, but

…

"Maddie wasn't your girl the last time you kicked Spencer's ass, but you did it for her."

He had a point.

I stared out the window at the house and tried to remember the plan again. Blaise had explained it twice on the drive over, but I hadn't been able to think clearly. Either I was worrying about Maddie, my parents, Oliver, or kicking Spencer's ass.

Not how we'd actually do it.

"You good?" Blaise asked, standing outside of the car and looking in through the open door.

"Yeah," I said, clearing my throat and stepping out of the car, my stomach in knots.

We walked right up the sidewalk to his front steps and knocked on the front door. My mind was so cloudy with regret and … with the thought of how stupid this was, but there wasn't any turning back now.

Not after I had just knocked.

Especially not when Spencer was opening the front door.

"I didn't think you'd actually show up," Spencer said, smirking at me.

I balled my hands into fists. "Where's—"

"Knock, knock, motherfucker," Blaise said, slamming open the door.

When Spencer stumbled back, Blaise stepped into the house and grabbed a diamond lamp sitting on a side table. Blaise swung the lamp right at his head, sending him flying backward and into his parents' bookcase. Books flew across the wooden floorboards. Spencer scrambled to his feet, hurling his fist back toward Blaise.

But Blaise sidestepped him, grabbed him by the jacket, and slammed his head into a glass window so hard that the thick glass cracked. "That's for bullying Vera Rodriguez freshman year, you piece of shit."

"I didn't bully her, prick," Spencer spit, grasping his head.

While I fought during games, I didn't like it outside of the rink. And besides, before Blaise killed the guy, we needed to at least find out where Maddie's brother and my—ex?—best friend was being held. I wanted to be logical. Then, I wouldn't feel so bad about kicking the shit out of Spencer.

"Where's Oliver?" I asked.

"Probably fucking your mom," Spencer growled as Blaise hurled the lamp at him.

Spencer ducked out of the way, letting the lamp hit the wall behind him and shatter to pieces. I glared at him, not letting him get the best of my emotions. He knew how to play the manipulative game.

But how had he known about my mother and Oliver? Had Oliver told him?

"Where is he?" I repeated through gritted teeth.

"Doesn't matter." Spencer smirked, the scent of wildflowers drifting through my nose from behind. "You're here, which means Maddie's now mine."

My stomach twisted, heart racing. Something didn't seem right.

So, I twirled around just in time to catch sight of locks of blonde hair before the person swung a bat at my head. My vision blurred for a moment, and then suddenly, everything went dark. Blaise shouted in the distance, but then his body hit the ground beside me.

56

maddie

"IT'S SO LATE," Vera said, yawning on João's couch. "Blaise!"

I ran a hand over my face and stared down at a tablet that Kai —the tech wiz of Poison—must've programmed for João because I didn't think that João was smart enough to code anything like this.

For the twentieth time tonight, I rewatched the security camera footage that Kai had sent over to João earlier.

The cops had pulled Oliver over blocks from the school, but instead of any police officer exiting the car, Spencer did with a gun. When Oliver realized what was happening, he tried to get away, but Spencer shot out one of his tires and pulled him out of the car, tied him up with the help of ... someone I couldn't quite make out, and threw him into the back of his Jeep.

"Blaise?" Vera called again from the couch, yawning. After a moment, she hopped off it and padded into the kitchen. "We should get going."

"I need to find Oliver," I said desperately.

"It's almost three in the morning," Vera said. "We've been up for almost twenty-four hours, Maddie. We're not going to find him tonight, especially not when we're almost falling asleep. Let

Poison do the hard work for you. That's what you're paying them for."

"Yeah, get the fuck out of my house," João said, half-asleep while leaning against the wall near the kitchen table. He crossed his arms and yawned. "Ana is going to be up in two hours, wanting breakfast."

"Blaise!" Vera called again, glancing around the room. "Where did he go?"

"They left." João said.

"What?" she asked, furrowing her brow. "When?"

Ana padded from the back room, clutching her teddy and crying. "João! I want Imani!"

"About four hours ago."

"Where did they go?" I asked, glancing out the window to see Alec's car was gone.

I furrowed my brow because Alec would never hang out with Blaise just to bullshit. They had to be doing something together, right? But to stay out this late and not tell me at all? Not even a text?

"Don't know, but listen, I can't help you right now," João said, heading toward the hallway, where a wailing Ana stood. "You gotta figure out where your little boys went off to yourselves. Now, get out of my house."

After running a hand over my face—because I was stressed the fuck out—I tugged Vera out of the house and down the front steps toward Blaise's car, which was the only one left on the road. "Do you happen to have his keys?"

"No," Vera said, shielding herself from the light rain.

"I'll call an Uber," I said, whipping out my phone to catch a ride.

While we waited for our ride, Vera bounced on her toes. "So, did Mrs. Wolfe really …"

"Sleep with my stupid brother?" I asked between gritted teeth. "Yes."

She scrunched her nose. "Why? She's married."

I balled my hands into fists and glared at Blaise's car, wondering the same damn thing.

"Maybe his parents have an open relationship?" Vera suggested.

"Still, if they have an open relationship, they shouldn't be so open about it in front of Alec. They didn't tell him anything, and he walked in on his dad fucking Jamal and Carter the other night."

"Ew, Carter?" Vera asked. "He's gross."

"I know," I said. "Like, come on, Mr. Wolfe. There are hotter guys in Redwood."

Vera snickered, and I let out a small laugh, too, for the first time tonight.

She clutched her stomach and slumped against my shoulder, giggling like a maniac. "Literally anyone else in Redwood is hotter than Carter."

"*Carter* and *hot* don't even belong in the same sentence."

We laughed so hard in the rain until we were wheezing and no noise was coming out. I wiped the tears from my cheeks as headlights blazed through the darkness. I looped my arm around Vera's, still smiling.

"Is that our Uber?" she asked, cheeks rounded.

"Let me check the license plate," I said, pulling out my phone to double-check.

But all I saw was a text from Piper.

Piper: I'm sorry.

Piper: *Current location.*

"Is it him?" Vera asked, glancing over my shoulder at our group chat on my phone.

I ignored the car that pulled up to the curb, seeing Imani in the driver's seat, and tapped on Piper's current location.

Why the hell did she apologize? What is she up to tonight? Last I had heard, she had been doing something for her dad.

"Hey, guys!" Imani said, exiting her car and waving. "What're you doing here?"

"Hey, Imani," Vera said with a smile.

While I wanted to respond, I could barely lift my gaze off the phone trembling in my hand. "Oh my God," I whispered, eyes widening.

"What is it?" Imani said, hopping on to the curb.

"Piper?" Vera furrowed her brow. "Where is she?"

My mouth dried. "Spencer's new place."

57

alec

EYES FLUTTERING OPEN, I squinted at the fire blazing across the room. Spencer sat in a large, cushioned chair in front of it, one ankle kicked up onto his knee and his arms crossed over his chest, as if he had been waiting for me to come back around.

My head pounded from when the baseball bat had collided with it earlier, and while I remembered blonde hair ... I didn't think I'd actually seen who it was. But it hadn't been Spencer, which meant that he was working with someone.

A woman maybe.

"Let me fucking go," Oliver growled from the opposite corner of the room.

I blinked again, my vision becoming clearer as he came into view. Large bruises covered his face, down his neck, and all over his bare chest. His hands and ankles were bound together so he couldn't escape. Though ... the skin looked raw near the rope.

"Finally coming around, are we?" Spencer said, ignoring Oliver's pleas.

Deciding to annoy his stupid fucking ass, I glanced around the room to see Blaise lying in a different corner, completely passed out with his head swollen near his right eye. I closed my eyes and cursed myself for ever believing we'd be able to do something to Spencer.

I hadn't been thinking in my right mind, and now, we were Spencer's captives.

God, I needed to stop thinking off pure emotion. I had been good at it for a while, but seeing Carter with my father and thinking about Mom and Oliver and with everything that had happened so suddenly with the Glaciers ... it was too much for a kid.

In the fourth corner of the room, someone sat in another chair, completely covered in darkness.

Spencer stood from his seat. "Wonderful."

"What do you want? Money?" I asked, still refusing to look him in the eye. "I can give—"

Spencer's chuckle boomed throughout the room. "I want you to break, lover boy. Again. And again. And again. And again. As punishment for ever thinking that you could replace me and love Maddie."

"Maddie will never love you," Oliver spit at Spencer.

"She will, if I make her," Spencer said.

"You'd never make her," I growled.

"If I let her watch you sleep with another woman *again*, I could."

"I didn't sleep with anyone else while we were together," I snarled.

"Not even at Oliver's party?" Spencer chuckled. "I know you did. Because *I* watched it happen."

"He's just talking shit, Alec," Oliver said. "Don't listen to him."

"And I know who did it," Spencer said.

My mouth dried, heart racing. "You what?"

"It's just wonderful that she's here tonight too," he exclaimed, walking to a closet door and opening it up.

A young woman was slumped on the ground, as if she had been sleeping, and blinked her eyes open.

"C-can I go?" she whispered.

And I froze.

No ... no, it couldn't be.

"You got shit to do, bitch," Spencer said, kicking her. "Get up."

Piper scrambled to her knees and stared into the room.

I stared at her through teary eyes, still in disbelief. "It was you that night?"

"I'm sorry," Piper whispered, squeezing her eyes closed. "I'm so sorry."

My body jerked forward, and I tried desperately to escape my binds, rage rushing through me. "You fucking raped me?! You drugged me and raped me! And you acted like you didn't know shit about it every fucking day to Maddie's face!"

Piper's lips trembled, but I wasn't believing that shit. Tears burned my eyes, and I shook my head. Why would she do that? She had never once shown interest in me, never mind wanting to stab Maddie in the back.

When Maddie found out, she'd be crushed.

"My dad forced me," she whispered. "I-I'm sorry."

"Your dad didn't force you to do shit, you fucking bitch!" I shouted, my voice breaking. "You made the decision to slip the drug into my drink, climb onto me while I was passed out, and then ... then you fucking harassed Maddie?!"

"That might be true." Spencer chuckled. "But tonight's going to be a little different."

"P-please, Spencer," Piper cried. "Don't make me do it again."

Spencer held a gun to the back of her head and smirked at me from over her shoulder. "Why don't you show Alec what he missed that night when you spiked one of his many drinks after he fucked *my* girl?"

I shuffled back, my heart pounding against my chest and fear running my blood cold.

Tears streamed down Piper's cheeks. "P-please, Spencer."

Spencer pressed the gun against her skull harder. "Do it, bitch."

After crying out, Piper dropped to her knees in front of me. I scrambled back until I hit the wall behind me, memories of that night running through my head. I squeezed my eyes closed. My breaths came quickly. My throat drying.

Piper sniffled at my feet. "I'm sorry, Alec. I don't want to die."

"Please don't," I said, turning my head away from her and pressing the side of my face against the wall. My lips quivered, and I let my tears spill down my cheeks as I realized that I had failed Maddie *again*. "P-please."

"I'm sor—"

Spencer shot a bullet straight through the wall two feet from my head. "Quit stalling!"

Once Piper crawled up my legs and straddled my waist, she unbuttoned my jeans with trembling fingers. I stared up at the ceiling, lips trembling and tears trembling in my eyes. I didn't want to watch.

Maddie would never forgive me for this.

All I wanted was to have a life with her, but I ... I couldn't even stop her best friend from ... from ...

I bit my lip to hold back a sob. *Why is this happening to me again? Who will be there for me this time?*

"She'll forgive you," Oliver said from the opposite corner. "Maddie will understand."

"Not this time," I sobbed. "Not this fucking time."

"You know how big her heart is," Oliver said. "She loves you. She'll forgive you."

But all I could do was shake my head in disbelief. Maddie might love me, but I wouldn't be able to forgive myself after this. I wouldn't be able to *live* with myself after Piper—Maddie's best fucking friend—did this to me. *Again.*

"The two best friends reconciling," Spencer cooed. "How cute."

"Shut the fuck up, you asshat," Oliver growled, struggling against his restraints.

"Smile for the camera, you four," Spencer said, glancing over at a camera he must've set up for this exact reason before we made it to his house tonight. "Maddie is going to see the whole thing. That pretty little girl is going to be mine."

58

maddie

"MADDIE, PLEASE CALM DOWN," Vera said beside me, clutching my hand.

We sat in the back of Imani's car, next to Sakura and Nicole, with Imani and Allie up front. My knees bounced uncontrollably, heart racing. I didn't know *how* Vera could tell me to calm down right now. Piper was at Spencer's! *What if he does something to her?!*

Now, he had my brother and my best friend.

When we pulled onto his street, my stomach dropped.

"Why is Alec's car here?!" I exclaimed, staring out the window in horror.

Vera tensed.

Alec and Blaise both hadn't been answering any of our messages for the past hour that we had been scrambling to get our asses up here, and my stomach was in my throat.

What if ... what if Spencer kills them?!

Tears trembled in my eyes. I would never forgive myself.

As soon as Imani pulled up to the curb, I leaped out of the car and sprinted toward the front door. Adrenaline rushed through my system. And suddenly, someone's arms wrapped around my torso and threw me down.

I screamed and twisted in their hold to see Vera on top of me. "What are you doing?!"

"What are *you* doing?!" she whisper-yelled back at me. "Running into Spencer's house without a plan and without us? We don't know what he is up to there or who he is with. I'm scared, too, but if he takes us ... nobody will save us."

"We have to go in there, Vera," I cried through the tears and snot. "He has them!"

"I know," Vera said. "But we need a plan."

"We have a plan," I said, scrambling to my feet. "Kick his ass."

"What if he's in there with other people?" Vera said, clutching my elbow so I would stay rooted to the spot with her and digging her fingers into my flesh. She looked over her shoulder and at the dark house. "If he has all of them, he's working with someone."

"Or more than one person," Allie called.

Nicole, Imani, Allie, and Sakura hurried onto the grass, each armed with some kind of equipment that we had found in Mr. Avery's garage when picking up Sakura. Nicole held a battery-run pressure washer and tossed me a baseball bat.

"More than likely multiple people," Imani said.

"Well, we can't just stand here!" I reasoned, pointing the bat at the door.

"There aren't any cars in the drive—"

"I'll give you fucking anything," Oliver said, his voice drifting through the cracked window. "Let Alec go. Don't do this to him, Spencer. You're sick if you do, especially if you show Maddie. Do you think she'll ever love you?"

Show me what?

I waited and waited and waited, but there was no response from Spencer.

"Stop!" Alec cried from inside the house. "Please!"

Deciding that I couldn't wait any longer, I clutched the bat and stormed to the front door. My eyes stung, but I let the tears fall and continued marching up the walkway until I slammed my foot into the door.

"I will kill you, Spencer!" I screamed from outside, kicking the door again. "Fucking murder you if you lay a fucking finger on Alec." *Kick.* "I swear to God, I don't care if they throw me into prison for—"

Before I could finish my sentence, Imani hurled a rock right through the front window. As glass shattered everywhere, Allie jumped through the now-broken window and opened the front door for us. And then I ran into the room to save my man.

59

maddie

WHILE I HAD SPRINTED into the room, ready to swing at Spencer's stupid fucking face, I stopped mid-swing and stared at one of my best friends on top of Alec. The bat slipped from my hands, the tears building in my eyes.

"Piper," I whispered in disbelief. "Wh-what are you—"

Alec stared emptily up at the ceiling, lips trembling and tears streaming down his cheeks. I sprinted toward her, grabbed a fistful of her hair, and threw her halfway across the room by it, so hard that she slammed against the wall and fell to the ground.

"What are you doing?!" I shrieked. "He's my boyfriend!"

"I-I'm sorry," she cried. "I didn't mean it."

"You were about to fuck him!" I growled, lunging at her again.

But she made no move to fight back, and I couldn't bring myself to hurt her. I had no problem hurting the man who had basically raped me for a year and a half, but Piper … I had … told her so many of my secrets, had given her so much of me.

For the second time tonight, I stopped midway and dropped my fist. "It was you."

"I'm sorry," she said, her hair shielding her face. "I'm so sorry."

"Look at me!" I screamed. "Look at me and admit it! You raped him at Oliver's party."

Piper gazed up at me through trembling eyes. "I did."

My hand moved before I could stop it, and I smacked her across her face so hard that my palm turned red and stung like a motherfucker. Tears welled in my eyes, betrayal rushing through my veins.

"How could you?" I scolded, shielding Alec from her. "How fucking could you?!"

"I didn't want to do it, but my father ..." Piper started, hiccuping. "My father ..."

"What? What did your father do?" I screamed. "Because he's not the one who drugged and raped my boyfriend at a party. He's not the one who lied to me for weeks, who threatened me over text, who acted like nothing was wrong!"

"He made me do it," Piper sobbed.

"How'd he make you—"

"She's not lying," Nicole said suddenly.

I snapped my gaze to her and realized that she, Vera, and the guys were the only others left in the room with me. Even Spencer had vanished. But I didn't have time to worry about him right now. Not after my best friend was about to fuck my boyfriend in front of me.

Nicole paused, swallowed, and glanced down at Piper. "Your father is an officer, right?"

Piper nodded.

After another moment of silence, Nicole lifted her gaze to me. "There's a sex trafficking ring. I don't know if you know about it, but Imani and Allie do. The police traffic high school girls and force them to do things for information."

"How do you know?" I asked Nicole.

Tears trembled in her eyes. "Because I am—*I was* part of it since I was thirteen."

My chest tightened, and I didn't know what to say to her. *She's been sex-trafficked since she was barely a teenager? What the fuck wi wrong with the people in this town?! How screwed up are they?*

"Is that what this is?" I asked Piper. "Is that why you slept with Alec? And that teacher …"

"I know I fucked up," Piper cried. "But if I didn't, they threatened to hurt you and Vera."

"That's why you spent so many nights with your father? When you couldn't hang out and told us that he was teaching you to code?" Vera asked, lips trembling. "He was forcing you to … to sleep with people in Redwood for information?"

"It's more than just that." Piper sniffled. "There are videos, pictures, people …"

"I didn't think you were part of it," Nicole whispered to her.

All Piper could do was whimper beside me.

While I wanted to wrap my hands around her neck for fucking Alec up big time, I couldn't bring myself to do it after what she had just admitted to me. I could barely even think straight, and I didn't want to do something to her that I would come to regret.

"Get out of here," I said through gritted teeth. "I never want to see you again."

"You should punish me for what I've done," Piper said.

I forced myself to turn away from her. "No."

"Please," she pleaded, her voice filled with desperation.

"You didn't rape me. I shouldn't choose your punishment."

"Maddie," Piper said, crawling closer to me, "please, I deserve it."

"Leave!" I shouted through the tears.

After Piper ran out of the house, I glared at the open door for some long, tense moments with my hands balled into fists. *How can she do this to me? To him?! And how can she live with herself day and night? How can she look me in the eye? Pretend like nothing happened?*

"Maddie," Alec whispered behind me.

I snapped out of it and looked over at him, tears streaming down my cheeks. Once I quickly pushed them away, I dropped to my knees and wrapped my arms around Alec's shoulders, pulling tightly.

"Don't you ever run out on me again," I cried into the crook of his neck. "Don't leave me."

"I'm sorry," he whispered, lips trembling.

I pulled back slightly and took his face in my hands. "Don't apologize."

"I-it almost happened again," he whispered. "I wouldn't have forgiven myself."

"It's not your fault," I reassured.

"B-but s-she's your best friend," he said. "How could I have lived with myself if she had done it again? Spencer was going to send you a video. He was going to use it against me to break you, and I couldn't do anything about it."

"Shh. Shh. Shh."

And while I tried to soothe him, he broke down and sobbed uncontrollably. "I'm sorry."

"Here," Vera said, handing me a knife that she must've found in the kitchen. "I couldn't untie Blaise's binds, so I had to cut through them. You should take them off Alec before he loses circulation. Blaise's were tight."

I gripped the knife and crawled behind Alec to cut through the ropes, watching each thread break one by one. My heart was pounding so hard inside my chest that I could hear it in my ears. I didn't know what a panic attack felt like, but this had to be close to it.

When his restraints were released, Alec wrapped his arms around me and pulled me onto his lap. "God, I don't know what I would do without you, Maddie. I love you with everything that I have left."

60

alec

"CAN YOU CUT THESE ROPES?" Oliver asked Maddie.

She scowled at him. "Why? So you can run off again?"

"I'm not going to leave," he said.

"Like you did—"

"Let him go," I said to Maddie. "It's fine."

"It's not fine," Maddie grumbled to herself, cutting his rope. "We're going to talk later."

After nodding, Oliver rubbed his wrists and turned toward me. "I'm sorry."

I stared emptily at him because I didn't have shit to say to him anymore. I had wanted to talk to him for so long, but now, I wasn't in the right mind, and even if I were, I didn't think I could come up with a response.

He hadn't believed me, but now, he had to. Because he had almost watched it happen.

"I should've believed you," he said.

"Yeah, you should've."

"I'm sorry," he repeated.

"He doesn't have to accept your apology," Maddie said, curling her arm around mine.

Oliver gazed down at the floorboards and dropped his voice. "I know."

"Where's Spencer?" I asked, mouth dry and body aching so badly that I could barely move.

Murmurs erupted through the room, but Spencer was nowhere to be f—

Imani shoved open the door and grabbed someone's ankle.

"Damn, Sakura, you're psycho," Imani said to Sakura, who held Spencer's other ankle as they both dragged him into the room.

Allie marched in behind them.

They dropped him in the middle of the living room. His arm was cut to the bone by what looked like a saw, and deep puncture wounds across his ripped shirt, his flesh bleeding underneath. He wasn't struggling, yet his eyes were open.

"I gave him something to paralyze him for a bit," Imani said with a smirk, stepping back. "He's all yours, ladies and gents."

But Maddie didn't move.

Instead, she sat next to me and stared at that asshole who had hurt her for years.

When nobody moved toward Spencer, Nicole cleared her throat and walked over to him. "This is for Maddie. You piece of literal dog shit!" Nicole hollered, blasting a pressure washer into Spencer's eyes.

I didn't know where she had gotten the pressure washer, but I couldn't seem to care anymore. I sat back, breathing heavily, and watched Maddie's ex-boyfriend, turned stalker and apparently kidnapper, scream out in pain.

Allie jumped in next with a metal thatching rake. Then, Imani crawled on top of him with large pruning shears. Oliver stumbled to a standing position and hobbled over to Spencer, kicking the living shit out of him.

For a brief moment, I closed my eyes and blew out a low

breath. If Maddie hadn't shown up, then Piper would've … hurt me again. Spencer would've recorded it and shown the one woman I loved. And we would've been ruined forever.

I clasped my hand around Maddie's and glanced over at her. "Thank you."

"You should've let me handle it from the beginning," she said. "Why'd you run off?"

"Because I don't want you in trouble with Poison."

She frowned. "They would've taken care of all this."

"At what cost?" I whispered, shaking my head. "It doesn't matter."

My gaze shifted to Vera, who held Blaise to her chest tightly, scolding him, too, for being so stupid. But Blaise was smirking like a dumbass and commenting about how he had watched the dark side of Vera tonight. Sakura stood alone near the door, staring nervously down at the girls.

Using all my strength, I crawled over to Spencer's body—*his life*—hanging on by a thread. The girls moved off him, giving me room to finish this fucker off. And while I knew that I shouldn't get involved, it was too late.

After straddling his waist, I used what energy I had left to hurl fist after fist after fist into his swollen and bruised face. Layers of eye tissue had burned off, the blood vessels shot. I doubted that he could even see anymore.

But that didn't matter. Because I couldn't stop myself.

I continued to punch him until Oliver pulled him off me.

"He's dead."

"He's dead?" Vera repeated.

"What are we going to do with him?" Allie said.

"Bury him?" Imani suggested.

"Burn him maybe?" Sakura said. "That will leave the least amount of—"

"What the hell is Avery teaching you?" Blaise asked Sakura as I collapsed onto my ass.

Sakura's cheeks reddened. "Oh, I just, um, read that in a book."

I snarled at Spencer's body and gritted my teeth. If anyone found out that I had just killed a man, then all my chances of being in the NHL would be ripped from underneath my feet. But I had done it to protect not only me, but also Maddie.

And not only Maddie, but also everyone involved.

Spencer had been completely unhinged. If worked up enough, he might've killed everyone here. And while the girls had been doing a good job with keeping him down, he had been working with someone else.

After glancing toward the fourth corner, I saw the shadowy figure was gone. "There was ..."

"Someone else," Oliver finished. "In the corner."

"Probably left during the chaos," Blaise said.

"Spencer wasn't the only one who ran out of the house," Allie said.

I winced and leaned back onto Maddie, who gently clutched my head near the swollen flesh. "There was someone in the corner. I didn't get a glimpse of her." I glanced over at Blaise, then Oliver. "Did you?"

"Bro, I was blacked out the entire time," Blaise said.

"No," Oliver said, gazing down and frowning.

"Did you see her?" I asked Allie.

"No."

"I'll look at the security footage later with Kai," Imani said. "But it was a woman."

Cursing to myself, I closed my eyes and racked my brain for *anyone* who could have it out for me. I never would've thought of Piper, so maybe I needed to be a bit more open.

What women are close to me who want to hurt me? Who could do this? Who wants to see me and Maddie break up?

And only one person continued to pop into my mind.

Sandra.

61

maddie

"WHAT THE FUCK do you want me to do with it?" João growled at Imani.

We sat in Imani's living room while Mrs. Abara, her mother, checked out Alec, Oliver, and Blaise. The girls chatted quietly to themselves by the door, probably waiting to be picked up by their boyfriends.

"Get rid of him?" Imani said, like it was obvious.

"You want me to take care of another"—he glanced over at Mrs. Abara and lowered his voice—"body for you? I already told you that I wasn't doing this again. We can't be doing your dirty work after you kill a man."

Imani crossed her arms and glared at João, who matched her stare.

"Another successful night with the Redwood Girl Gang," Nicole said, slinging her arm over João's shoulders.

"Get the fuck out of here," he said to her between gritted teeth, shoving her back a couple of feet. "And don't pick up a fucking water pressure again. Shit's too messy to clean up from the carpet."

"So ..." Imani rocked forward on her heels and batted her lashes. "You'll clean it up."

After glaring at her for another moment, João shoved by her to the front door, slipped out into the night, and slammed the door behind him. Imani dusted her hands off and smirked as she turned toward us.

"Told you that I have him wrapped around my finger," she said. "He's whipped."

Allie snickered, then sat down beside me. "How're you doing?"

"Okay. Glad that Spencer is finally gone."

"That asshole deserved more than what we gave him," Nicole said.

Someone banged on the door, and Imani walked over to answer it. Callan Avery stood in the doorway with his arms crossed over his chest and scanned the room, his gaze landing on Sakura, who stood with her hands full of his gardening supplies.

"Damn, Avery!" Blaise called. "Should've seen your girl earlier."

Callan grabbed the supplies from Sakura, jaw clenched hard. "You could've hurt yourself, Sakura," he scolded, his gaze dropping to her belly. "Or the—"

Sakura slapped him in the center of the chest, cheeks reddening. "Shh."

"Or the what?" Nicole asked.

The girls all looked at each other, then at Sakura, who blushed even deeper. Callan blew out a heavy sigh and exited the house with all the gardening supplies to put them into his car.

Sakura rocked back on her heels. "You girls promise not to say anything?" she whispered.

"Come on. We basically just kill—" Imani stopped short and glanced over at Mrs. Abara, who arched her brow hard at her daughter. "We basically did all that bad stuff tonight, which definitely didn't involve murdering anyone ..."

"Yeah, we won't say anything," Vera said.

Sakura gulped, then pulled up her baggy sweatshirt enough for us to see a small bump.

"Shut up," I said breathlessly, my eyes widening. "You're not pregnant."

"Holy shit," Allie said beside me.

"You guys can't tell anyone!" Sakura begged. "Please."

"How many months?" Imani asked.

Sakura smiled. "I'm due a few weeks after graduation."

Nicole shrieked. "Oh my God. I'm so excited!"

"Me too!" Vera grinned.

Callan cleared his throat by the door. "You told them?"

"Avery, why haven't I heard about this?" Blaise shouted across the room while Mrs. Abara checked him out for potential head injuries. "I should've been the first person to know. We're besties."

The disgusted look that crossed Avery's face nearly made me shit myself. I bit back a snicker and turned back toward Sakura, who had pulled her sweatshirt back down to hide her bump. If she was due at the end of June, that meant that … they'd been banging for a while.

"Sakura wants to keep it a secret," Callan said, eyes narrowed at his nephew. "If you tell anyone, Harleen, I'm not afraid to kick your ass like your father should've a long, long time ago. So, keep your mouth shut."

Blaise held up his hands in defeat. "I won't say anything. But Vera might."

"I will not!" Vera said, crossing her arms and turning toward Sakura. "I promise, I won't."

After Sakura smiled, Callan grabbed her hand and pulled her out of the house. I loved having Sakura around, but I didn't want her to get into any trouble or put herself in any danger for us anymore with the gang-related activities, especially if she was having a little babe.

When the door closed, Nicole clapped her hands together. "We have to have a baby shower for her in the spring! We can rent out Grand Hall by the beach and throw her a huge bash with all these cute lil' baby gifts."

"I want to decorate too," Allie said.

"Do you think they know if they're having a boy or a girl?" Imani asked.

"If she doesn't know now, she'll tell us when she does," Vera said.

"I hope it's a girl," I said.

"Oh my God," Oliver said, rubbing his forehead. "You're all giving me a headache."

"Cover your ears then," Blaise said. "They just saved all our asses."

When the boys began arguing with each other, I glanced over at Alec, who Mrs. Abara was checking out for injuries. He winced when she gently moved her fingers over the egg forming on his forehead.

"All right, boys, you all look fine to me." Mrs. Abara said after a couple of moments. "Just make sure that you go easy tonight and tomorrow, Alec." She glanced over at me. "Make sure he doesn't go to hockey practice. He needs to rest."

"Thanks," Alec said, leaping up. "Because I have something to take care of."

Before he could run out of the house, I grabbed his elbow. "Where are you going?"

"I need to see Sandra."

"Why?"

"Because if I find out that bitch did this …"

"No," I said, yanking him back toward me. "The only place we're going is home."

"But—"

"I said, no. You need to rest. You can talk to Sandra tomorrow at school."

"Maddie …"

So he couldn't argue with me anymore, I grabbed his hand and pulled him out the door. I didn't care who he wanted to see tonight for whatever reason. My boy needed rest, and I wouldn't let him do anything else after the day he'd just had.

62

maddie

"YOU'RE STAYING THE NIGHT HERE," I said to Alec as we walked into my bedroom. "And every single other night for the rest of your life. You don't need to go back to your house ever again if you don't want to."

Alec stayed quiet and dumped his belongings—which were essentially just his keys—on my desk and slumped down in my comfy gaming chair.

I kicked off my shoes and headed for the door. "I'll go grab some clothes from Oliver."

I slipped out of the room, headed down the hallway, and pushed open Oliver's door because that was what that annoying asshole usually did to me. Plus, we had just saved his ass, so I didn't really give a fuck about knocking right now.

"What're you doing in here?" Oliver asked, glancing into his full-length mirror and over his shoulder at me. He had his shirt pulled up over his abs and was gently touching huge bruises on his ribs, where it looked like he'd been kicked repeatedly.

After grimacing, I walked toward his closet. "Grabbing clothes for Alec."

"For Alec?"

"That's what I just said, isn't it?"

Once I grabbed a bunch of clothes that Oliver didn't wear anymore, I walked out of his closet and over to him. I slammed my finger into his chest. "And you'd better fucking apologize to him tonight."

"Maddie—"

"I'm serious, Oliver. He's hurting, and we just saved you."

"I already apologized. What else do you want me to do?"

With his clothes tucked under my left arm, I grabbed him by the shirt and slammed him against the mirror. "I want you to fucking mean it, Ollie. If I'm important to you, then he should be too. He's not only your best friend, but he's also my boyfriend. And I love him."

Oliver growled. "You don't—"

"I love him," I said, cutting him off. "And one day, he's going to be your family."

After a moment of tense silence, he pressed his lips together. "You're serious?"

"Fuck yeah, I'm serious." I twirled around and headed for the door. "Apologize to him."

Once I finally slipped out of his room—but not before sending him another pissed glare—I walked down the hallway with fresh clothes for Alec to wear tonight. I would grab his belongings from his house tomorrow, but it was far too late tonight.

"Here," I said, walking into my room and tossing him the clothes. I closed the door behind me. "You can wear these tonight and tomorrow for school. There's also an extra toothbrush in my bathroom."

While I could tell that his mind was elsewhere, he smiled softly over at me. "Thank you, Cupcake."

I jumped onto my bed and shamelessly watched him strip off his jeans and sweatshirt to put something more comfortable on. Alec and Oliver were about the same size, but the sleeves of Oliver's shirt tightened around Alec's biceps.

"What're you thinking about?" I asked as he placed his dirty clothes in my hamper.

"Tonight."

Part of me wanted to scold him again for being so stupid and going out to find Spencer alone, but I didn't want him to hurt more. Piper—that fucking bitch—had almost raped him for a second time. I couldn't even imagine the pain he must be in.

"What are you going to do about Piper?" I whispered.

"What do you want me to do about her?" Alec asked, crawling onto the bed with me.

"Hurt her back?" I suggested even though I felt sick to my stomach for even thinking that.

If what Nicole had said was true, then Piper was already hurt. But that didn't erase the fact that she had raped Alec the first time and had almost done it again. And she would've if we hadn't stopped it. I didn't know what hurt worse—that she had done it or that she hadn't even told me about it.

She was supposed to be my best friend.

"Me hurting her won't take away the pain she caused me," he whispered, shaking his head. "Plus, I don't want to get in trouble. We were invited to check out hockey practice this weekend instead of in the spring."

"What about after we get back?"

"Maddie," Alec said, his voice harsher than usual. Then, he cursed underneath his breath and tucked some hair behind my ear. "Sorry for raising my voice. I don't want to hurt anyone, but I saw that pain in your eyes today. I saw the way that *you* wanted to hurt her, to hurt Spencer. And that asshole deserved what he got, but …"

"But what?"

"But I don't want you turning into someone who runs around Redwood, killing people." He wrapped his arms around my waist and pulled me on top of him, his fingers dancing underneath the hem of my shirt. "You're my cute little girlfriend who loves playing video games and watching anime." He chuckled softly. "Maybe even some hentai."

Cheeks flushing, I curled my fingers into his taut chest. "How'd you know about that?"

He cracked a smirk. "I have my ways."

He grasped my hips and pressed his up into mine, staring at me with those sad eyes.

"Don't," I whispered, gently pushing myself off of him. "You're hurting."

While he hadn't said anything, I knew he wanted to have sex. Or ... maybe *want* wasn't the right word. *Need* felt better for this particular instance. Guys like Alec didn't like showing their emotions.

"But—"

"It almost happened a second time," I said, referring to Piper. "Let me hold you this time. I don't need sex as a form of you validating your love for me, Alec. I know your guilt would've killed you if that had happened again." I took his hands in mine and brought his knuckles to my lips. "And I know you love me."

He curled his lips into a soft smile, but it didn't reach his eyes. "You're more important to me than anyone in this entire world, Maddie. You know me better than anyone. I don't know what I would fucking do without you."

I lay back on the bed, curled up into the crook of his arm, and pulled him tight to me. "Come here. Let me hold you tonight because you're mine to protect. And I already promised you that I wouldn't let anyone hurt you."

63

alec

ONCE MADDIE FELL asleep on my chest, I gently placed her on the other side of the bed and shuffled to the door. I had been parched all night since we had left Imani's house, but I hadn't wanted to say anything to Maddie. She loved caring for me, and I loved that about her. And I had just wanted to hold her all night until she fell asleep because we both needed it.

So, I walked down the hallway, then down the steps to the kitchen. My gaze lingered on the huge living room, where Oliver's wild parties had taken place many times over. Where I had gotten so drunk that I could barely see.

I wished I could say that I'd ever had fun at his parties.

But I hadn't. Not once.

The only reason that I had come to them—most times—was to see Maddie, to make Maddie jealous enough that she'd make the first move, or to get myself drunk enough to flirt with her, like I had a few weeks ago.

Who knew that night would be so shitty?

After turning on the light in the kitchen, I grabbed a glass from the cupboard.

"You're up late," someone said from behind me.

I jumped back slightly and turned around to see Oliver sitting on the island, drinking from a glass that definitely didn't have water in it. I could smell the booze halfway across the room. I turned back toward the fridge and poured myself some water.

"Yeah, that's what happens when you don't want to close your eyes because you fear having another nightmare."

"I'm sorry, dude," Oliver said. "I should've believed you."

I set down my glass, placed my hands on the counter, and stared out the window over the sink. "It's a bit too late for that, Oliver. I needed you to fucking believe me weeks ago. And all you did was"—I sucked in a shaky breath—"make everything worse."

Oliver didn't say anything.

"You made everything worse," I repeated, voice cracking at the end. "I fucking needed you." Rage rushed through me, and I whipped around and grabbed him by the collar, balling his shirt in my fist. I pulled him off the counter and slammed him against the wall. "I needed you, and you made fun of me with the rest of the school."

"I know," he said quietly.

But I wasn't nearly finished. I wanted him to hurt as badly as I had. He had done nothing but betray me, almost get me thrown off the hockey team, which would've made me lose all my chances at getting out of this shithole.

"I would've fucking believed you!" I sneered, tears burning my eyes. "I would've brought you to the hospital, helped find the girl who did it to you, been there if you needed someone to cry to, but I had to do all those things alone."

Tears glistened in his eyes, and he dropped his gaze to our feet.

I slammed him against the wall harder, my grip slipping from his shirt. "Do you know how hard it was to suffer in silence for weeks, feeling like nothing but a piece of shit because I woke up to you filming me, drugged out, after she raped me?!"

"No, I ... I don't know how hard that must've been."

While I wanted to slam him up against the wall once more, my fists slipped from his shirt. I dropped to a crouched position in front of him, wrapping my arms around myself and shaking my head. I didn't have the energy anymore.

"And even after you didn't believe me," I whispered, pain shooting through my chest, "I went and found you to protect you from Spencer. I didn't need to do that. I could've let you rot there with him until he killed you. But I did because you're fucking important to me."

"I'm sorry."

But sorry didn't make up for everything that I had sacrificed for and everything that had happened because of him. I drew my tongue across the tips of my teeth, anger rushing through me.

"Did you really sleep with my mom?" I asked.

"Alec, please, do—"

I snapped my gaze to him, seething. "Did you sleep with my fucking mom?"

Oliver ran a hand through his hair and turned his back toward me. "Once. That's all."

"Man, fuck you, dude."

"I was pissed that you liked my sister," he reasoned. "I've always seen the way you look at her."

"It's my mom!" I exclaimed. "My fucking mom, who is married to my father, who also can't keep his dick in his pants anymore either. God-fucking-damn it. I wouldn't give a fuck if you'd slept with a sibling—if I had one—but my mom?!"

"It just sorta happened."

"How the fuck does something like that *just sorta* happen?"

Oliver placed his forefinger and thumb on opposite sides of his forehead and furrowed his brow. "One night after practice, I went to grab a bite to eat at Escape down by the beach. Your mom was there, drinking alone ... and one thing led to another."

I arched a brow. One night after practice?

"When?" I asked.

"What?"

"When was this?"

"A couple of weeks ago."

"So, before you found out about me and your sister."

Another low sigh left his mouth. "Alec …"

"Stop fucking lying to me," I growled, shoving him. "I give you a chance to be honest …"

And he continued to fuck up. Chance after chance after chance. Had he ever really been my friend? I'd always thought we'd get through everything together, but he had betrayed me multiple times when I needed him the most.

"I'm sorry," he whispered. "I've been a shitty friend."

"Yeah."

"I won't let it happen again."

"What, you fucking my mom?"

"Piper—or anyone else—doing that shit to you."

I shook my head and walked out of the room. "Fuck you."

64

alec

"THAT BITCH ISN'T HERE TODAY," Maddie said through her teeth.

"Who, Sandra?" I asked, shutting my locker and heading toward Spanish with Maddie.

"No, Piper." Maddie arched a brow. "Why do you want to talk to Sandra anyway?"

"Because she's the only person who's had a thing for me," I said.

I had been thinking about it all night, and I couldn't stop thinking about the blonde wig that Sandra had stuffed in the back of her closet. She had bought it last Halloween for a costume that she didn't end up wearing.

"And?"

"And what if it was her?"

"I don't think it's her," Maddie said. "Half the school's population likes you."

"Maddie," I grumbled.

She tucked some hair behind her ears and matted down the frizziness. "What?"

"You know that's not true."

Cue the longest and most dramatic eye roll that I had ever seen. "Are you serious?"

"Yes."

"Do you not see *everyone* staring at you?" she exclaimed, pointing toward a group of freshman girls who were huddled by a locker and giggling, their gazes locked on me.

They turned away, all embarrassed, and hurried down the hall in the opposite direction.

Honestly, I hadn't even realized they were staring. All I cared about was Maddie.

"It could be anyone," Maddie whispered.

"No," I said. "It has to be someone that Spencer knew."

"So ... literally anyone with a vagina?"

"Maddie," I sighed. "I'm trying to find the person who did this to us. Plus, you hate Sandra."

She pressed her lips together and continued down the hallway of lockers. "I'm not trying to stop you from finding her, but I'm just telling you that Spencer used to sleep around with a lot of girls"—her voice dropped—"believe me." Another sigh. "He even used to have a thing for Mrs. Dawson."

"Our math teacher?"

"Yeah," Maddie whispered. "She was extra flirty with him around me."

"You think that they were sleeping together?"

"Think?" Maddie scoffed in disgust. "I walked in on it."

"Cupcake ..."

"It's fine," she said dismissively. "I'm over it. But it's why I got so angry when I heard about your parents sleeping with guys from our school. It's triggering, and I wanted to protect you because I love you."

My lips turned into a small smile as I curled my fingers around the belt loops of her jeans and pulled her closer to me. I rested my head against hers and shook my head. "I don't deserve you."

"Shut up, Wolfe," she said, playfully smacking my chest. "You deserve the fucking world."

"Excuse me!" Mrs. Dawson called from across the hallway. She stood at her door, freshly highlighted hair curled around her shoulders, dressed in a blinding bright Lilly Pulitzer teal shirt with some equally bright dress pants. "You know physical affection is against school rules."

Maddie tightened her grip on my shirt and growled underneath her breath, "Sure. Sorry about that, Mrs. Dawson. I'll save the physical affection for when I'm fucking him after school." Maddie—while she was pissed—threw me a wink. "Gotta get to class."

Once Maddie turned around to head in the opposite direction of where her class was, I grabbed her hand and pulled her back toward me. "Won't happen at school again, Mrs. Dawson. But no promises about after hours."

"Excuse me, Mr. Wolfe. I'm not going to have to keep you after school to—"

"I'm not interested in fucking you, like Spencer Katz did."

"Oh shit." Jace Harbor, high school football star, chuckled down the hall.

Flushed in the face, Mrs. Dawson crossed her arms over her belly and stepped back. "I—"

"Serves you right, bitch," João said, giving her the finger as he and Jace continued toward their class. "That's for giving Landon a D last year because he didn't want to sleep with your crusty ass."

After Mrs. Dawson marched back into her room and slammed her door, Maddie chuckled next to me and pulled me toward the staircase to walk to our class. "She's going to hate you now. You didn't have to do that."

"Of course I had to do it for you," I murmured, intertwining my fingers with hers and squeezing. "I'm not going to let her tell me when I can and can't kiss my own girlfriend. She can go fuck herself for all I care."

When we reached the third floor, I spotted Sandra lingering

outside her locker with Jenny. I cleared my throat and nodded to my ex-girlfriend. "Is it okay if I go talk to her for a couple of minutes? I'll be in class soon."

Maddie glanced at Sandra and sucked in her cheek. "Sure. But be quick."

Once Maddie disappeared into the classroom, I walked over to Sandra. Jenny gave me a half-smile and hurried down the hallway as the first bell rang.

Sandra crossed her arms over her chest. "What do you want?"

"Did you kidnap us?"

She laughed and twisted a piece of hair around her finger. "What?"

"I'm not fucking playing around. I saw the blonde hair."

"Are you being serious?" she scoffed, grabbing locks of her hair and holding it toward me. "What're you, blind now, Alec? Does this look blonde to you? Anyone with eyes can see I have the blackest hair on the face of the planet."

"What about Jenny?"

"What about her?"

"You both had those blonde wigs you picked out for Halloween last year."

"I didn't kidnap you," she said through gritted teeth. "Why would I do that?"

"Because you still like me."

She rolled her brown eyes. "I might still like you a little, but I wouldn't kidnap you! Besides, I had a sleepover with Jenny for the past two nights in a row." She bit back a smile as she stared at the ground. "It was fun."

I snapped my finger in her face. "Hello?"

She lifted her lip in disgust. "As I was saying, I might still have a crush on you, but I was too busy with her. And if you would really like the details of what happened, then I can tell you, but it involves vaginas, and I doubt that your girlfriend would like you talking about that with me."

After massaging my forehead between my thumb and forefinger, I exhaled. "Then, who was it?" I mumbled.

"Someone actually kidnapped you?" she said in a burst of laughter.

"Sorta."

"I don't know," she hummed, snorting. "Have you thought about Mrs. Dawson?"

"Why would Mrs. Dawson kidnap me?" I asked, but she was the second person to bring it up to me today. And while I didn't think that Mrs. Dawson had the damn strength behind that harsh force that had knocked me out ... I didn't know.

She shrugged. "Because I always see her flirting with freshmen who don't know any better. She probably has a thing for you too. And she's blonde."

I scrunched my nose. "Ew."

"Yeah, ew." Sandra slammed her locker. "It's gross how handsy she is with kids."

"What would she want with me?" I asked. "I have never once shown interest in her in my entire life here. She used to flirt with me, too, in freshman year, but I had always had my sights set on Maddie that I ignored her most of the time."

"Don't know," Sandra said. "And it's not my problem. But rumor has it that she's gotten possessive and jealous of guys she used to flirt with in past years. I heard that she slept with a couple of students three years ago and ... paid them to keep quiet."

That wasn't even the worst of it, especially if Maddie had walked in on her and Spencer ...

"Anyway, gots to go," Sandra said. "Class time. Have fun with your little investigation."

65

maddie

"FINALLY," I whispered to myself on Friday night, settling into my plane seat. "Some downtime."

These past few weeks, Redwood had been nonstop drama. We both needed some time away from everything. And I was ecstatic that Alec wanted me to come along to oversee practice with a professional hockey team!

While I wanted Alec to have the full support of his family and I had even encouraged him to mention to his parents that we were leaving, they hadn't seemed to care. I mean, his parents said that they *wanted* to come, but their responses sounded so dry. And if they had *really* wanted to come that badly, then they could've grabbed some tickets on this relatively empty flight. They had enough damn money to rent a private jet for the weekend.

After closing my eyes, I growled to myself. I hated them too. So fake.

I just hoped that Oliver wouldn't try any more shit with Alec's mom. If he did while we were gone, then I had made sure that I would know. I might've gone behind Alec's back to keep tabs on Oliver.

Imani had an in with Poison, which meant that she could send me security footage of Alec's street. And if I caught that damn bastard sneaking around with Mrs. Wolfe again, I would punch his teeth in—for real this time.

When the overhead cabin lights turned off, Alec laid a blanket over our laps and rested his head on my shoulder to use me as a pillow. This kid had a neck pillow and still wanted to use me as a—

He slipped his hand between my legs.

I arched a brow and glanced over at him.

Here I am, thinking he wanted my shoulder to fall asleep on. SMH.

"What are you doing?"

"It's an overnight flight, Maddie," he mumbled into my ear. "And we're in first class."

"Alec," I whispered, glancing around nervously and hoping nobody was watching, "if you tell me to relax with people around us, I'm going to knock you into next year! We only have this sheet covering us."

"That's enough for my fingers."

"You can't be—"

"You're lucky that I don't sit you on my lap and shove my cock into you, Cupcake."

Sucking in a breath, I pressed my lips together and glanced around to make sure that nobody else had heard the profanity that just came out of his mouth on a public plane. *What is he even thinking?! Does he want to get caught by the flight—*

"How're we doing?" the flight attendant asked. "Do we need anything over here?"

I tensed and crossed my thighs, squishing Alec's hand in the process. But his fingers were already buried so deep inside me, massaging my G-spot, that I couldn't even think straight anymore. So, I sat there, smiling back like a dumbass, head in a daze.

She looked at me quizzically, then at Alec, who gave her his signature smirk.

"Maybe some water with ice?"

After snapping my gaze to him, I narrowed my eyes.

"Wonderful," she said. "I'll be back in a moment."

Once she disappeared, I sat back in my seat and stared at the headrest in front of me, attempting to act as cool as humanly possible. Like my boyfriend's fingers weren't buried deep inside me at this very moment.

"Alec—"

"Here is the glass of water with ice, sir," the flight attendant said, handing him the glass over me. Her fingers lingered on his longer than they had with the other passengers, and jealousy ticked inside me.

"Thank you," Alec said, placing it in his lap.

"Is that all?" she asked.

Alec moved his fingers back and forth against my G-spot. "You sure you don't want anything, Cupcake?"

I cut my glare to him and cleared my throat. "No, that's fi—holy."

Alec chuckled softly, moving his fingers faster inside me. "Sorry about her. She gets cranky when she's tired. That's all we need right now. We'll turn our light back on if we need anything else from you."

After smiling at us, she headed back to her station.

"What do you think you're doing with that water?" I asked.

"The water?" he repeated. "Nothing. But the ice ..."

He fished an ice cube out of his cup, then straight-up dropped it between my cleavage. I slapped a hand over my mouth to muffle a scream, body jerking in the first-class seat. One of Alec's arms wrapped around my waist to hold me still, the other gliding the ice cube around against my breast and to my nipple from outside my shirt.

My nipple hardened as the ice cube slowly melted against it. I gripped on to his thigh, my breath catching in the back of my throat. Alec pressed his mouth against the column of my neck, then to my ear.

"Touch yourself for me while I play with your tits, Cupcake."

"Alec," I whimpered.

"Don't make me say it again, or another ice cube goes down your shirt."

Once I sucked in a sharp breath, I pushed my hand between my thighs and drew my forefinger across my slit. Alec pinched my nipple through my wet shirt and tugged. Warmth exploded through my core, and I pressed two fingers against my clit.

"Good girl," he praised into my ear. "Just like that."

"Nmpft," I whimpered. "Alec …"

"You're doing so good for me," he whispered. "Rub your clit faster."

Squeezing my eyes closed, I moved my fingers faster and faster against my clit and bit back another moan. He captured both my nipples between his fingers and pulled on them, harder this time.

"Have I ever told you how much I love your tits?" he growled into my ear.

He released my nipples and dropped his hands to underneath my full breasts, his thumbs still on my sensitive buds, moving back and forth and back and forth as he bounced my tits. I rubbed myself faster, building myself up quickly.

"Look at these titties bounce," he murmured. "You're a filthy little slut."

A moan escaped my throat, and I slapped my hand over my mouth, pleasure exploding through my entire body. My legs shook uncontrollably, the orgasm rushing through me.

He kissed me softly on the neck. "Good girl."

66

alec

"I CAN'T BELIEVE we're actually here," I whispered to Maddie.

She *had* to be annoyed with me because that had to be the twentieth time I had said it during the past hour and a half of watching the Glaciers play in a game. But she sat in the stadium next to me, right outside the penalty box, and smiled.

No eye roll. No, *Alec, stop it.*

Just a supportive smile with a thigh squeeze.

"I'm so excited for you," she said, gaze flickering across the ice as the puck glided to the other side. "I can't wait until I'm watching you play in professional games." She placed her head on my shoulder and sat on her hands, kicking her legs back and forth. "When we have a little family of our own someday."

"Someday soon."

Cheeks tinting red, she glanced up at me through those long lashes and giggled softly. "We're still in high school, Alec. Not anytime soon. I want to get through college and have a stable life away from Redwood first."

But I didn't want to wait.

I had waited for years to have a family that wasn't fucking

dysfunctional like both of ours were. I had wanted Maddie for so many years, had been planning out what our lives could be together if I ever got up the courage to talk to her.

Maddie glanced down at her phone as it buzzed. *Vera.*

After turning off the screen, she glanced back up at the game when the buzzer sounded.

Another buzz. *Vera.*

"Aren't you going to answer her?" I asked.

"I'm here with you right now," she said with a grin. "Vera will understand."

She slipped the phone into her purse, stood up, and took my hand. "Come on! Game's over, and didn't the coach say he wanted to talk to you before we headed back to the hotel tonight? This is the last chance you'll get to impress him before we fly home tomorrow."

Warmth spread through my chest, and I let Maddie lead me out of the stadium. Instead of waiting like everyone else did, she pushed her way through the crowd for us, throwing elbows in drunk men's sides and stepping on feet.

"Maddie," I murmured, grasping her hips, "if you're not careful—"

"You can fight, can't you, Wolfe?" she hummed.

A low chuckle escaped my throat as I smiled at people Maddie had pissed off so I wouldn't *have* to fight anyone who decided she was being a bit too rough with the crowd. And thankfully, we made it out into the hallway without a scratch.

Once the crowd dispersed, we walked toward the head coach's office. And I finally gathered the courage to knock on the door. This was the last time I would have to make a good impression on him. I wanted this so badly.

"Alec Wolfe!" someone called. Head Coach Welker walked down the hallway from the locker room toward us, a grin painted across his face from the Glaciers' win tonight. "I hope I didn't keep you waiting long."

After he unlocked the door, we stepped into his office.

"It was great, having you this weekend," he said, shaking my hand and smiling. "The team loved having you around. And"—he paused and glanced at Maddie—"hopefully, you'll both be back soon."

Maddie grinned and tightened her grip on my opposite hand.

"I hope so too," I said, barely able to contain my excitement.

"Be expecting a call from us soon."

Biting back a grin, I nodded. "Thank you, sir."

"And, Maddie," Coach Welker called, "take good care of him."

"I will," Maddie said, tugging me to the door. "We really appreciate this opportunity."

After one last good-bye, we slipped through the door and headed down the hallway toward the exit of the stadium. Butterflies fluttered through my stomach, and I broke out into a full-on grin as excitement rushed through my body.

Is this really fucking happening? Has he alluded to making me an offer?

"I can't believe it," Maddie whispered, glancing over our shoulders and back toward the head coach's office door. She tightened her grip on my hand and pulled it up to her lips, kissing my knuckles. "I can't fucking believe it!"

"Thank you for coming with me," I said once we made it out the double doors.

When we reached the top of the staircase that descended into the parking lot, Maddie wrapped her arms around my shoulders and pulled me down into a kiss. Her fingers tugged on the ends of my hair, and her lips were curled into a smile the whole time.

"You don't have to thank me, sweetheart," she murmured against my lips once she finally pulled away. She rested her forehead against mine as I felt her phone buzz in her purse again. "I would do anything for you."

"You know, you should get that," I hummed. "Vera's probably pissed."

"Vera? Pissed?" Maddie giggled. "Those two words don't even belong in the same sentence." She reached into her purse and turned on her phone to see almost a hundred messages in the last twenty minutes from Vera.

Then, the phone rang.

"Hey, Vera," Maddie said through the phone. "Can I call you back? We're finishing—"

The soft look on Maddie's face shifted into one of horror, fear, and sadness. I gripped her hand, brow furrowed, and wondered what the hell was going on with Vera back in Redwood. She hadn't called all weekend.

"What do you mean?" Maddie said, stiffening. "Slow down, Vera. I can't understand you."

While I tried to listen to Vera through the phone, I could barely hear anything over her sobs. Maddie's eyes filled to the brim with heavy, trembling tears. She clutched my hand as the phone slipped from her hand and onto the ground.

"Maddie, what is it?"

A stray tear rolled down her cheek. "I'm sorry. We have to go home."

I grabbed Maddie's hand before she could fly down the stairs to the parking lot, trip, and crack her head on the concrete. "What's going on? What happened? Is Vera okay? Your brother? Tell me something, Maddie. Tell me—"

Before I could finish my sentence, she wrapped her arms around my torso and pulled me to her chest. She buried her face in my shirt and sobbed. "Vera told me that Piper …" Sniffle. "And I don't know what to think …" Sob. "This is my fault."

After taking her face in my hands, I lifted her head so she'd look at me, and I pushed some tears off her cheeks with my thumbs. "Slow down. I can't understand you."

"Pip-p-per …"

"What happened to her?" I asked.

"She hung herself."

67

alec

SOLEMN MUSIC PLAYED through the funeral home. I grasped Maddie's hand and guided her to the back of the line, where Redwood Academy students were lined up to see Piper one last time before she was buried.

Since the plane ride back to Redwood, everything had been a blur. Maddie had woken up countless times from nightmares for the past three nights and had been pulling away from me. Not because she didn't love me, but because she was dealing with shit.

We both were.

When Vera and Blaise found us, Vera hugged Maddie tightly as they both sobbed. Blaise kept his mouth shut. And I stared emptily in front of us with my hands in my pockets, stepping forward unconsciously. My mind was numb from the feelings inside me.

Part of me thought that Piper had gotten what she deserved, but the other part was upset.

I hadn't wanted anyone to die or to kill themselves. I just hadn't wanted to get raped.

The line shuffled forward again, and we moved along with it. I gazed at the students bent over the casket, my eyes burning with tears. *Why did this happen? Why would she fucking kill herself over this?*

My gaze landed on Allie Hall, Jace Harbor, Imani Abara, and Poison about halfway to the front. Poison looked uncomfortable in suits, or maybe they were uncomfortable from being here. Who wanted to go to their dead classmate's funeral?

"I'm sorry I'm late," Mom said, cutting the line to stand beside me.

Maddie glared at her through tears but then turned back to Vera. I side-eyed her, wondering why the hell she had decided to come to Piper's funeral. They hadn't known each other at all. Mom had maybe seen her at a couple of hockey games.

"What're you doing here?" I asked quietly.

Mom pressed her lips together, her eyes soft. "I'm here for you."

"You don't give a fuck about me, Mom. Why don't you leave?"

"Alec," she whispered, looping her arm around mine, "I'm sorry."

"This isn't the place to talk about our problems," I said.

"When you get home," she whispered, "can we talk?"

After a moment of silence, I gulped and nodded. "Sure."

We waited for twenty more minutes until the couple cleared ahead of us. I urged Maddie to go first with Vera because Piper had been her best friend and because I didn't know if I would be able to look down at Piper and feel anything pitiful.

Maddie collapsed at the foot of the casket as Vera stood behind her and wiped tears from her own cheeks. I stared at the girls, my stomach tight in knots and my thoughts rushing through my head at lightning speed.

The girls cried for what seemed like hours but was only several minutes.

And when Blaise finally tugged them along so other people could pay their respects to her, I froze in my spot. A sudden chill rushed over me, my mind blank. It had just been rushing, just been hurting, but ... now, there was nothing.

"Come on," Mom whispered, taking my hand and pulling me toward the casket.

I almost didn't let her pull me up there, but I stumbled forward with shaky hands. Mom didn't know what Piper had done to me. She didn't know the fucking pain that Piper had caused me and Maddie that night at the party.

When we stopped in front of her pale body, Mom wiped a tear from her cheek. I peered down at her, a hole still in my heart. Just because she was dead, nothing changed inside me. I still hurt, still feared that it'd happen again if I wasn't careful.

I didn't heal.

I had hoped and hoped and hoped, but it didn't happen.

Once Mom finally pulled me away, I walked with her to the side of the room, where Maddie, Vera, and Blaise stood. While I wanted to stay with Maddie and support her, my mind was all over the place. I couldn't stand around in this room anymore while the woman who had raped me lay in a casket, dead because she couldn't live with the things she had done.

If anyone should've killed themselves, it should've been me.

I balled my hands into tight fists. Piper had taken the easy way out.

"I'm sorry," I whispered into Maddie's ear.

She gave me a quizzical look through her tears, but I walked through the crowd and toward the exit of the room. Mom went to follow me, but I shot her a glare because I was still pissed at her, and she stayed put near Maddie.

Once I left, I walked through the quiet hallway toward the exit of the funeral home. My chest tightened by the moment. I didn't know what all these feelings were, but—

Fuck!

I hurled my fist at the wall, smashing right through the drywall and bruising my knuckles. My chest heaved up and down, and I clasped my bleeding hand as I shoved my shoulder into the door to leave this place.

It wasn't fair! It wasn't fucking fair.

I had never done anything to her, and she had hurt me *and* Maddie. All these emotions, I had pushed them to the side and tried to forget about them, but they had seemed to fizzle over the edge and … and come out now.

Now, of all fucking times.

"Wolfe!" João called from the sidewalk outside.

Landon leaned against the funeral home while Kai sat on the edge of the curb.

João tossed a cigarette onto the ground and stomped it out with his heel. "We need to talk."

I blew out a breath and ran a hand across my face. "What'd you want, Rocha?"

João hopped off the curb and walked toward me. "We have some information for you."

"About what?"

"Piper."

Stiffening, I arched my brow at him. "I didn't ask you to find any shit on her."

"You didn't."

"Maddie did?" I asked.

"No," he said. "But we found it, and it could be useful to you."

After sighing through my nose, I narrowed my eyes at him. "How much?"

He smirked, threw an arm around my shoulders, and guided me toward his car. "We can talk numbers on the ride back to my place. We can't talk about it here, especially not with half of the Redwood Police waiting to bust us."

68

maddie

"LET me know when you want me to bring you home," Blaise offered.

I sat in Vera and Blaise's apartment and stared emptily out the window. I had gone to the funeral with Alec, but he had left, so I hadn't had a ride back home. And honestly, I understood the reasons for him leaving. I would've, too, if that had happened to me. He had seemed so distraught, and I wanted to give him space.

"Thanks," I whispered, grasping on to one of their pillows and clutching it to my chest.

Vera sat beside me with her head on my shoulder and her body trembling. She had kept it together for most of the service, but it seemed to actually hit her now. Piper might've betrayed us, but we had been best friends for over a year now.

Even if she had felt bad about what had happened and if what Nicole had said was true, she hadn't had to commit suicide. We didn't hate her that much. She could've gone to therapy and worked on herself or even asked one of us for help to get out of the situation that she had been trapped in.

Guilt rushed through me. As her friend, I should've seen the warning signs.

But everything had seemed so perfect with her. Sure, she might've been at home a lot or with her father, but she always had a believable excuse. I hadn't even thought that anything could possibly be wrong.

Someone knocked at the door, and Blaise answered it. Nicole, Imani, Allie, and Jace walked into the apartment, all the girls teary-eyed, but not as badly as we were. But still, them going to the funeral and then coming here afterward meant the world to me.

"How're you holding up?" Allie asked, sitting on the couch across from us.

"Why did she do it?" Vera sobbed suddenly, clutching on to me tighter. "I don't understand. She hid this from us for so long. Didn't she think that we would help her out the best that we could?!" She bundled her dress up into her fists and shook her head. "W-why?"

Nicole frowned and sat on the ground at Vera's feet, gently squeezing her knee, as Imani took a seat next to Allie, and Jace lingered near the kitchen with Blaise. Nobody could answer her question for many reasons.

But I had the same thoughts, the same questions and doubts. How could she have done such a thing? It was selfish. So selfish. And I didn't forgive her for it. Though I understood why she had done it, I still didn't agree with it.

The room filled with Vera's sobbing until Blaise finally came over and pulled her into his arms. She grasped on to him with everything she had, and part of me wished that Alec had stayed around so he could do the same with me.

"Did you notice that Piper's father wasn't there?" Nicole asked, breaking the silence.

"That's his own daughter," Allie whispered. "How could he not show up?"

Jace glanced at Blaise, who grimaced. Vera shook her head, as if she knew what they were thinking. And honestly, I thought we all knew what they were suggesting had really happened. But nobody wanted to say it out loud and make it real.

"Do you think she actually killed herself?" Imani finally asked.

Nobody spoke a word.

"I can find out," Nicole said after a long pause.

"How're you going to do that?" Allie asked.

Nicole's gaze faltered for a moment, and then she swallowed. "Don't worry about it."

Allie sat up and shook her head. "Whatever you're thinking, don't do it."

While I didn't know the extent of what Nicole had done or been through, she had mentioned that she was part of the ring and pimping that the police did with girls at Redwood Academy. And her father was the police chief. She had to have done some … shit.

"It's the only way to know," Nicole said, straightening her back. "I'll do it."

"At what cost?" Allie asked. "I refuse to let you end up like her."

"Allie, it's fine," Nicole reassured her. "I won't end up like her."

I cleared my throat. "How're you going to do it?"

Nicole dropped her gaze. "My father … likes me. Not in a way that a father should. He's trained me to get information out of important people at Redwood. Who says I can't use that against him? That I can't get the same information out of him?"

Tension sat heavily in the air. She didn't have to explain any more for us to understand.

"You don't have to do that," I said.

After standing, Nicole shook her head. "My mind is already made up. If her own father killed her to hide something, then we need to find out what it is, and we need to take care of them all before something happens to another one of us."

69

alec

I SWALLOWED down a mouthful of bile and stared through the windshield of my car. The garage door opened, and Mom walked out into the bitter cold with her arms crossed over her chest, her mouth moving, but the words not making it into my ears.

Finally, she pulled the door open and hid behind it to shield her face from the searing wind that had rolled in sometime after Piper's funeral. "Alec, you've been sitting in the driveway for the past fifteen minutes. What're you doing?"

Honestly, I wasn't sure how long I had talked to Poison, but it must have been a few hours. Maddie had attempted to call me a couple of times, but I'd directed her calls to voice mail and texted her that I'd call her soon.

"Come inside, sweetheart," Mom said.

After another moment, I shrugged my shoulders forward and slumped out of the car. I couldn't believe what Poison had told me. I had known that this town was fucked up, but how could … how could someone murder a student?

Sometimes, girls went missing from Redwood Academy—like Skylar last semester—but it was always swept under the rug, and the students found something new to talk about the next day. Must've been the police's doings.

But this time ... things were different. This time, people cared.

"So, with all that said—"

"What?" I asked quietly, kicking off my sneakers at the door.

"Were you not listening?" Mom asked.

I pressed my lips together and shook my head. "Sorry."

She sighed softly, then pinched her lips into a small smile. "It's okay, sweetheart."

As we entered the house, the scent of freshly cooked chicken noodle soup drifted through my nose. I eyed the dining room table that had two bowls sitting atop it and clenched my jaw. *Did I interrupt her lunch with another student from Redwood?*

"I thought we could have lunch together," she offered, her smile strained, as if she feared how I'd respond. "And you can finally tell me how it went with the Glaciers. I ... I don't know how good the food is. I made it myself."

Swallowing all the nasty things I wanted to say, I took a seat at the dining room table and picked up a spoon. She sat down in front of me and glanced down at the table, two lines forming between her brows.

"I wanted to apologize for everything that's been happening around here," she whispered. "Your father and I wanted to keep you out of it as much as possible, but I think it's finally time that we come clean."

I stiffened. "Come clean about what? What's happened now?"

Between Spencer and Piper and what Poison had just told me about the police force—the extent and detail of what some of the girls had gone through—I couldn't even begin to imagine anything anymore.

Everything I knew about this town ... had turned on its head.

"Your father and I have an open marriage."

I snapped my gaze up to hers. "An open marriage?"

She grimaced and dipped her spoon into the soup. "Something like that."

"So, that's why you both are fucking students from my school?" I asked, balling the spoon into my fist and glaring at the soup. "And don't try to deny it again. Oliver told me what happened last week."

Mom reached across the table and grabbed my hand. "I really am sorry, Alec."

"Why?" I asked. "Why'd it happen?"

"Because ... your father asked for an open marriage years ago when you were about ten. I didn't know what to think, but I didn't want to break this family up, so I agreed to it. But he stayed out later and later as the years went by, and sometimes, he didn't even come home. And it broke me." Her voice cracked. "It broke me to pieces, Alec."

Tears streamed down her cheeks, and it took everything inside me not to wipe them away and tell her that everything was fine. Because it wasn't. Both her and dad had hurt me, and I wasn't ready to forgive anyone.

"When I found out that he had been sleeping with *men*, I ... I lost it." Her bottom lip quivered. "I would've been fine if he had told me from the beginning that he was having doubts about his sexuality, but to expect him being out with women and finding out that ... that he wasn't even attracted to me at all anymore ..."

"So, you fucked my best friend to get back at him."

"Alec ..." Mom whispered. "It wasn't like that."

"Well, that's what you did."

"I was so lonely," she cried. "Your father hasn't touched me in years."

I dropped my spoon into the bowl, making the soup splatter everywhere. "So, why Oliver? You could've slept with any other person in the entire town. You could've *paid* any other man to sleep with you. But you chose my best friend."

"He was there," she whispered. "And always flirting with me. He made me feel ... sexy."

For the second time tonight, bile rose in my throat. I swallowed it and closed my eyes, wishing I could close my ears, too, and never have to continue this conversation with my mother ever again. Because, *fuck*, it hurt.

"Mom," I grunted, swiping a hand across my face.

"What?" she asked. "You wanted me to be honest with you. This is me being honest."

"You telling me this doesn't make up for what you've done."

She dropped her head. "I know it doesn't, but I just want the best for you."

"The best for me would be if you hadn't slept with my best friend."

"There's nothing I can do about it now, except apologize," she whispered.

"Are you going to keep fucking him?" I asked, hands balled into fists.

"No."

"Are you sure about that? Because Oliver thinks—"

Mom looked me directly in the eye. "It won't happen again."

I pressed my lips together because I didn't know if I could even trust her. She had broken my trust so fucking badly this past month. *What if she does it again? What if she feels lonely again and finds Oliver as an easy option?*

"What if it does?" I asked.

"Then, you have every right to never talk to me again," she whispered. "I just want us to be the family we once were. I want your father to love me and you again. I want to take those family pictures we used to do every Christmas by the Overlook. Back to being the Wolfe family. That's all."

"That's all?" I asked.

"Yes," Mom said. "I'd do anything to bring us back together."

70

alec

AFTER LISTENING to Mom cry for thirty minutes straight about how Dad didn't love her anymore and that she would do anything to get her family back, I drove to Blaise and Vera's apartment.

If she wanted her family back, then she would have to do a lot more than cry. Trust wasn't earned overnight, and she had shattered mine to pieces after it came to light that she and my idiot best friend—if I even wanted to call him that anymore—had fucked. More than once.

Once I parked my car in the lot, I pushed open the door, and a blast of cold air seared my face. I wrapped my coat tighter around my body and sank into the Redwood Hockey–branded wool scarf around my neck.

Ice cracked underneath my dress shoes that I hadn't changed out of since the funeral, the salt beginning to stain the edges. After hopping up onto the curb, I yanked open the door and let the heat from inside the building envelop me.

I rubbed my numb fingers together and checked in with the security at the front desk. Once he nodded, I tugged on my scarf and headed toward the elevators for a short ride up to Vera and Blaise's apartment. The doors began to close.

"Hold the elevator!" a familiar voice called, jogging from the front entrance to the lift.

I slipped my arm between the closing doors to stop them and stared at Oliver entering the elevator with me. Halfway inside, he paused. We stared at each other for a few moments before the doors began closing again, and he finally hopped on.

After gritting my teeth, I moved closer to the metal wall. With ragged breaths from running toward the elevator, he stood on the opposite side in silence. I stared up at the glowing numbers above the door, wishing they'd move faster.

The lift ascended, but not fast enough. I balled my hands into fists by my sides and wondered what the hell he was doing here. As far as I knew, he didn't know anyone here from school.

Is he following me around? Wondering when I'd talk to him? Forgive him?

When the elevator dinged and the doors opened on the fourth floor, we stepped out at the same time. I clenched my jaw and peered over at him to see him walking the same way down the hall with me.

He stopped at Blaise's door.

"What're you doing here?" I asked before knocking.

"I'm here to pick up Maddie."

"*I'm* here to pick up Maddie."

"Hate to break the bad news to you," Oliver said, pounding his hand on the door. "But she called me to swing by and get her. Said that you were too busy with your family. Had to call in the big bro to—"

The door opened, and Blaise stood in front of us.

"Alec," Maddie called, hopping up from the couch and running toward me. She threw her arms around my shoulders and pulled me into a tight hug, her face buried into the crook of my neck and her vanilla scent drifting into my nose. "What happened?"

"I talked to Poison," I mumbled. "Then my mom."

Oliver stiffened to my right.

God, I honestly didn't have anyone in my life besides Maddie that I could talk to and not completely lose it. Everyone I'd trusted and everyone I'd wanted to trust, besides her, had stomped on me. Repeatedly.

After biting my tongue, I glared at the wall ahead of me. All this time, I had been trying to keep my cool with Oliver and Mom and Dad and everyone else on my list who had betrayed me, but after seeing Piper lying in a casket tonight … I wanted to fight.

I was so sick and tired of everyone pushing me around, of hurting me, of thinking they could make things up to me with a few crocodile tears and a half-assed apology. Maybe Maddie was right. The only people we could trust to get shit done and not fuck it up were Poison.

As sour as their name sounded, they didn't disappoint.

"Oliver, what are you doing here?" Maddie said, deadpan, finally turning toward him.

I stifled a dead chuckle caught in my throat.

"You called me to pick you up," Oliver said.

"In an hour," she said. "Not now. You can go."

"Maddie, I'm not going all the way back to the house now."

"Don't worry. Alec can bring me home."

Oliver pressed his lips together, jaw twitching. He didn't like to be told no, but Maddie wasn't going to take his shit anymore either. I was proud of her for sticking up for herself. Sometimes, I envied the strength she had.

"The fuck happened to you not liking Poison?" Blaise asked me. "You working with them?"

"No, I'm not working with them," I said. "They jumped me."

Maddie snorted. "They jumped you?"

My lips curled into a small smile for the first time today. "More like harassed but …"

"What'd they want?" Oliver asked.

"They told me that they strongly believe that Piper didn't kill herself."

Maddie and Vera shared a long gaze.

"Where'd they hear that?" Maddie asked.

"I don't ask questions," I said. "And if I did … I'm not sure if I would *want* to know."

"How much money did you fork over for that information?" she asked.

"Too much," I murmured.

"They charged you?!" Imani asked, leaping up from her seat and heading toward the door. "Oh, those boys are going to get it real good tonight. Come on, Allie. Let's go beat them up."

After grumbling, Jace shuffled behind Imani and Allie out the front door and into the hallway toward the lift.

Nicole stood up, too, and frowned, hands stuffed into her pockets. "I should get going too."

"Oliver, you're stinking up the place and making people leave," Maddie sneered.

"Come on, Maddie. We're going too," Oliver said.

"I'm not going anywhere with you," Maddie said, crossing her arms and shuffling closer to me. "Alec and I will see you at the house later tonight. Thanks for coming over an hour before I wanted you to and ruining the day."

71

maddie

"HEY, BOYS!" Mrs. Dawson shouted, waggling her fingers at a couple of freshmen the next school day.

I had been in and out of it since I had woken up this morning, my mind hazy and my heart still so sad over Piper's passing.

Mrs. Dawson wasn't even looking at me, but I shivered in disgust from the look she gave the kids. The freshmen shifted uncomfortably by their lockers, ignoring her outward flirtatious remarks, and continued talking to each other.

Mrs. Dawson strolled across the hall to them and twirled her finger around a strand of the junior varsity athlete's hair, her perfume so strong that I could smell it all the way down the hall. "Hey, handsome. You starting in the game tonight?"

He awkwardly scratched the back of his head. "Um, I don't know yet."

After *playfully* smacking his chest, she giggled, the sound like a shrill. "I bet you are! I'll be there, cheering you and your cute butt on, Holliday." She leaned in so close that her lips almost met his ear and whispered something that made him turn red and recoil.

"What the hell is she—" I started, storming toward her.

Vera grabbed my hand. "Maddie, I don't know if …"

Before she could finish her sentence, I yanked my hand out of hers and rushed down the hall toward the bitch herself. My hands were balled into tight fists, and I had to physically hold myself back from hurling one at her.

"Get away from him," I snarled, pulling the freshman boy, who stood a foot taller and wider than me, behind me. I glared at Mrs. Dawson. "Stop being a perv and flirt with men your own age."

Mrs. Dawson laughed like this was some joke. "Don't be jealous, dear."

"I'm not jealous," I said through my teeth. "Can't you see he's uncomfortable?"

"Nonsense," she said, smiling at him again. "I'm just being friendly."

"No, you're not."

"Maddie, are you sure this isn't about Spence—"

"Get back to your classroom!" I shouted, my voice echoing through the dead-silent halls.

She paused for a moment, then looked around at the students recording this interaction on their phones, ready to post whatever was going to exit her mouth next. Probably something predatory. But then everyone would know how fucking weird she was.

After smoothing out her neon-green pants, she marched down the hall toward her classroom, her heels clacking against the tiles. Once she shut the door, the athlete behind me sighed a breath of relief.

I swallowed some bile in my throat and grimaced at the nasty woman's classroom. She reminded me of Alec's mom. They seemed like they'd be best friends if they knew each other, could go to all the proms and hockey games to see some underage boys.

Disgusting.

"Thanks," he said from behind me.

"It's fine."

The lunch bell rang, and I walked to the cafeteria with Vera. I looped my arm around hers and headed to the table we normally sat at with Imani, Allie, Nicole, the guys, and sometimes Sakura. Usually though, she had lunch in Mr. Avery's room.

Students buzzed with chatter. A group of guys passed around a phone with a girl's tits plastered right in the center. I scrunched my nose at how disgusting they were sometimes and continued through the crowd, still pissed about Mrs. Dawson.

Poison, Allie, and Imani sat at our table, giggling and sharing a bag of Ruffles chips.

"Kai said that it happened," Imani said.

"Really?" Allie said, her gaze and mind seemingly far away from the conversation.

"What happened?" Vera asked.

"Remember that one teacher who hacked into her students' parents' bank accounts last year?" Imani said, chomping on another chip. "Well, she was just released from jail, and that woman is back at it again. Can't catch a break."

"Tell me about it," I mumbled, picking at my food.

Between that crazy and Mrs. Dawson, nobody could catch a break, huh?

"I feel like the only nice teacher at Redwood is Mr. Barnes," Imani said, nudging Allie. "What about you?"

"Huh?" Allie said, glancing over at Imani. "Oh, yeah."

"Girl, what is wrong with you today?" Imani exclaimed. "Stepbro didn't dick you down—"

"Have you heard from Nicole?" she finally asked.

Nobody at the table said a word.

"She was supposed to talk to her dad," Allie whispered, readjusting her glasses and chewing on the inside of her cheek. She placed her burger down on her tray. "And she didn't show up for school today."

Imani turned toward João.

"No," João said before Imani could ask for a favor. "We have shit to do."

"But—" Imani turned toward Landon. "Will you help me?"

"Sorry." Landon shrugged. "We have something to take care of tonight, Imani."

"What is it?" she asked.

"None of your business. Don't worry about it," João growled, grabbing his tray and standing. "Let's go before she asks any more questions and starts sticking her nose into other people's shit."

João, Landon, and Kai all headed out of the cafeteria while Imani followed them with her gaze, brow arched hard.

She mumbled something incoherent underneath her breath and whipped out her phone. "If they don't want to help us, then we can do it ourselves."

"Do it ourselves?" Vera repeated.

"Let's go to Nicole's house," Imani said.

"And skip?" Vera exclaimed, glancing nervously over her shoulder at the deans.

"Make it less obvious, Vera!" I whispered.

"But—"

"We're just skipping for a period. Nobody will know," I said.

Imani threw her arm around Vera's shoulders and pulled her to her feet. "We'll be in and out in no time. Don't worry about it." Imani glanced down at Allie. "Is that okay with you? We'll just make sure Nicole's okay?"

Allie smiled softly at her best friend and nodded.

While Vera was a pack of nerves, I pulled her along to the exit of the cafeteria, where the deans stood. They had let Poison saunter right out of the room without question, but stood in front of the doors to block us.

"Where are you girls going?"

"Just to the library." Imani smiled.

"To finish up a bit of studying before our test in Bio today," I added.

After sharing a glance, they smiled and stepped out of the doorway.

"Honestly, you girls are some of the best students I've seen come through Redwood," the dean said. "I wished those Poison boys would take some notes, learn how to be studious like you. Have fun. And I'd say make Redwood proud, but you already do."

72

maddie

IMANI ZOOMED OUT of the student parking lot and to the ritzy side of Redwood. Vera and I sat in the back, chatting quietly about how disgusting Mrs. Dawson was, while Allie sat in the passenger seat, knees bouncing.

While I had been to Nicole's house a couple of times before to pick her up with the girls, I had forgotten how nice it actually was. The winding streets were surrounded with huge mansions, and the grass was always green, even in the wintertime.

"Didn't Nicole live in your neighborhood years ago?" I asked Vera.

"Yeah, but she moved in middle school."

"Her family got quite the upgrade," I noted.

"It's from her father's shady deals with the police," Imani said from the driver's seat.

Large, trimmed shrubs lined the sidewalk in front of her house. Imani parked on the side of the road and glanced over at Allie.

Allie nodded to Nicole's car in the driveway. "She's here."

"Maybe she's sick," Vera offered.

"She hasn't texted me back."

"She could be sleeping in?" Imani said, turning off the car.

"We need to make sure she's not hurt."

When Allie went to tug on the car door, I grabbed her elbow. "What're we going to do if her dad answers the door? I don't know if it's a good idea for us to bang on her front door in the middle of the day and demand answers."

"Well, we can't just sit here," Allie said.

After a moment of silence, we all exited the car. While I wasn't sure this was the best choice, we had done this at Spencer's house, and it'd worked relatively well. At least, we had … rescued Alec, Blaise, and Oliver.

As we walked to the front door, my phone buzzed in my back pocket. When I pulled it out and tapped on the notifications, my heart stopped. I opened and closed my mouth a handful of times, unsure if I was really seeing this right now.

It … it couldn't be.

"Maddie," Vera whispered, "you're pale. What is it?"

I blinked my eyes a few times. I had to be seeing things.

But no matter how many times I blinked, no matter how many times I read that message over and over and over again, it said the same exact thing and was from the same exact number. A number from a girl I swore had died.

Unknown: Watch your back, Weber.

Vera looked over my shoulder and stiffened. "I thought …"

"That this number belonged to Piper?" I whispered. "Me too."

"You don't think she is …"

"Still alive?" I finished, my stomach twisting. "No. She can't be."

We had seen her dead body in that open casket. She hadn't moved, hadn't taken a breath for hours upon hours when everyone was there. She couldn't be alive, and if she was, then she wouldn't have done this. Right?

I mean …

A shiver coursed through my body.

She couldn't … I hadn't …

What if this really was her?

With everything going on in Redwood, I honestly wouldn't put it past a dead person coming back to life. Hell, Poison had recorded themselves slashing off Principal Vaughn's head and throwing it on the football field for all to see, and they hadn't even gotten in trouble for it! Mrs. Dawson openly flirted with boys ...

Who the hell knew what could happen in little old Redwood?

"Maddie?" Vera asked.

"No," I whispered, though I didn't even believe myself. "This can't be her."

"Then, who is it?"

"Are you guys coming?" Imani whisper-yelled to us, halfway up the sidewalk.

I shrugged at Vera. "I'm not sure—"

Suddenly, the silence in the gated neighborhood was shattered by the sound of a gunshot. We all froze as the sound bounced off one mansion to the next to the next in a jarring symphony.

Birds flew from branches. Dogs began barking wildly across the street. Squirrels scampered up trees to find shelter. And we stood there like a bunch of deer waiting to be picked off by a hunter, one by one.

The air suddenly filled with the scent of gunpowder as the sound came a second time.

Or maybe it was a third. I thought my ears had stopped working because Vera's mouth was wide open, her face scrunched up, as if she was screaming at me. Allie and Imani had fallen to the ground, and I finally caught the sight of a black Jeep driving past Nicole's house with the back window rolled down just enough.

Another bullet whizzed through the air.

This time, it was aimed right at me.

73

maddie

A SHARP PAIN pierced through my arm, and I fell to my knees behind the car, screaming at the top of my lungs. My front smacked hard against the ground, my wound oozing blood between my fingers.

I whimpered out in pain, clutching the hole in my arm and wanting comfort. "Vera!"

Lying on the cold concrete as the car continued down the road like nothing had happened, I rocked my head back and forth, tears streaming down my cheeks. Vera was right. We shouldn't have come today.

"Vera," I cried again, "call the police."

When I didn't get one of her frantic answers back, I used all my strength and rolled onto my back, finally able to see Allie crouching over Imani with blood splattered all over her face. Imani was clutching her abdomen with shaky fingers.

Another scream left my mouth. "Ver—"

When my gaze landed on Vera lying still beside me with a blood-soaked shirt, I scrambled to my knees and crawled over to her, forgetting about all of my pain. Horror rushed through me, my heart pounding.

"No. No. No. No. No. No. No!" I shouted, placing my hands on her chest to find the wound. But the blood continued to pour out of her body from somewhere. My hands shook uncontrollably as I grasped her face. "V-V-Vera! Stay with me. Please, stay with me."

While she wasn't moving, her eyes were wide open and staring up at the white sky. I crawled closer to her so I could be in her field of vision and so Vera knew that someone was here for her. Because she wasn't going to die.

I refused.

I fucking refused.

Tears sprang from my eyes. "Someone, call 911! Please! Nicole! Someone!" I screamed at the top of my lungs because I didn't know if Allie could hear me.

She was too busy hovering over Imani, helping her hold her wound closed, and crying. When Nicole didn't run out the front door, I reached into my back pocket for my phone, only to find that it was gone. Missing.

I scanned the surrounding area for it. When I found it sitting on the ground near the car, I crawled over to it as quickly as I could and dialed 911 with shaky fingers, making my way back to Vera on my knees, the concrete splitting open the skin on my knees.

"Nine-one-one. What's your emergency?"

"I need an ambulance!" I cried. "She's been shot."

"What's your location?"

"I ..." I glanced around, terrible with street names. "I don't know the address. We're at the police chief's home. Front yard. Please send someone now!"

Vera coughed up some blood underneath me.

"Please!"

"Calm down," the operator said over the phone. "Tell me what happened."

"Th-there ... we were ..." I sobbed, unable to get anything out, a pain piercing through my chest and my vision tilting for a second. "Someone drove by and shot at us. At least three of us are w-wounded. Two ... two d-dying."

Heavy tears burned my eyes as the words left my mouth. I threw my phone down, refusing to answer any more questions because I wouldn't let my best friend die after I had convinced her to skip school with me.

"Vera, please," I cried, wiping the blood that dribbled down her chin. "Stay with me."

Staring with wide eyes up at me, she parted her lips. "Maddie." Her voice was hoarse and strained, more blood seeping out as she attempted to talk.

When she parted her lips again, I shook my head.

"Stop talking, Vera," I whispered through sobs. "Please."

"You're hurt," she said again, gaze dropping to my arm.

"Vera, please, save your breath," I murmured, shaking my head. "Someone's coming."

"My ... chest hurts," she said, tears welling in her eyes. "Am I shot?"

Not knowing what to say, but not wanting to upset her, I shook my head. "N-no."

The corner of her lips twitched, but then her brown eyes widened even more, and she coughed up more and more blood. A stray tear rolled down her cheek. "I want to see Blaise again, Maddie."

My eyes burned, guilt and sadness rushing through me. "Vera, stop it."

"I love him so much," she whispered.

I rested my forehead against hers. "You're going to see him again, V."

"If I don't ..." she whispered, as if she knew I had been lying to her about being shot. "If I don't see him ever again, please tell him that I love him with all my heart. He's been the best ... the best boyfriend that I ... that I"—her words became slower—"that I ..."

"Vera!" I cried loudly, fingers trembling as they grasped her face. "Vera, stop. Please."

The faint sound of sirens drifted through my ears, becoming louder by the moment. I stumbled to my feet and headed toward the street, waving them over as they approached. Two police cars and one ambulance skirted up to the curb, paramedics hopping out immediately.

One pulled a stretcher out of the back while the other hurried with me toward Vera. Imani and Allie both looked over at us, Imani at least looking like she was awake and with it. They placed Vera onto the stretcher and lifted her into the air.

Another wave of dizziness washed over me, but before anyone could stop me, I rushed toward the ambulance, where they were taking Vera. She couldn't be alone. I'd promised her that I would be there with her through anything. And this … this was all my fault.

"Miss!" the policewoman said.

I shoved her off me because I didn't believe that the officers here would be of any help. They hadn't been when Oliver was kidnapped by Spencer, and they really wouldn't be after someone had tried to kill us in front of the police chief's home.

"Get off me," I growled when she reached for me again.

After her hand slid off my shoulder, I stumbled forward and hit the ground, the world spinning around me. I pressed my hands into the ground, but the dead grass, mixed with bloody snow, seemed to move around my vision so it was above me and the gray sky was below.

Needing to make it to Vera before they separated us, I squeezed my eyes closed and pushed myself off the ground. Only for my arm to give out, and I face-planted into the dirt. I cried out in pain as I stared through a teary and streaky gaze at the ambulance lights disappearing down the street.

"You've lost too much blood," the policewoman said, on her knees beside me and her hands wrapping around my left arm to hold the wound closed. "There's another ambulance coming for you and your friends."

"M-my friends," I murmured, my energy draining by the second. "Where are my friends?"

She lifted one arm and pointed to the front of the house, but my gaze didn't make it all the way there before everything went dark.

74

alec

I SAT NEXT to Maddie's bedside with my hand wrapped around hers, impatiently waiting for her to wake up. When she shifted in the bed, I leaned forward and grabbed her hand even more tightly.

"Maddie, are you awake?"

Her eyes fluttered open. "Alec?"

After drawing my fingers across her cheek, I let a tear fall down my cheek. "You're awake."

She smiled softly, and then she slowly scanned the room. Confusion washed across her face for a moment, replaced with horror. She leaped out of bed, half-dressed with her hospital gown hanging open in the back, and hurried toward the door. "I need to find Vera."

"Vera's not here," I said, grabbing her wrist. "You should lie back down."

"No," she said, tearing herself away from me. "I need Vera."

After she pushed through the door, she hurried down the hallway and gazed into each of the rooms, tears building in her eyes. I grabbed her hospital gown and tied it closed so she wouldn't run naked down the halls, and I tried hard to convince her to lie back down.

"Where is Vera? Imani?" she exclaimed.

"They're both in surgery right now," I said.

"Where are our friends?" Maddie asked.

"If you mean Blaise and Allie, then *your* friends are in the waiting room."

Maddie stared at me blankly, then frowned. "You're mad at me."

"Maddie, you skipped school," I whispered, knowing that I shouldn't be pissed at her for getting shot.

But why the hell had she skipped school in the first place? What had they been up to? Allie hadn't said anything about it yet, but continued to call Nicole on her phone.

After I didn't say anything else, Maddie shook her head and hurried down the hall in nothing but her hospital gown. "Alec, I will explain everything later. We need to find *our* friends, especially Allie."

With frizzy red hair, she walked toward the elevators. I ran my hand across my face and released a long sigh, shaking my head and eventually following after her before the doors could close.

"Maddie, wait up," I said, grabbing her hand as the doors closed. "Are you okay?"

"I'm fine," she whispered. "Do you know how Vera and Imani are doing?"

"I'm not sure," I said, tightening my grip on her. "I've been too worried about you."

When the elevator doors opened at the bottom floor, near the waiting room, Maddie hurried out and spotted Allie pacing back and forth near the seating area while Jace sat in one of the seats, grimacing.

"Allie!" Maddie cried, running over and hugging her. "You're okay."

"I didn't get shot," she whispered, opening and closing her mouth a handful of times. "But it should've been me. It should've fucking been me, Maddie." Allie sobbed into Maddie's shoulder as someone shouted from the entrance doors.

João slammed his hands on the front counter. "Where the fuck is she?!"

"Sir, I don't—" the nurse began.

"Hey!" I called so he—and the rest of Poison—wouldn't harass the poor nurse.

João stormed over to us and grabbed me by the collar. "The fuck is she?"

"In surgery," I said, shaking him off.

He picked up an empty chair and hurled it across the room at the wall. The chair dented the wall, nearly hitting someone in the process, then fell to the ground. João went to pick up another chair, but Landon rushed into the waiting room and caught it from him before he could hurl it.

João grabbed his shirt collar, too, like he had with mine, and shoved him back by it. "I will kill them. I will fucking kill who did this to her. I don't give a fuck who it is. I'm going to snap their fucking neck."

Kai walked in a moment later, holding an open laptop in his hand, staring down at them and shaking his head. He collapsed next to Jace and rubbed his forehead. "Will you let me fucking concentrate?" Kai growled at João. "Please."

As Poison began quarreling with each other about God knew what, I collapsed in the seat across from Jace and Kai, gaze on Maddie. My hands tightened into fists by my sides, and I shook my head, still in disbelief that this had happened.

Why did she even leave school today? Why did she put herself in danger?

Tears welled in my eyes. I could've lost her.

And if I had lost her, then there would have been no point for me to go on in this life anymore. I would have no reason to live. She was the only woman who could've ever gotten me through what she had, and I'd almost … I'd almost fucking lost her.

"Man the fuck up and stop crying," João growled at me. "This is fucking serious."

Landon punched João square in the jaw, sending him backward. "Shut the fuck up and sit down. I remember you crying your fucking eyes out when your mom died. His girl almost died today. Why don't you worry about finding out who the hell did this to Imani?"

A door near the front desk opened, and Mrs. Abara stepped out.

"Vera is out of surgery and stable," Mrs. Abara, Imani's mother, said softly. "Room 401."

Immediately, Blaise and Maddie hurried toward the elevators. Mrs. Abara lingered in the waiting room, pausing for a moment, and then a wave of distress washed over her face when her gaze met Poison's.

"We didn't do anything this time," Landon said to her. "She skipped herself."

Mrs. Abara sucked in a sharp breath, glancing at Kai, who nodded, and João, who paced the waiting room with a pissed-off expression written all across his face.

After nodding, she headed toward the back. "Imani will be out soon. She's fine."

Once she disappeared behind the door, Landon slumped his shoulders forward and hung his head. "Thank fuck."

"We're not thanking fucking anyone," João growled, grabbing Landon by the front of his jacket again and pulling him forward. "Imani was shot, and we're going to find out who the fuck did it so we can kill them."

Landon shoved him away. "You think I don't fucking know that?"

As they began to quarrel again, Kai turned back to his laptop and continued typing away on it. And I had a feeling that he *wasn't* trying to finish any essay or schoolwork. His brightness was all the way down, so I couldn't even see his screen.

Allie crossed her arms and paced the waiting room near the

entrance, the doors opening and closing, letting cold air into the room. I ran a hand across my face and wished that Maddie had just stayed in school and forgotten about this Girl Gang that they were trying to run.

Because if she wasn't careful, she'd get killed one of these days.

75

maddie

VERA HAD BEEN LYING unconscious in the hospital bed for the past few hours. Time passed so slowly in the hospital, every moment feeling like an eternity until she came back around. I sat next to her on one side of the bed, Blaise on the other, Vera's mom and Blaise's dad by the door.

I tore some skin off the inside of my cheek and gnawed on it.

"Ms. Rodriguez," a nurse said, frowning. "Can I talk to you?"

Ms. Rodriguez, Vera's mom, nodded and followed her out into the hall, leaving the door ajar. Keeping my gaze on Vera, I inched closer to the door to listen in on whatever this nurse was about to tell Vera's mom about Vera's condition.

Their voices were muffled, so I couldn't quite hear clearly what they were saying, but I caught the word *insurance* tossed around a couple of times. I rubbed my sweaty palms together, playing with my fingers, because I knew that Ms. Rodriguez couldn't afford good insurance.

Ms. Rodriguez would forever be in debt because of me. This was my fault.

After about five minutes of them chatting back and forth and seemingly getting nowhere, Mr. Harleen—Blaise's father—stepped into the hallway and shut the door behind himself so that we couldn't overhear their conversation anymore.

Blaise sat on the other side of Vera's bed, clutching her hand tightly, tears in his eyes.

"This is my fault," I whispered. "I convinced Vera to skip school with me."

"Maddie," Blaise growled from across the bed.

I hung my head. "I'm sorry."

While I had never really been left alone with Blaise because he wasn't much of a talker to anyone but Vera, I had seen how much they loved each other. And though he didn't show his emotions on a regular basis, they were written all over his face right now.

Blaise brought Vera's hand up to his lips and drew his thumbs across her knuckles.

"She wanted me to tell you that she loves you with all her heart," I whispered.

The room was quiet for a long, long time, Blaise tensing by the moment. And then, suddenly, he burst out into a sob, his cries breaking my heart even more than Vera's words while she had lain on the concrete, bleeding out.

The door opened, and Ms. Rodriguez and Mr. Harleen walked into the room. Ever since Blaise and Vera had started dating, their parents had become closer and closer, like they used to be years ago.

"Ethan," Ms. Rodriguez said, staring at Blaise's father, "you don't—"

"Luciana, don't fucking tell me that I don't have to do anything for your daughter."

I stared between them, heart pounding. Ms. Rodriguez worked multiple jobs to support Vera and Mateo, her children, and she didn't like taking money from anyone. But Ethan Harleen wasn't just anyone to her anymore.

"Thank you," Ms. Rodriguez finally whispered. "Thank you so much."

Blaise glanced up from Vera's bedside. "What happened?"

"Don't worry about it, Blaise," his father growled at him.

From what Vera had told me, Blaise and his father had never had the best relationship, but I was glad that he had come to at least support Blaise. Or maybe he was only here for Ms. Rodriguez. Hell, it didn't matter to me, but Vera was the only person that Blaise had.

"Blaise, why don't you take Maddie and Mateo to the cafeteria?" Mr. Harleen offered.

"I'm not leaving Vera's side," Blaise said.

"You've been here all night," Ms. Rodriguez whispered to him. "Can I spend some time alone with my daughter?"

After another moment of silence, Blaise sighed softly and stood up from his seat. He placed a kiss on her forehead, one last tear dripping down his cheek, and then walked to the door, where Mateo had been standing all night, crying.

"Come on, punk," Blaise said to him, grabbing on to his shoulder and squeezing.

I stood. "Are you going to be okay?"

"I'll be fine, sweetheart," Ms. Rodriguez whispered.

"Do you want anything from the cafeteria?"

"No, but thank you."

Once I pulled her into a hug because she needed it, I followed Blaise and Mateo into the hallway. While I expected them to head to the café, Blaise stopped at Imani's door, where Poison was gathered outside with Alec.

"Why don't you pick us up something in the cafeteria, kid?" Blaise offered Mateo, gently nudging him down the hallway. "Heard that chocolate pudding is good. I gotta talk to Poison for a bit, okay?"

Mateo glanced at me. I shook my head.

"I'll come down in a couple of minutes. I promise," I said. After Mateo disappeared down the hallway toward the elevators, I cleared my throat and turned toward Poison. "What's the plan?"

"The plan is that you're not getting involved anymore," Alec growled.

My eyes widened at how aggressive he suddenly was in front of everyone else. "Alec—"

"No, Maddie," he said between gritted teeth. "You almost died today."

"But I didn't."

"But you fucking will," Alec said, "if you keep trying to solve everyone's problems."

"To solve everyone's problems?!" I exclaimed. "We were looking for Nicole because she hadn't been answering any messages and hadn't shown up at school after the funeral. We thought something had happened to her."

"And what would have happened to her?" he said. "She's the police chief's daughter."

Blaise stiffened next to me while Poison feigned surprise. Did Alec not know about Nicole? I thought I had told him or that he had heard it from someone else. Maybe he had heard it but didn't remember because his life had been just as crazy lately.

"Alec," I whispered, moving forward, wanting to tell him so he could see that what I had done was justified. But I should've done it alone and not dragged Vera along with us because I was the one who had gotten her in this mess.

"Not here," Landon growled, glancing at the cops lingering at the other side of the hall.

"We can talk about specifics back at my place," Kai offered.

"I'm not leaving the hospital," I said, arms crossed.

"God, you're as annoying as Imani," João said, rolling his eyes.

I snapped my hand around his collar and yanked him toward me, not giving a damn about the consequences. "I get that you think we don't know what we're doing, but at least we give a fuck about our friends. We're smart, and we have connections too. Let us work with you—at least until the end of the year. Nobody will suspect a thing from a group of good girls. We can take down this shitty town forever."

76

alec

"WOLFE!" Landon called from down Redwood's hallway, jogging to catch up with me. He kept my pace as we headed for the cafeteria and nodded toward a side hallway. "We're meeting with Avery in five. You're coming with us."

"Me?" I asked. "What happened to you agreeing to work with the girls?"

Not that I actually wanted them to work with Poison. But João had finally cracked yesterday while sitting in the hospital and told Maddie that if she kept her mouth shut, they would work with them. And I was still pissed.

"Fuck that," João growled from behind me.

I glanced over my shoulder to see him pulling out a pack of cigarettes and walking alone toward Landon and me, heavy bags under his eyes, as if he hadn't slept.

"They're not getting involved."

Thank fuck.

"You need to control your girl, Wolfe," João said, lighting up in the middle of the hallway and blowing smoke out through his nose. He pulled the cigarette from his lips and shook his head. "She's fucking crazy."

"She's passionate," I said.

And a little crazy too—which I loved about her, but it'd get her hurt one of these days.

"Where's Kai?" I asked. "Blaise?"

"Kai's at home, working on figuring out who shot at the girls," Landon said. "Blaise is …"

"At the hospital," Jace said, leaning against Mr. Avery's closed door. With a football in his hands, he tossed it back and forth. "He texted the group this morning and said that he was staying with Vera today."

"The group?" I asked, brow furrowed. "What group?"

"The group chat," Landon said.

"What group chat?"

"The one we added you to last night," João said. "Come on. Stop being fucking stupid."

After pulling out my phone, which I had turned off to ignore Mom's nonstop texts about the dinner that she was making for me and Dad tonight, I turned it on and saw a bunch of texts from unknown numbers in a group chat called *No Girls*.

I rubbed my forehead. *Damn, these guys are trying hard to get themselves in trouble with their girlfriends, huh?* Because if any of the girls saw a group chat labeled *No Girls*, they'd immediately become god-tier hackers to get into their phones and figure out what we didn't want them to know.

"Don't listen to him," Landon said, following João into Mr. Avery's room. "He's just pissed off about what happened to Imani."

Mr. Avery looked up from his desk, where he sat with Sakura, eating lunch, and grimaced at us. After wrapping Sakura's grinder, he stuffed it into a brown bag and handed it to her. "Why don't you eat lunch with the girls in the cafeteria?"

While Sakura couldn't be more than a few months pregnant,

her belly had already grown so much since the last time I had seen her.

After setting down the grinder on his desk, she glanced back at us and pulled on an oversize sweatshirt to hide her stomach, then grabbed her belongings. "I will see you after school."

Mr. Avery kissed her on the lips, guided her toward the door, then locked it behind her.

João whistled. "Baby mama doesn't want anyone knowing that you're the father?"

"Doubt that Imani would ever want anyone to know that *you* were the father of her baby if she had one either," Landon said.

And I mean, I didn't disagree with him because João was so explicit and hard to get along with.

"What do you want, Rocha?" Mr. Avery said, heading back to his desk.

"Information," Jace said.

Mr. Avery leaned against the desk and crossed his arms, brow arched as he looked between Poison and then at Jace and me. "Has Poison finally accepted new members into their little clique?"

"Fuck no," João growled. "But this has to do with all of us. Even you."

"Me?" Mr. Avery said, shaking his head. "I'm not getting involved with this shit anymore. I have Sakura to protect and a baby on the way. If anyone realizes that I've left the mob to work with Poison, they'll be in danger."

"Well, the girls got shot yesterday, and Sakura could've been one of them," Landon said.

Mr. Avery drew his tongue across his teeth, his gaze faltering for a moment. "What is it?"

João handed Mr. Avery a slip of paper. "Do you know any of these guys?"

Mr. Avery sat down at his desk and kicked his right ankle up onto his knee, scanning the sheet. "Are these the guys who did it? Because ... they don't look familiar to me. I can ask around to find out who they are, but no promises that I'll come up with anything."

"You'd fucking better find something or—"

"Or else what, João?" Mr. Avery asked, looking up at him. "You'll kill me? No. You won't do that. You only kill people if you're getting paid for it." He forced out a breath. "I'll do what I can, but nothing more."

João lunged at Mr. Avery, but Landon caught him and threw him back so hard into the desks that three of them tumbled to the ground on top of João. "Step the fuck back and settle your ass down, Rocha."

Yep, they were still in the same fight as yesterday.

I leaned against the whiteboard, stuffed my hands into my pockets, and pursed my lips, not wanting to get involved in their drama too. I had way too much of my own right now. Maddie had barely said two words to me since our argument at the hospital yesterday.

While I knew that she just wanted to fight for her friends, it was too dangerous. Because the enemies were brawling with bullets and willing to kill a group of good girls, and neither one of us knew how to properly hold a gun. Never mind how to shoot to kill.

"You hear anything, message Kai," Landon said to Mr. Avery. "We'll make sure that nothing happens to Sakura in the meantime."

"The girls are supposed to go to the hospital after school," Jace said.

"Maddie is probably going to talk Sakura into going with them," I said.

"Allie too." Jace nodded. "I'll keep an eye on her if you need extra time, Avery."

"Don't let anyone touch her," Mr. Avery said. "I'll be at the hospital for Sakura's doctor's appointment at five thirty. And if I'm even two minutes late"—he looked over at João—"that'll mean something happened to me, and you'd better take Sakura and the girls somewhere safe."

77

maddie

ALLIE and I sat alone at our table during lunch. Blaise had skipped school to be with Vera in the hospital. Imani had stayed home to heal up a bit more. The guys were nowhere to be found. And Nicole still hadn't answered us.

I pushed around some mashed potatoes on my plate and frowned. "You think ..."

"Hmm?" Allie asked in a daze, peering up at me.

"Forget it," I mumbled, not even knowing what I had planned to say.

My eyes were heavy, and I wanted to sleep for days without having to worry about someone trying to take me out with the rest of the good girls at Redwood. I drew a hand across my face and glanced down at my phone when it buzzed on the table.

Unknown: Meet me at the park tonight. Alone.

Did this bitch really think I was stupid enough to meet her—or him—at the park in the dark?! Especially after we had all just gotten shot at in the police chief's front yard and yet nobody at Redwood seemed to know about it?

Seemed fishy to me.

Unknown: 8 p.m.

When the second message rolled in, I bit my tongue and replied.

Me: No, bitch.

Then, I blocked the number, which I should've done a long, long time ago. Sandra had done it once, but this shithead had still texted me from a second number. Besides, I didn't have time for this absolute bullshit and this nonstop drama. First, Alec being assaulted. Then, Piper and us getting shot at. I didn't need an insecure asshole trying to distract me.

Or plotting to kill me.

A couple of moments later, Sakura wandered into the cafeteria in a large sweatshirt that covered her growing belly and a brown-bagged lunch. She slid onto the seat next to Allie and frowned. "The guys are talking to Callan right now, if you are looking for them."

"Thanks," I said with a half-smile.

Though I wanted to know *what* they were talking about. While Alec had stayed with me last night, we'd barely talked to each other since our fight at the hospital. He didn't like that I wanted to help take charge, and I understood his reasons.

But my friends had almost been killed yesterday while we were just checking on Nicole. We hadn't even been trying to hunt anyone down, beat anyone up, or kill the rich. We'd wanted to do something nice, and we'd gotten fucked for it.

"How're the others?" Sakura whispered, lips trembling. "Callan said that they were shot."

"They're recovering in the hospital," Allie said.

Suddenly, Sakura burst out into a fit of tears, sniffling with her head hanging. Allie moved closer to her and gently rubbed her back while I frowned and thought about Vera sitting in the hospital room without me. Sure, she had Blaise, but I wanted to be with her too.

"We're going to the hospital after school," I said. "You're welcome to come with us."

"Really?" Sakura said, teary eyes wide.

Allie smiled. "Of course. Imani will be there too. She stayed home today."

"I don't know how long I'll be able to stay," Sakura said, wiping her tears and placing her hand on her belly underneath the table. "Callan is bringing me to a doctor's appointment today for the"—she paused, glanced around, and lowered her voice—"baby."

"When will you know the sex?" I asked.

Cheeks rounding, she smiled. "Hopefully today."

"No way!" Allie exclaimed, grabbing her hand. "You have to tell us right away."

I beamed at them because while all this shit had been going on, we finally had something to smile about. I just hoped that Sakura and Mr. Avery would stay out of the drama as much as they could. I didn't want anything to happen to Sakura or the baby.

"Of course I will," Sakura said. "I really want a girl."

"Me too!"

"What does Mr. Avery want?" Allie asked.

"He wants a girl too."

"God, I'm so happy for you," I said, grinning, my gaze shifting from Sakura to behind her.

Nicole stood with the dean of students near the cafeteria doors, her blonde hair shielding her face and her arms crossed over her chest, as if she wasn't comfortable in her own body—very unlike the bubbly, flirtatious Nicole.

After a moment, Nicole turned toward us and kept her gaze on the ground. Once she reached our table, she slid next to Allie, buried her face into the crook of her neck, and burst out into quiet tears.

"I'm so sorry that I didn't text you earlier," she sobbed. "It's my fault that you ... that ... it happened." She sniffled. "I should've ... I should've sucked it up and come into school yesterday so you didn't come looking for me."

"You're not to blame, Nicole," Allie whispered. "We're just glad that you're safe."

"I am to blame," she said. "If I had just … texted you, then nobody would've gotten shot."

When she lifted her head and her hair fell out of her face, I stiffened. Bruises the size of someone's hands decorated her neck, and her bottom lip had split open and scabbed over. I glanced at Allie, who fumed.

"Who did this to you?" she asked.

"Don't worry about it, Als," she said. "You should be worried about Imani and Vera."

"One of these days, your dad is going to kill you," Allie said.

Everyone stayed quiet, even Nicole because I think she actually believed it to be true too. A shiver ran down my spine, and I shook my head, hoping that we could get her out of this at some point. She might've been captain of the cheer team, but she didn't have any support.

"On the brighter side, Poison was right," she said with a half-smile that didn't meet her eyes. "Piper's father had something to do with her death. From what I gathered, Piper saw the face of the woman who had been working with that other idiot."

"Spencer?" I asked.

"Yes," Nicole said. "I don't know much more than that, but I'm assuming she didn't want Piper to say anything, so instead of threatening her, she decided that it'd be best to get rid of her for good with Piper's father's help."

"Which means that …" Allie paused. "Piper must've recognized the woman."

"Hey, boys!" Mrs. Dawson shouted through the windows as she walked from her car and toward one of the side doors with a brown bag, probably filled with her lunch. She wiggled her fingers at them and swayed her hips from side to side, her teal pants blinding me.

"Do you think it's someone from school?" I asked.

Nicole followed my stare and frowned. "I don't know. Could be."

I scanned the cafeteria for anyone who might be suspicious and caught Sandra staring at me from across the room, her eyeliner so sharp that it could cut me, and her lips curled into a sinister smirk. I balled my hands into fists underneath the table.

No more hasty decisions, Maddie.

Yet my hands ached to wrap around their throats. If either of them had been the one to do it, to hurt Piper and Vera and all of my friends, then they would pay for it. I didn't care what kind of trouble it would land me in. They would get everything that was coming to them.

78

alec

"YOU'RE COMING WITH US, WOLFE," João shouted across the parking lot after school.

Maddie, Allie, Sakura, and Nicole, who had apparently come back to school today, had gone straight to the hospital after the last bell rang while I stayed after for hockey practice with Oliver. I sighed and tossed my belongings into my car's trunk.

"Kai wants to talk to you about something," Landon said. "Follow us."

Sweat dripped down my forehead from drills during practice, and I wiped it away with the back of my hand and slid into my driver's seat before following them. João and Landon drove down into the slums and parked outside of a run-down house.

After eyeing the boarded-up front door, I turned off my car and followed them to a side door that led down into a basement. Landon held the door open for us to walk down the creaky steps, then shut it, flicking on a dim hanging lightbulb.

"This is Kai's place?" I asked.

Neither of them responded. João placed his finger on the electronic lock, and then the door clicked open. I walked into a small room with about twenty television monitors or more on the wall, and Kai was in a swivel chair, staring at a bunch of code.

"You look like shit," Landon said to Kai.

In the midst of a yawn, Kai side-eyed Landon.

João lit up a cigarette and leaned against the doorframe. "You always look like shit, Landon." After taking a long drag on the cigarette, he pulled it out of his mouth and drew his tongue across the scab on his lip, where Landon had punched him yesterday during their fight at the hospital. "Hit like a bitch too."

Landon scowled at João and headed for a back room while I sat down at the table next to Kai and hoped that Landon and João wouldn't drag me into the middle of their fight. Kai set one of his laptops in front of me, a video on the screen.

"I found out who did it," Kai said.

I snapped my head toward him, eyes wide. "You did?"

"Took me all night and all day, but I did it." Kai paused and looked over at João, who glared at the room that Landon had disappeared into.

Then, in a burst of anger, João followed him and slammed the door, yelling.

Kai cleared his throat. "Don't worry about them. They're pissed at each other for what happened to Imani."

"But they didn't do anything," I said.

"Yeah, well, that's how they are."

"So," I said, glancing at the video, "why'd you want to talk to me about it?"

Instead of answering me, Kai pressed play.

On the screen, the girls pulled up to the side of the road in front of Nicole's house. For a few moments, they lingered by the car, then began walking to the front door as a car slowed down on the street.

I clenched my jaw when the girls began falling to the ground, one by one. Anger rushed through me, my nostrils flaring and my fists tightening by my sides.

Kai took note and paused the video as the car began driving away. "You good?"

"I want to kill whoever did this to them." I was seething. The words tumbled out of my mouth before I could stop them.

I'd had so much pain these past few weeks, but I hadn't wanted to kill anyone before I saw what had happened to Maddie and the others. How could someone do this to them? All they had wanted was to check up on their friend.

Unlike João or Landon, who would've both said something to me, Kai stayed quiet and continued playing the video that he had scraped together. The next clips were from other cameras, following the car through Redwood.

"It disappears here," Kai said, pointing to the screen where the car disappeared into the woods. "I searched what I could from other town security systems and couldn't find the car again since the shooting. So, I grabbed what I could from the license plate and ran it across all potential matches for cars registered in Redwood and nearby towns."

"What'd you find?"

Kai handed me a single slip of paper that had a bunch of names I didn't recognize on it.

"Are these supposed to mean something?" I asked.

"Aliases for some members of the Redwood mob. Callan Avery confirmed it this afternoon during his free period. I searched for footage of the days leading up to the incident to see if they had met with anyone." He paused, lips pressing together. "And I found this ..."

After another pause, he pressed play, and a new video appeared on the screen of Escape, down by the beach. People walked in and out of the restaurant, chatting with each other, and then the door opened once more, and three guys walked out.

"Those are the men who were in the car," Kai said.

The video continued with them lingering by the door until a woman followed them outside into the cold, her blonde hair shielding her face. A gust of wind blew locks of her hair back, and I froze.

"No," I murmured. "I-it can't be her."

Kai paused the video so we had a clear view of her, then hopped up and disappeared into a back room. A moment later, after I agonized over it and attempted to talk myself out of what my eyes were really seeing, Kai came back with a gun and placed it in front of me.

"I don't care what you do with it," Kai said. "But if I were you, I would kill her."

With a shaky hand, I seized the gun. "How do I use it?"

After Kai gave me the rundown of it, I stood up and shook my head, feeling so betrayed.

How can she do this to me? How can my own damn mother do this to her son? She had said that she'd do anything to get her family back, but the only way that'd happen was in her dreams, in her nightmares, in that magical, fictional place she called heaven.

But she wasn't going to heaven for what she had done.

I tightened my grip around the gun and headed straight for the door, my bones and body empty and devoid of all emotion.

I'd make sure she went straight to hell.

79

alec

WHIPPING ONTO MY STREET, I slammed on the accelerator. When I spotted Oliver's car parked at the bottom of my driveway, I clutched the steering wheel and sped up the driveway to the garage, blinded by rage.

How could Mom do this? How could she fucking do this?!

I hopped out of the car, and Oliver grabbed my shoulder.

"Can we talk?"

"Later."

"Please, dude," he reasoned. "You ignored me all practice."

After leaning over the center console, I grabbed the gun that I had shoved into the glove box and stuffed it into the inside of my jacket. Adrenaline rushed through my system the more I thought about that bitch.

"Get the fuck out of my way, Oliver," I growled, slamming my door and pushing past him.

He stumbled back, his gaze on my jacket, then hurried after me into the garage. "Alec."

"Go home."

"Dude, was that a gun?" he asked. "What're you doing with *that*?"

"Taking care of a problem," I gritted out. "Now, leave."

"The only person home is your mom," he said in confusion.

"I know."

"The fuck? This isn't you, Wolfe." He stepped in front of me as soon as I entered the house and grabbed my shoulder. "The hell are you doing with a gun? You planning to kill her? For what? Because I slept with her? I already apologized for it. If you want to take it out on anyone, take it out on me."

I shoved him to the side so hard that when he slammed into the wall, picture frames fell onto the ground at my feet. Images of all the happy days we used to have together as a family on vacation stared up at me. All that happiness, and Mom had still betrayed me.

"Get the fuck out of here, Oliver. And don't come back."

Before he could rip me back again, I stormed through the house and to the living room. Fury rushed through me the more and more I thought about the video.

How could Mom do this to me? How could she betray me? Betray Maddie?

What the fuck is wrong with her?!

"Mom!" I shouted in the living room. "Where the fuck are you?"

"Alec?" she hummed, skipping down the staircase with a huge grin. "Dinner's almost ready. I just have to—" When she stepped onto the last stair and saw the gun in my hand, she stopped and shuffled back against the railing. "What are you doing with that?"

"Get down here," I growled, gesturing with the gun for her to walk forward.

Mom raised her hands and slowly walked toward me.

Oliver grabbed my shoulder from behind. "Come on, Alec. Think about this."

As if Mom hadn't seen Oliver before now, she glanced over at him, eyes widening even more. "Oliver, what are you doing here?

You should be at home. I'm having dinner with my family tonight."

"What? Were you two planning on meeting up?" I growled, moving the gun between him and her. "Did Oliver show up when he shouldn't have? Is he only a little late-night fuck buddy for you, Mom?!"

Oliver raised his hands and stepped back. "The fuck, dude? Don't point that at me! I already told you that I cut it off with her. But she won't stop texting me and asking me to come over. We haven't done anything together since you found out."

I nodded aggressively. "Hmm, is that right, Mom? Did you want to get rid of him too? Is that why you kidnapped him after Maddie uncovered the truth about you and him? Were you pissed at her for that?"

"I don't know what you're talking about," she said.

"Did you use Oliver to get closer to Maddie?" I snarled.

"Sweetheart, you're scaring me," Mom said, faking surprise. "You're talking nonsense."

"Stop fucking stalling!" I shouted. "Did you fucking use Oliver to get closer to Maddie?!"

The innocence dropped from Mom's face, her perfect facade wavering. "No."

"You're lying."

"I'm not lying, Alec. I told you why I was with him."

"Stop fucking lying to me!" I shouted. "That's all you've done my entire life!"

"Put the gun down, Alec."

"No. I want answers."

"Answers? Why don't you tell me why you're pointing a gun at your mother?"

"I have a gun pointed at my mother because I'm going to do to her what she tried to do to Maddie," I said through gritted teeth, stepping toward her. "I'm going to shoot her dead because *she* ordered the mob to kill the woman I love."

"What?" Oliver said to my left.

My arms shook, but I kept the gun pointed at Mom. "Admit it!"

Mom stayed quiet for a long, long time, and then she dropped her gaze to the ground. "Alec, you don't understand. It was the only way I could get us all back together. She was pulling you away from me. I told you that I'd do anything to get my family back. Let's talk about—"

"You ordered the hit on Maddie?" Oliver whispered, almost to himself.

"There isn't shit to talk about, Mom!" I shouted, finger hovering over the trigger.

If I killed her, if I fucking killed her … all my dreams would be dust. I'd be sentenced to prison for the rest of my life, and I would leave Maddie all alone in this world and in this shitty town without protection.

"Put the gun down, Alec," Mom said. "I know you, sweetheart. You won't shoot—"

Before she could finish her sentence, Oliver snatched the gun from my trembling hand, aimed it at Mom's head, and pulled the trigger three times in quick succession.

80

alec

MY ARMS DROPPED by my sides, my eyes widening with tears as the pops echoed through my ears. Mom collapsed to the ground, a puddle of blood forming underneath her as the light left her eyes for good.

"You tried to kill my fucking sister?!" Oliver screamed, dropping the gun and snatching Mom's corpse from the ground. He hurled her to the other side of the room, her blood splattering all over the white walls. "I fucking loved you, and you tried to kill her?!"

I stared at them in horror, not knowing what to feel. Oliver had loved her? Mom was dead. I could barely process what had just happened. But all I could think now was that Maddie was safe from the people who had tried to hurt her.

At the thought, I relaxed my shoulders and let out a low sigh. *Maddie is safe.*

While Oliver continued shouting at Mom's corpse, I pulled back one of the accent chairs and slouched down into it, throwing my head back against the cushion, my nerves coming out in a belly laugh. I must've looked—and sounded—crazy, but I didn't care.

If Mom had really been behind all of this, then had she planned my rape? Had she planned for it to happen again and wanted to watch? I had so many questions that I would never find the answers to now that she was gone.

I would have to live with the unanswered trauma.

But at least Maddie was safe.

Another laugh escaped my mouth. She was all I cared about.

After a couple more moments of letting this all sink in, after staring emptily at Mom's paling body, I finally raised my gaze to Oliver, who paced around the room while running his hands through his hair.

"Go clean up," I said to him. When he didn't make a move toward the bathroom, I stood and gripped his shoulder. "Oliver, go clean up. Wash the blood off your hands and take a shower if you need it. It's going to be okay."

Tears welled in his eyes. "I thought … I thought she loved me."

"She was using you," I whispered. "She was using all of us."

"Why?" he choked out. "Why'd she want to kill Maddie? Why would she do that?"

"I don't know," I said, nudging him toward the bathroom. "Go clean yourself up."

A sob escaped his mouth, and he dropped his head. Then, suddenly, his arms came around my shoulders, and he pulled me into a hug. "I'm sorry for everything, Alec. I'm sorry I screwed up our relationship and yours with your parents."

"You didn't ruin anything," I said even though he had.

But I didn't want him to feel bad about this. I needed him to think clearly because I needed his help with our next steps.

How do I explain this to Dad? Should I hide her body? Burn it? Bury her? What happens next?

After another moment of clutching me hard, Oliver walked to the bathroom. As soon as the door closed, I let out another breath and stared down at Mom, who had three holes in her forehead, the blood seeping out of all of them.

"What's going on here?" Dad asked, freezing.

I whipped around and stared at him through wide eyes. *When did he get here?*

"Alec?"

The gun sat at my feet, Mom's body smeared with blood on the floor.

I stared at Dad, who wasn't innocent in any of this either, and stepped back with my hands raised. "Dad, I … I can explain. I didn't—"

Dad's gaze dropped to Mom, his eyes widening. "Alec! What'd you do?!"

"Nothing!" I said, taking another step back. "I didn't do anything."

Within a moment, he crouched next to her and pulled her into his lap. "She's dead!"

I continued to back up, my legs moving on their own until I hit the nearest wall. My heart and mind raced uncontrollably. I hadn't planned on him returning home tonight, and I had completely forgotten about Mom's stupid dinner.

What am I going to do? What can I say to him?

I had planned to kill Mom, but I couldn't do it myself. Hell, I hadn't even had the chance to do it before Oliver swiped that gun out of my hand and shot her dead.

"You killed her!" he sobbed.

"No, I didn't," I said, shaking my head. "I didn't kill her."

"Then, who did, Alec?" he growled, snapping his gaze to me, Mom against his chest.

I hated the way that he held her now because he hadn't held her like that when she was alive in a long, long fucking time. If he had cared about her while she was living, he wouldn't have slept around with other men. He would've broken up with her to respect her if he really did want to cheat.

Hot, angry tears burned my eyes. I balled my hands into tight fists by my sides. I hated him almost as much as I hated Mom and Piper. Dad didn't give a fuck about his wife. This was a lie, a facade, shock.

Not love.

"Huh?" Dad shouted. "If you didn't do it, then who did?"

Oliver walked out of the bathroom, wiping his bloody hands on a rag, his hair sticking up from how many times he had run his hand through it. Dad looked from him to me and then back, a bewildered expression crossing his face.

"You?" Dad asked in disbelief. "You did this?"

Oliver stared at him, then at Mom's corpse, his jaw twitching.

"Call the police, Alec. We need to get justice for your mother."

But when I hadn't had the balls to murder my own mother, Oliver had. He had shot her to protect his sister and the woman I loved. And I couldn't throw him under the bus. While we'd had a falling-out, he had still been there for me more than Dad ever had.

"Oliver, call Poison," I started, staring in guilt at Dad.

"Screw Poison. We need the police!" Dad shouted, clutching his wife like he'd ever cared about her. He might have at one point, but he couldn't love a woman that he never saw. He couldn't love a woman who was now dead, one that he hadn't cared about in life.

"Once you're finished calling Poison, get the police on the phone." I pressed my trembling lips together. "Tell them that we walked in on my father standing over my mother's dead body with a gun in his hand."

Dad snapped his gaze up to me. "Alec, you wouldn't. You did this!"

While I didn't believe in fate, this was the closest damn thing to it.

"You had a secret love affair with two guys from Redwood," I whispered. "You didn't love your wife anymore. You hadn't loved her for years now. She found out about your affair, and you wanted to keep it a secret. You had to get rid of her, Dad."

"Alec!" Dad shouted through tears. "You can't do this to me! Nobody will believe you."

"I believe him," Oliver said, squeezing my shoulder. This time, it wasn't to hold me back or to convince me to think through what

I had planned to do with that gun. This time, it was to support me. "I fucking believe him."

81

maddie

"ALL RIGHT, VERA," Mrs. Abara said, leaning against the hospital door, "you're free to go. Just make sure you get a lot of rest these next few weeks and keep your bandages clean. I'll have Imani come over and check on you throughout the week. If you have any questions, you know who to ask."

Vera nodded and sat up in her hospital bed, smiling softly. "Thank you."

After helping Vera out of the bed, I closed the curtain around her bed and gently helped her out of her hospital gown and into some sweatpants and an oversize Redwood Academy T-shirt that wouldn't rub up against her wound.

"There you go," I said, rolling her shirt down her stomach so she was covered.

Wincing, Vera grabbed her coat and slung it over her forearm. "Could you grab my overnight bag from the chair? I don't want to forget anything. Blaise has been itching to get home since I checked in."

Once I grabbed all her belongings, I thrust the curtain apart and opened the hospital door. Nicole, Imani, Allie, Blaise, and Jace walked down the hallway toward us with goodies from the cafeteria.

"Why're you up?" Blaise asked, walking over to us.

"I can leave," Vera said, gesturing to the overnight bag in my hands, her movements much slower than they once had been. She winced again, stiffening her muscles and standing straight. "Can you take this from Maddie?"

"I can hold it, V," I said.

Blaise took her bag from me anyway, then grabbed her other hand to lead her toward the elevators.

Imani held out a pudding to Vera. "I got you an extra, if you want it. They have banana cream today, which is a total score!"

"No thanks," Vera said, stepping into the elevator.

We all piled in after her and rode the elevator down to the lobby.

"Do you think Sakura is almost finished with her appointment?" Nicole asked.

"They've been gone for the past thirty minutes," Allie said. "Maybe."

The 1 button lit up on the elevator, and the doors opened on the main floor. I helped Vera out of the lift and through the hallway. But instead of heading toward the exit, she walked to the waiting room.

"We should wait for Sakura," Vera said. "I wanna know what she's having."

"What we need is to get you home," Blaise said to her. "You need to rest."

"Rest and write smut," I hummed. "Sounds like everything you've ever dreamed about."

Vera giggled and tucked some dark hair behind her ear. I wrapped her jacket around her shoulders and zippered it so she wouldn't be cold once we left the hospital. She smiled softly at me and rested her head on my shoulder.

"Come on," Blaise said, nudging her. "I want to get you home."

Honestly, I would bet that it was more than wanting her to

rest. After what had happened, we had all been on high alert. Who knew if those fuckers would try to kill us again? We still didn't know their motive. Was it a coincidence? Or had it been planned?

"Please," Vera said, pushing him back. "Sakura should be out soon."

After muttering under his breath, Blaise stood between the lobby and the exit, his gaze on the sliding doors. I gulped down the tinge of fear that whoever it was would try to hurt us again and smoothed out Vera's jacket.

"So, what's going on with your mom and Blaise's dad?" I asked Vera.

Imani smirked. "Do I smell another stepbrother-stepsister relationship stirring up?"

Allie playfully rolled her eyes at Imani.

Vera shrugged. "I'm not sure. They have mostly kept to themselves lately."

Nicole wiggled her brows. "You think they're hooking up?"

"Whatever it is"—I smirked at her—"Mama Rodriguez was *glowing* earlier."

"Ew," Vera said, scrunching her nose.

A couple of moments later, Sakura bounced down the hall next to Mr. Avery, both grinning at each other. My lips curled into a smile, and I waved them over to us, desperately wanting to know the baby's sex.

"So?" I said. "Don't leave us waiting!"

Sakura gazed up at Mr. Avery, who tugged playfully on her ponytail. "It's a girl."

"Yes!" Nicole exclaimed, jumping up and throwing her hands into the air. "I knew it!"

"I am so excited!" Allie cheered.

"We're already planning a baby shower for you," Imani said.

Sakura blushed and buried her face into Mr. Avery's arm, giggling. "You don't have to."

"Of course we do," Vera said, cheeks rounding.

"How are you doing?" Sakura asked Vera. "Are they letting you leave?"

Vera nodded as Mr. Avery's phone buzzed.

"I have to take this," Mr. Avery said, stepping toward the side of the room.

After he began talking, Imani's phone rang. She stared down at it quizzically, then lifted it to her ear. "What the hell do you want, João? I'm in the middle of celebrating Sakura's gender reveal."

Then, a moment later, my phone buzzed. Alec.

What the hell is going on? Why is everyone getting calls at the same time?

"Maddie," Alec whispered over the phone, voice shaky, "where are you?"

"At the hospital. Why? Where are you?" I asked. Alec paused for a long moment, and then I heard someone, who sounded like Oliver, in the background. I furrowed my brow, wondering when they had returned to being best friends again. "Is that Oliver?"

Mr. Avery returned into the room and whispered something to Blaise, who tensed.

"Come with me," Mr. Avery said, glancing around the room. "All of you. We have some cleaning up to do."

I followed the girls toward the exit of the hospital.

"Alec?" I asked through the phone when he still hadn't responded to me. "What is going on? Why is Mr Avery bringing us back to his place? What happened?"

"My mom is dead."

82

alec

WHEN OLIVER HAD KILLED MOM, I hadn't thought I'd be burying both of my parents at the same time.

I stared down at the two six-foot holes that my parents had been lowered into hours earlier. The rain had started pouring twenty minutes ago, but Maddie hadn't left my side as she held an umbrella over my head.

Teeth gritted and hands balled into fists, I tried to bite back my frustration. But it came out in a loud, rugged shout as I fell to my knees at the foot of their graves. "I hate you both! For everything you did to me and for everything you were too busy to do. I hate you for all of it. Every single last bit!"

My fingers dug into the mud, and I ripped the wet grass right from its place in the ground.

"I deserved more," I said, voice dropping to a sob. "I fucking deserved more!"

"What happened to Mr. Wolfe?" Oliver whispered to Maddie behind me.

"Not now, Oliver," she shushed.

"Did he—"

"He killed himself." I dropped my gaze to his casket sitting in the dirt. "Asshole."

Dad had had enough money to get out of almost anything, but he must've had secrets that he had been hiding, even from Mom. Secrets that he would much rather, quite literally, take to his grave than have them spill out while on trial for murder.

"Alec," Maddie whispered, grabbing on to my sleeve, "you're shivering."

"Wait in the car for me," I said.

Because I wasn't done giving them a piece of my mind. I had always been the good kid, always worked hard to get perfect grades and be Redwood's top hockey player, and all they had done was fuck up my life. I had never talked back to them. I had let them do whatever the hell they wanted. And when I'd had that gun pointed at Mom, I still couldn't pull the trigger.

But now, they deserved to hear everything that I had to say about them.

Now, it didn't matter what they heard because they couldn't talk back, they couldn't judge me, and they really couldn't destroy my life any more than they already had. I finally had the autonomy and the power to myself.

"Go, Maddie," I urged, gently nudging her toward the car. "It's cold."

"I'm not going anywhere," she said, still standing next to Oliver. "I'll stand here with you for as long as you want to stand here. You're the person I love the most in this world, and you're not going through this alone."

My chest tightened, and I intertwined my fingers with hers.

The low hum of a motor switched off behind me, the rain still falling hard around us. Oliver glanced over his shoulder and stood up taller, giving someone a small smile and moving out of the way.

"Thought I'd catch you here." Coach squeezed my shoulder from behind. "How're you doing?"

"Fine."

"People who are fine don't say they're fine."

I pressed my lips together. "He barely showed up to my birthday parties, growing up. He came home every other weekend, if I was lucky. Didn't know about anything that I was going through. Cheated on my mom, which screwed all of us the fuck up." I paused. "So, I'm fine."

Instead of releasing me, like everyone else had, Coach pulled me into a tight hug. "You've always been a son to me, Alec. If you ever need to talk or want to have dinner or anything, come find me. You're always welcome in my home."

"Thanks," I croaked out, my voice cracking. "I appreciate it."

And while my arms dropped by my sides because I couldn't hold them up anymore, he held me tightly and refused to release me. It was a hug from a man I had always wished were my father.

"There's something I need to tell you," he said, glancing at Maddie and Oliver. "Alone."

After handing me the umbrella, Maddie gave me a supportive smile and headed to the car with Oliver. I stood in the rain, still soaked, no matter how long Maddie had held this umbrella over my head, and lifted my gaze to Coach.

"I don't know if this is a good time to tell you," Coach said, grimacing and gazing down at his feet. "And I don't know what you'll think of me when I do, but it feels right. We're both all alone now, and … you deserve to know the truth."

"What is it?"

"Your father—"

"Cheated on my mom?" I asked, almost knowing what he was about to say.

He raised his brows. "She told you?"

"Yes."

"Did she tell you anything else?"

I shrugged emptily. I didn't know what was the truth anymore and what was a lie. She had said so much shit—*done* so much shit—to me that I … I didn't even want to think about that bitch anymore. I hadn't cared about her since I had found out she tried to kill Maddie.

"What'd you come here to tell me, Coach?" I asked.

He ran a hand across his face. "Alec, a while before your parents married, they split up for a bit because your mother suspected that Wolfe was cheating on her. She never found evidence of it at the time, but during their split …"

"What happened?" I asked blankly, not really giving a shit.

"We were together."

I snapped my gaze up to him. "What?"

"She didn't want to stay with me because I never had the kind of money Wolfe did, so she left me about a month later and …" He took another long pause. "And a week after that, she announced her pregnancy."

My jaw slackened. "She … are you?"

"I'm sorry," he whispered. "I just couldn't let you go off to college and never come back to Redwood without telling you. I've watched you grow up away from me for so long, and getting the chance to coach you, *son*, has been my proudest moment."

Tears welled in my eyes, and I found myself throwing my arms around him and pulling him into the tightest embrace of my life. "I'd never think of you any differently. Being coached by you has changed my fucking life. Thank you. So much."

83

maddie

AFTER THE FUNERAL, we headed to Poison's place with all our friends from the group. João sat on a dirty white plastic chair with an unlit cigarette in his mouth while flicking a lighter in front of him. I nestled on the couch next to Vera.

Alec had been acting weird since he had finished his conversation with his coach, but I attributed that to him having to bury both of his parents today. Even though he hated both of them, it must have been hard.

"Gotta give it to you." João lit the cigarette. "Didn't think you had the balls, Wolfe."

"What're you talking about?" I asked, glancing between Alec and João.

Alec stiffened. "It's nothing, Maddie."

João chuckled. "No shit. You didn't tell her, did you?"

"There's nothing to tell her," Alec growled. "Drop it."

"What happened?" I asked, looking from Alec to João to a suspicious Kai and back.

What aren't they telling me? And what is this big hush-hush secret that Alec has with Poison, who he supposedly hates?

After twisting his chair around, João sat backward in it and leaned forward, cigarette between his fingers and a smirk written across his face. "Your little boyfriend took Kai's gun and killed his mama."

My eyes widened. "What?"

"I didn't kill her," Alec gritted out between his teeth.

"What did she do?" I asked him.

Tears trembling in his eyes, Alec dropped down onto the couch and stared emptily at the wall that was decorated with holes the size of fists. "She was the one who sent you those messages, who put you in danger, who ordered Piper to ... do what she did to me."

"Wh-what?"

Mrs. Wolfe was behind all of this from the very beginning? What in the fucking world possessed her to be batshit crazy? What kind of drugs has she been taking? What kind of business has she been into?

"But I didn't do it," Alec said, almost as if to reassure himself. "I swear I didn't."

"Yeah, yeah. Your daddy did it." João waved dismissively again. "I don't give a shit what kind of story you tell the town. I just didn't think you had it in you to kill both your shitty parents. Easier to clean Redwood's billionaire row for us."

"I didn't do it," Alec repeated, this time more firmly.

Alec didn't have to say who had actually killed her because if he hadn't done it, then the only other person with him during that time had been Oliver. I highly doubted that Alec would kill anyone, but if pushed enough ... Oliver would.

Especially if it was for me.

"Drop it." I cleared my throat. "It doesn't matter anyway. We're not here to talk about who killed who. We're here to discuss how we're going to fix the problem that we have."

"We're not going to leave it in your hands," Imani said to Poison, more specifically to João, while crossing her arms. "Someone tried to kill us, and I don't feel safe with them running around town."

João leaned back, blowing out smoke through his nose. "What do you want me to do about it?"

"Let us help you," Imani said. "Like you agreed to do at the hospital."

"I wanna take down those fuckers," Allie said, crossing her arms.

"Me too," Nicole said.

"Um ..." Vera glanced at Blaise, gently drawing her fingers over her wound. She was *supposed* to be sleeping now, but Blaise had said she had dragged them out to see us. "I'll bake you guys some cookies and cheer you on from the sidelines while I recover."

Sakura leaned back on the couch, one hand on her belly. "Can you *please* make raisin oatmeal?"

"Fuck no." João scrunched his nose. "You'd better make chocolate chip cookies if you want us to do your dirty work."

Sakura's eyes filled with tears. "B-but I've been craving them."

Vera gently rubbed Sakura's shoulder. "I'll make raisin oatmeal and chocolate chip. Don't worry, Sakura. I got you."

"So, does that mean you're in?" I asked João.

João glanced at Landon and Kai, who nodded, and then he turned back to us. "We're in. Let's kill these motherfuckers."

Continue reading the Bad Boys of Redwood Academy with Science Project.

also by emilia rose

also by emilia rose

Scan the QR code with your phone to view all of Emilia's books!

about the author

Emilia Rose is a *USA Today* best-selling author of steamy romance.
Highly inspired by her study abroad trip to Greece in 2019, Emilia
loves to include Greek and Roman mythology in her writing.
She graduated from the University of Pittsburgh with a degree in
psychology and a minor in creative writing in 2020 and now writes
novels as her day job.
With over 18 million combined book views online and a growing
presence on reading apps, she hopes to inspire other young
novelists with her tales of growth and imagination, so they go on
to write the stories that need to be told.
Join Emilia's newsletter for exclusive giveaways, early chapter
releases, and more!

Milton Keynes UK
Ingram Content Group UK Ltd.
UKHW010636270324
440147UK00003B/45